one more day

one more day

A NOVEL

M. MALONE

one more day

For the lunchroom girls.
I miss you.

"YOU DIDN'T BRING your hot-ass sister with you?"

As soon as the words left his mouth, Jackson Alexander dodged the punch that came sailing his way. A chorus of laughter rang out around him as he playacted dodging blows while his friend, Matt Simmons, growled at him.

"I should give you the ass-kicking you've been asking for since freshman year."

Matt shoved the side of his lawn chair and Jackson tumbled down. He was laughing so hard by the time he hit the ground that it barely hurt.

Hanging out with his boys was his new favorite way to spend his weekends. After producing several platinum albums, suddenly everyone—from the kid who'd sat behind him in high school English class to the receptionist at his gym—wanted to be his best friend. Just a year earlier he wouldn't have believed the things people would do for a piece of the spotlight. His *real* friends kept him sane.

Giving one of them a hard time was part of the fun.

"Man, you know I'm only messing with you." Jackson righted

his chair and flopped back down. He kept a healthy distance from Matt though, just in case.

His brother, Nicholas, and their friend, Trent, stifled their laughter when Matt looked at them.

"You know we love Mara. Mainly because she keeps your crazy ass in line. She's coming to the barbecue, right? Or is she visiting your parents for Memorial Day weekend?" Nicholas asked. That was his brother, always the mediator.

They could have passed for twins with their golden-brown skin, dark eyes, and curly black hair, but they couldn't be more different in personality. Nicholas craved excitement whereas, more and more, Jackson just wanted solitude. It was hard to believe his playboy brother was actually twenty-seven, two years older than he was.

Matt took a swig of the beer he held. He rolled it across his palms a few times before answering. "Ask Trent. He sees more of her these days than I do."

All eyes swung to Trent. He shrugged but the look in his eyes was like that of a cornered animal. "She's great. She said to tell everyone hi."

Jackson picked up his lawn chair and then straddled it backward so he'd be facing the group. "Damn, you two aren't just playing with me? If I'd known she wasn't off-limits..." He stopped at the murderous expression on Matt's face.

Nicholas leaned over. "If I were you, I wouldn't finish that sentence."

Jackson shook his head as he looked back at Matt. "You are pathetic. I was going to say I would have married her. Mara is one of a kind."

Matt snorted. "You? Married?"

A hush fell over the group. Matt cleared his throat a few times before speaking. "Sorry, man. I shouldn't have said that. I wasn't thinking."

"You aren't saying anything that isn't true. I'm glad for once you aren't walking on eggshells around me." Jackson looked pointedly at Matt, then the other guys in the group.

"I gave up my chance to have a solo career when Cynthia got pregnant. I'll never regret that choice. She gave me the two best things in my life. I just wish she was here to see how amazing our boys are."

He stopped, frightened for a moment that his throat would close and he'd confirm their image of him as the tragic, broken widower. He just felt such anger, such impotent rage, that one twist of fate could take away his entire world.

"It's not too late. You could put out an album now," Nick suggested.

"I could. But it would mean a lot of time on the road away from the kids. I've let that dream go and I'm okay with it. Producing may not have been my first love but it's been good to me and I'm grateful. As for the marriage thing... Look, I know you guys think my life is just one party after another but I'm not making anyone any promises. I only date women who know the score and want the same thing. No strings and no drama."

"You're only twenty-five, Jack. You can't think you're going to be alone the rest of your life," Nicholas pointed out.

"I loved Cynthia more than life and when she died... Well, let's just say I'm not signing up for that kind of pain ever again."

It was so hard to remember his vibrant wife in that hospital bed, broken and bruised. Especially since he'd been as much at fault as the drunk driver who'd plowed his SUV into her car.

He'd gotten there before they wheeled her into surgery. There'd been just enough time to tell her how sorry he was and how much he loved her. She'd made him promise that no matter what happened, he wouldn't stop living. For their boys' sake, especially, that he not close himself off.

He ran a hand over his face wearily. It was the only time he'd ever consciously lied to her. But in that moment he'd have done anything, promised *anything*, to give her peace. Including the one thing he knew he couldn't do.

Love again.

"So, anyway, my point is that it doesn't make me an asshole because I'm not signing up for the whole 'til-death-do-us-part deal again. I just don't believe you can find that kind of connection more than once in a lifetime."

He looked at the ground, not meeting anyone's eyes. He couldn't stand the looks of pity. He was a composer, not a lyricist. He didn't have words to describe what it felt like to have the perfect family and then have it ripped in pieces. All he had were emotions that made him feel about as big as an ant and a sense of humor to keep his mind off the things he couldn't change.

He leaned closer to Matt. His friend clapped a hand on his shoulder, his expression grave. He almost hated to play a joke on him when he looked so serious, but this conversation was way too *kumbaya* for his taste. And joking around was easier than putting his emotions on a platter for everyone to rifle through.

"But I would definitely make an exception for your sister because she is fine as hell!"

He barely had time to duck when Matt swung on him this time, but hearing his friends laugh was worth a few blows.

"FINAL STOP—PORT OF NEW HAVEN!"

Ridley Wells leaned her forehead against the bus window and gazed at the boats bobbing in the water. The small shops lining the pier still had the same bright red awnings. Fat seagulls still swooped down from above, ready to waddle their way up and down the boardwalk begging for food. Everything looked exactly the same as it had the last time she'd been here. Fifteen years ago.

After waiting a few minutes so the other passengers could disembark, she grabbed her backpack and stepped down into the warm, briny air. She took a deep breath and closed her eyes, enjoying the cool breeze coming off the water.

She'd been traveling for two days and was more than ready to take a hot shower and sleep in a real bed. *If Raina doesn't slam the door in your face.* With her sister's temper, it was a distinct possibility.

"Is this your first trip to the peninsula, too?"

A middle-aged woman wearing a bright pink "Nowhere Like New Haven" tee shirt and a faded blue visor stood at her elbow. A group of other women, all wearing the same bright pink shirts, milled nearby chatting excitedly. *Tourists*, Ridley thought. Come to enjoy the beaches and the world-class seafood restaurants.

"No. I used to live here. A long time ago."

She smiled politely at the woman before walking past the others and pulling out her phone. She'd mapped out the distance from the New Haven bus station to her sister's house while on the road. Less than a mile away, it should be a relatively easy walk and a nice one. She hitched her backpack higher on her shoulder and set off to the south, toward the center of town.

The late-spring breeze carried the scent of saltwater and something slightly tangy like someone was having a clambake. It brought back memories of the two years she'd spent in New Haven in middle school. After years of moving around, an old friend of her mom's had told her about a waitressing position in the diner where she worked and offered to rent out her basement.

Ridley and her twin sister, Raina, were used to the schools in Washington, DC, so moving to some backwater town in southern Virginia seemed like banishment. Back then the town hadn't even had its own movie theater.

But their mom's friend, Miss Ruth, fixed up the basement so nicely it looked like something in one of the fancy design magazines Raina had always liked to flip through at the corner store. Their beds had been covered in pillows and not just the kind you slept on. Pretty little decorative ones with lace at the edges. Miss Ruth had told them she'd done the lace edging herself. It was the first time Ridley had realized everyone didn't live the way they did.

Her mother didn't do much after work that didn't involve a bottle.

They'd stayed there longer than just about anywhere else. Long enough for Ridley to get completely attached to Miss Ruth, her friends at school, and the sleepy little town itself. Driving away in their secondhand Buick had just about broken her heart.

College had become an obsession after that. If she had enough money, she could afford to make her own decisions. To make a place for herself somewhere, something no one could ever take away. Her sister had been just as driven. Raina had started modeling right after high school and never looked back. After years of working nonstop and traveling all over the world, she'd finally bought a house in the one place they'd lived that had felt like home. She'd sent Ridley a message containing her address, the security code, and a simple sentence.

You are always welcome.

Those four words had let her know that no matter what happened, her sister would always be there for her. When she'd found herself scared and in need of a place to stay, this had been the first place she'd thought to come. She'd always known she'd come back to New Haven at some point.

But not like this.

All she'd wanted was to locate her father. After her mother's death she'd become obsessed with finding the only family they had left. The private investigator she'd hired had *finally* gotten a lead. If only she'd pushed him to tell her what it was. Images of charred wreckage flashed through her mind and she shivered. She pulled the diamond pendant she'd been wearing since the accident from beneath her shirt and stroked it.

What had he found out that was bad enough to make someone sabotage his car?

Whoever it was had to have planned for him to die in the accident, but they probably hadn't counted on her witnessing the whole thing. She pulled back her sleeve to reveal the mottled bruises and scars on her forearms.

"You're just here to hide out until the police figure out what happened."

The officers working the case hadn't told her much, but she could tell something was up by what they hadn't said. When she'd asked directly, they couldn't tell her what she wanted to hear: that the accident was *truly* an accident. She planned to stay under the radar until they figured it out.

The arrow on her phone pointed to the left, so she turned onto the next street. An ornate, wrought-iron sign spelled out:

HAVENSBROOKE

Ridley walked past towering houses with lush, manicured lawns. Raina had been trying to convince her to move back to Virginia for ages and had claimed her new neighborhood was the perfect place for Ridley to launch her landscape-design business now that she was done with school. As she turned onto her sister's street, she gasped at the first sight of the house.

As girls, they'd always talked about what kind of homes they'd buy when they were rich and famous. It looked like her sister had managed to find a place that fit both their childhood dreams to perfection: a stately, three-story red brick with wide Palladian windows along the front.

"You really did it, Ray."

It made her sad that she hadn't been here when her sister

moved in. They'd always been there for each other during major milestones like this. Until recently.

Until David.

She knocked on the door and then rang the doorbell. It was completely quiet. Raina had told her there were two security panels but to use the one behind the house so she could get the spare key. As she climbed the stairs to the back deck, she peered through the rear window into the kitchen. There was a long, oak farmer's table covered with a cheerful, red gingham tablecloth. It looked cozy and inviting.

She walked over to the deck chair farthest from the door and squeezed the edges of its cushion until she felt a hard lump.

"Gotcha."

She unzipped the side of the cushion and rooted around until her fingers closed around the key. The alarm panel was mounted to the side of the door. She dropped her backpack on the deck and then punched in the security code. Three red lights flashed.

Access Denied.

"Okay. Let me try that again." She wiped her hand on the leg of her jeans and carefully typed the numbers in again.

Access Denied.

"Crap. I know I'm typing this right." She tugged her phone from her pocket and pulled up the e-mail from her sister. It was possible she'd forgotten something. It had been a few months since she'd gotten the note.

- - - - - - - - - - - - - - - - - -

From: Raina Winters
      (rwinters@modelco.net)
To: Ridley Wells (riri7@gigimail.com)
Subject: Just in case

- - - - - -

Here's my address:

1616 Crescent Drive
New Haven, Virginia 23665.

The security code is our birthday
(4 digits, the month and day).

You are always welcome.
xRaina

- - - - - - - - - - - - - - - - -

The message had been pretty straightforward, so Raina must have forgotten to tell her one of the steps. Her sister hadn't responded to any of her text messages and calls since she'd left two days ago.

Probably still mad at me, she reasoned. Not that she could blame her. Their last argument had been one for the record books.

"I guess I'm on my own."

She let out a breath and pulled out her cell phone again. It was getting close to lunchtime. It was already pretty humid and she wasn't even in direct sunlight. Her shirt clung to the damp skin between her breasts. She couldn't wait to take a shower.

As soon as she figured out how to get in the house.

Maybe she was supposed to hit the Enter button or something afterward. She walked back to the security panel and typed the code followed by Enter.

Access Denied.

"Great."

A door slammed next door and she shrank back out of sight as an older man came out on his back deck and walked around the yard. He looked over her way but didn't seem to notice her. After a few minutes, he went back in his house.

"How do I always get myself into these situations?"

This was the kind of neighborhood where everyone looked

like they belonged in a golf advertisement. Her rumpled tee shirt and well-worn jeans made her look like a reject from one of those Survivor-style reality programs. With her luck, her sister's neighbors would call the police if she hung out too long, and she'd had enough of dealing with the police to last her a lifetime.

She looked back at the yard. The house directly behind was just as imposing but made of a beige brick. There was a wide patio on the back and a gorgeous little gazebo. Their yards were separated by a small creek.

Water.

The grass was spongy beneath her feet as she crossed the lawn. Half-convinced she was imagining the sight like a delirious desert traveler; she dropped to her knees and cupped her hands in the cool, clear water.

Multicolored fish darted beneath her hands as she scooped up handful after handful and rinsed her face. She'd been traveling with single-minded determination and hadn't made many stops. A proper shower was going to feel like nirvana. Water dribbled down her chin and across the front of her shirt but she didn't even care. Nothing had ever felt so good.

"Hey, what are you doing?"

She whipped around. Two little boys watched her curiously from a few feet away.

"My daddy said we're having a cookout. That means I get hot dogs!" The older of the two boys spoke hurriedly, all his words running together in one large breath. The smaller boy just stood watching, his thumb bobbing up and down in his mouth as he sucked on it.

The oldest boy took a tentative step forward. He reached into his pocket and produced a ragged napkin, which he offered her with a hesitant smile.

She took it and used it to wipe the water from her face. "Thanks. A cookout sounds like fun. What's your name?"

"It's me. Chris." He frowned. "Are you okay?"

"Oh, I'm..." A wave of nausea made her double over.

She took a few deep breaths. After two days of constant travel, she needed to rest and eat something that didn't come wrapped in cellophane. She'd done her best to travel without leaving a trail but she was hardly a super spy. It was time to face reality. Whatever David had discovered had been enough to get him killed. If she didn't want to be next, she had to get it together and fast.

She would try the security code one more time and if it didn't work, she still had enough cash left to pay for a night at a hotel. Not the best plan, but it would do for now, at least keeping her out of sight until she could get in touch with Raina.

"I'm fine..." She stood and the world spun crazily.

Tiny squiggly lines passed through her vision. God, it was hot. *Why was it so hot?*

She dimly felt it when she hit the ground but there wasn't any pain. The last thing she saw was two tiny faces peering down at her.

Then everything went gray.

———

JACKSON MOVED his chair farther away from his friend. "I couldn't resist! If we sit around talking about our feelings too long someone's going to come and take my man card."

"Oh, that's right. I forgot you have an image to uphold. Mr. Big Shot Producer." Matt started clapping. The other guys chimed in and chanted his name.

He shook his head and then took a mock bow. It didn't bother him when they teased him about his sudden fame. They'd been with him since college when he was still using a closet as a makeshift recording studio. They'd earned the right to clown him a little.

"Daddy! Daddy! Miss Raina ate the fish!" His youngest son, Jase, ran up and jumped in his lap. "She's in the water!"

Jackson gazed down at his son affectionately. His sons were the best things that had ever happened to him and he knew his late wife had felt the same way. Cynthia had gotten pregnant their second year in college, derailing her plans to be a lawyer. She hadn't agreed that getting married was the best option, but the idea of only seeing his child on weekends and holidays had left him cold. He'd done everything he could to convince her that he was worth taking a chance on.

Cynthia had finally agreed after a lot of influence from her mother, and they'd been married in a civil ceremony at city hall as soon as the school year ended. They'd decided to have their second child shortly after the first so she wouldn't have to interrupt her schooling again later with another pregnancy.

They'd had their issues in the beginning, both too young and headstrong to have any idea how to navigate marriage and parenthood. But in the end, no matter what problems they'd had, raising their sons right had been the one thing they'd always agreed on.

Not everyone believed in the old-fashioned methods, but he wanted his boys to grow up with memories like the ones he had: playing outside with his brothers, eating dinner together as a family each night, and having respect for his elders. He intended to raise his kids the same way.

Even if he had to do it alone.

"Are you guys playing in Miss Raina's yard while she's out of town?"

Their newest neighbor, Raina, was a fashion model. She'd walked up one afternoon and introduced herself before inviting the boys to come see her fish. Jackson had been so stunned at first that he hadn't even responded. Most women who looked like Raina weren't overly fond of rambunctious, messy little boys.

That was something Jackson had learned through experience over and over again in recent years.

Raina, however, actually seemed to enjoy their energy. Once he'd recovered enough to give his consent, she'd answered the boys' million and one questions with aplomb as they walked to her yard. Most impressive of all, she didn't even blink when Jase jumped in the pond fully dressed, splashing them all in the process.

It was no surprise to him that both of his boys had become instantly fascinated with her. They had a new story about *Miss Raina* every other day it seemed.

"Yeah, Daddy. She ate the fish. Then she fell down." Jase put his thumb in his mouth and bounced excitedly in his lap.

Matt leaned closer. "Did he say she fell down? Wait, here comes Chris."

They watched as his oldest son, Christopher, came tearing across the yard. He skidded to a stop right in front of them.

"She won't wake up!" He took a deep breath, his chest heaving after his mad dash across the yard. "Miss Raina's hurt! She fell down and she won't wake up!"

Jackson got up and the other guys followed. Raina's yard wasn't directly behind his, rather two yards over and separated by a small creek. As soon as he got to the end of his yard though, he could see the small figure slumped on the ground.

"Look!" He pointed toward Raina's yard.

"There she is." Matt vaulted over the creek and Jackson followed. He could hear the other guys behind him and the kids shouting. By the time he reached Raina's yard, Matt already had his fingers on her pulse point.

"Her heartbeat is strong." He looked over his shoulder at Jackson. "She doesn't look like she's having any trouble breathing, either. But we should definitely call for an ambulance. People don't just pass out for no reason." Matt was a sergeant in the Army and trained in first aid, so Jackson was more than willing to trust his judgment.

Trent pulled his phone from his pocket. "I'll call 911."

Jackson knelt down next to Matt. "Look at her arms," he whispered.

Matt lifted her arm and pulled back her long sleeve to expose her skin. Bruises wrapped around her wrist, extending halfway up her arm.

"Is Miss Raina okay?" Chris's voice wobbled.

He turned around. Usually the boys were right underneath him, but even they could sense the gravity of the situation and were a few feet back, holding Nick's hands. When he caught his brother's eye, he was surprised to see that Nick looked deeply shaken.

"She's okay. Maybe you should take the boys back to the house."

Nick nodded mutely but didn't move. It was odd to see his usually jovial brother so disturbed. Although, if he was honest, he was disturbed as well.

Violence wasn't something they'd ever had to deal with. Seeing the effects on a woman he knew, even if it was only a casual acquaintance, made his stomach turn.

"Raina isn't even supposed to be in town. She told me just a few days ago that she'd be gone for two weeks straight. She had a bunch of modeling jobs booked in Asia. She seemed really excited about—"

Matt held up a hand and he halted mid-speech. "She's waking up."

They all watched as Raina turned on her side and exhaled a long, slow breath. When her eyes opened, they darted around wildly. When she noticed Matt right next to her, she started scrabbling backward.

"Easy, it's okay." Matt backed away.

She got to her knees and blinked rapidly.

"Raina?"

She held up a hand as if the sunlight was too bright. He wondered if she could even see them.

"It's Jackson. Are you okay?"

Her wide, brown eyes locked on his face. She stared at him for a minute, then glanced away before looking back. Then her lips curled up into a small smile.

His stomach dropped. The sensation was like falling while standing still.

Shock forced him to take a step back. He'd never had this reaction to Raina before, despite the fact that she was an extremely beautiful woman. When she was dressed impeccably and made up like she was going to a photo shoot, he'd only felt the general attraction that most red-blooded men feel around gorgeous women.

But in that moment, as her eyes held him captive, she was more beautiful than he'd ever seen her. With her hair wild and a streak of dirt on her cheek, all he could think was...

Wow.

two

RIDLEY HAD ALWAYS BEEN the good twin. The one who followed the rules. Her sister was the one who seduced, cajoled, and manipulated to get her way. She'd never understood why her sister did the things she did. Lying seemed like more work than just telling the truth.

So when she realized the man in front of her thought she was Raina, she knew what she needed to do. Correct him. Tell him who she was.

Then she looked at him and forgot all of it.

Good Lord, he's gorgeous.

He crouched down and met her gaze. "I'm sorry if we scared you. The kids saw you passed out in the grass. We've already called 911, so don't worry."

"No! You can't." Ridley jumped up, then swayed when another wave of dizziness hit her.

He caught her and lowered her back to the grass. "Don't try to stand yet. Just take it easy."

In that one instant, she understood her sister's dishonesties better than ever. Because she was willing to allow this man to think she was Raina if it meant she got more time with him treating her like this.

Like someone he cared about.

"I traveled overnight to get here and I must have been more tired than I thought. Please don't call for an ambulance. I'm fine."

Her voice failed and heat flooded to her face as she noticed all the people standing around watching. There was a man with a buzz cut on the ground near her. A blond man stood off to the side on a cell phone. The two boys she'd seen earlier were there, too. They were holding the hands of another man who looked a lot like the guy in front of her.

Jackson, he'd called himself.

Despite how bad she felt, all she could think was that she needed to stay under the radar. Her name in some sort of incident report was hardly incognito. If someone was looking for her, she wasn't going to make it that easy for them to find her.

"I thought you were supposed to be out of the country for two weeks?" Jackson asked. "Did something happen?"

Ridley sighed. That explained why no one had answered at her sister's house. The last time they'd talked had been a month ago and it hadn't ended well. Her sister had always been bossy but she'd been unreasonable lately. They'd both said things they shouldn't have and hadn't spoken since. She'd assumed that Raina was just ignoring her calls. But if she was out of the country, then she'd come all this way for nothing.

There was no one here to help her.

"Are you sure you're okay?" The guy with the buzz cut looked at her arms. She pulled her sleeves down further to cover the bruises on her wrists.

"Yeah, I was in a car accident. But I'm fine. I actually should be going." Something in the back of her mind warned her not to give out too much information. Being too trusting was how she'd gotten in her current situation in the first place.

"I'd really be more comfortable if we took you to the hospital."

Jackson gestured toward the one with the buzz cut. "Matt's trained as a medic but he's not a doctor."

"It's really not necessary. I'm slightly anemic and it's worse when I haven't been eating well. This isn't the first time I've fainted after skipping meals. I'm more embarrassed than anything."

He nodded once before turning and walking over to the man on the phone.

"Did I interrupt a party?" she asked.

Matt shrugged. "Not exactly. The actual party isn't until Monday. We just like coming over early to help out. Or to give Jackson a hard time. Both are fun."

Ridley smacked her forehead with her hand. "Oh, right. I forgot it was Memorial Day weekend. You're lucky to have such a big group of friends. I've only got..." She glanced back at the house and sighed.

"So, you just got back from a modeling job?"

She heard the disbelief and wasn't even offended by it. She'd never bothered with straightening her hair or wearing makeup anyway. Considering that she'd been traveling for the better part of the last two days and felt like hell, she was sure she looked nothing like a supermodel.

"Not exactly."

"Well, you're welcome to hang out with us. It's just us guys right now but my sister will probably come over later. Mainly because her new boyfriend is here, the blond guy over there, who happens to be one of my best friends." Matt's face twisted as he said it.

Ridley looked at him and couldn't think of anything to say other than "Oh. Well..."

"Yeah. That pretty much sums it up," Matt deadpanned.

She burst out laughing just as Jackson walked up. He looked

between the two of them curiously, which just made them break out into another round of laughter.

"Well, I've canceled the ambulance but we should at least get you inside and cleaned up." He held out a hand.

She hesitated a moment but then allowed him to pull her up. He was even better looking up close, all golden-skinned and masculine. She was suddenly hyper-aware that she was wearing a ragged old tee shirt and hadn't showered in the past twenty-four hours. After a few gentle tugs he released her hand, which she immediately tucked in her pocket.

"I can't. I'm locked out."

Jackson took her arm gently. "Well, that settles it. You'll come to my house."

Ridley looked between them awkwardly. "You're going to let me stay at your house?"

"Well, yeah." He looked at her strangely. "We're neighbors. In New Haven that means we're practically family. You can take one of the spare rooms upstairs and relax until a locksmith can make it."

Ridley watched, openmouthed, as Matt jogged over to the deck and picked up her backpack. She looked back at Jackson who stood patiently waiting. He didn't rush her or seem pissed that she was holding him up, either. He seemed to understand that she needed a moment.

What had seemed like a simple plan had turned into a tangled mess. Not that she'd thought her plan was perfect. Run and hide was about as far as she'd gotten. But now she was stranded, possibly being stalked, and her sister was clearly angrier than she'd suspected if she'd changed the security code. Her plan had taken a huge nosedive, and Jackson had unwittingly just offered her the perfect solution.

There was no better way to hide than in plain sight.

If she went to Jackson's house, she'd be completely off the grid.

It was a much better plan than checking into a hotel, at least until she got in contact with Raina. She'd be on her way before long and no one had to be the wiser. She could travel and leave no trail.

Going off with a stranger probably wasn't ideal, but he seemed so sincere, and Raina wouldn't be friends with this guy if he was an axe murderer, right? If she was lucky, Raina would call back tonight and then she'd be on her way. Raina was mad at her but she'd still help her until the police figured things out.

She hoped.

In the end she couldn't see any reason not to trust him.

"Okay," she said at last. "Lead the way." She followed the guys to a section where the creek was narrower and they took turns hopping over it. Then they walked down a couple of houses to a sprawling, white-brick colonial.

Holy cow.

She didn't have to worry about him having bad intentions toward her. Gorgeous men with this kind of money in the bank usually had more women than they could handle. Not that it mattered. This wasn't a social call. She was staying just long enough to get some sleep, charge her phone, and get in contact with her sister. Then she was gone.

We're practically family.

She ignored the thrill those words made her feel. The only family she had was a father she'd never met and a sister who was halfway around the world. These were hardly normal circumstances and, even if they were, the last thing she had time for was a handsome man.

Especially since the last one she'd liked had ended up dead.

———

AFTER SHOWING Raina to a guest room, Jackson retrieved his cell phone from his office. He'd had his security company on speed dial ever since his youngest son had gotten tall enough to reach the door handle. He'd been locked out plenty of times.

Although he doubted anyone would be willing to come out on a holiday weekend without charging an outrageous amount, it was still worth calling. The Raina Winters he knew probably wouldn't even blink at the price. She no doubt spent thousands a month just on the fancy clothes she usually wore.

You're going to let me stay at your house?

Not that she wasn't usually polite, but she'd seemed stunned and incredibly grateful at the offer. He softened, remembering the look on her face. Why was she having this effect on him now? They'd been neighbors for almost six months. His boys adored her and she was always very friendly, but he'd never felt anything more than passing interest. But she'd seemed different. Approachable, even. Which was dangerous, in more ways than one.

He hit the last speed dial on his phone and waited as it rang. As expected, it went to voice mail.

"Hey, Len, it's Jackson Alexander. One of my neighbors is locked out. You're probably out of town for the long weekend but if not, let me know. She's staying with me in the meantime. Thanks."

He called a few other companies for good measure, then tucked his phone in his pocket. All they could do now was wait. It was a long shot, hoping that anyone would be able to come out on a holiday, but the alternative was spending the long weekend with a supermodel. Raina Winters was the kind of woman he usually stayed far away from.

After the dark year following Cynthia's death, his friends had pushed him headfirst into the singles scene, determined to draw him out of his depressed state. He'd gone out with singers, actresses, athletes, and socialites. Blondes, brunettes, and every shade in between. Curvy and slender, feisty and giggly, he'd been on a mission to feast on all the female delights he'd missed out on by marrying young.

Somehow, he'd thought if he could bury himself in female attention, he could forget that the only woman he wanted was gone forever.

Then he'd met Alana. She'd seemed like everything he could want in a woman: sexy, talented, and ambitious. A jazz singer, she'd been someone he could talk to about the business and bounce around his ideas about producing a new kind of album. She'd been excited about the project and even volunteered to sing. When she'd started pressuring him for more of his time and commitment, he'd actually felt guilty that he couldn't give her what she needed.

Until the day he found her ass-up over his assistant's desk. In the end, Alana wasn't special. She was just another singer looking for her big break and she'd been willing to do whatever or *whoever* it took to get there. They'd broken up, but he'd learned a valuable lesson. He'd been in love with a fantastic woman once and the odds of it happening for him again were somewhere between "not gonna happen" and "a snowball's chance in hell."

Since then he'd only dated women who knew the score and had just as much to lose as he did. Starlets who needed someone on their arm for a film premiere and models who needed an escort who wasn't prettier than they were.

But in that moment, when he'd seen Raina on the ground with those big wounded eyes aimed at him, he'd experienced an almost startling sensation of *longing*. In the past three years no other woman had tempted him to break his no-strings rule. And none had roused the instinct to comfort and protect. Until now. Until Raina.

Which meant she *really* had to go.

He walked down the hall to his sons' room where Nicholas was helping Chris with one of his toys.

"Daddy, look at what Uncle Nick did. He fixed my robot. It lights up and everything!" Chris held up a toy that had been broken for weeks.

Jackson looked at his brother, shocked. "I've been trying to fix that one for ages. What did you do?"

Nicholas grinned. "I hit it. Hard."

Chris picked up the toy and flew it around the room making beeping noises.

"Figures."

His phone chirped and he pulled it out to see there was a message. "Hopefully this is the locksmith."

He hit the button to play his messages.

BEEP

"Um, yes, hello. This is Linda Taylor-Whiting. I'm scheduled to interview for the nanny position this afternoon." She paused and cleared her throat a few times. "I was reading the agency's notes on your children and it mentioned that one of your boys particularly likes insects. I'm not sure I would be the best candidate in this circumstance."

Jackson shook his head as she stumbled through an apology before hanging up. He'd been blessed for years because Cynthia's mother had been able to care for the boys during the day. But she'd recently gotten remarried and moved to Massachusetts.

The boys hadn't made it easy to find a replacement for the grandma they adored. He was proud of his children but also completely aware that they weren't choirboys. Between Chris's penchant for playing practical jokes and Jase's current fascination with insects, they definitely didn't make his task any easier. He hadn't met a woman yet who could deal with them for more than a few hours at a time.

"Damn. Another nanny bites the dust."

He just needed someone who could watch the boys during the afternoons while he was working, at least through the summer.

Once the school year started, Chris would be in kindergarten and Jase would be in preschool. He'd be able to get by on his own then. Of course in an ideal world he'd find a caregiver he could retain all year, maybe even one who could also run errands, such as grocery shopping, for him.

Nicholas looked up. "You *still* can't find a nanny?"

"Every time I think I have a candidate there's a catch. The first one was excellent at running a household, but stiff with the boys. She didn't even last a whole day. The one after her was more interested in baby-sitting *me* than the kids. Her skirt barely covered her ass."

He knew that type and avoided it like the plague. Gold diggers and groupies were a part of life in the music business, but he'd learned his lesson about needy women. His ex-girlfriend had made sure of that.

He hadn't realized when he started looking for nannies how difficult it would be or that there were women who'd apply for the job hoping to catch his eye. If he had, he would have asked his mother to handle screening the candidates.

Although, considering how much his mother wanted him to remarry, that might not have been the wisest plan either.

"Then there were the two after that who looked more like convicted felons than Mary Poppins. Now we have the one I was *sure* was perfect, who was scheduled for this afternoon, but she just canceled." He hung his head in defeat.

Nicholas shook his head in sympathy. "I don't envy you. Unless you need someone to interview the ones with the short skirts? No? Okay, well just keep me in mind."

Jackson clapped his hands until he had both boys' attention. "Aren't we having fun with Uncle Nick? As a matter of fact, who wants to spend the night at Uncle Nicholas's house?" Jackson asked in a singsong voice.

Jase, who'd been watching his brother from his perch on the

bed, took his thumb out of his mouth and yelled, "Me, Me, Me!" while Chris danced in the background in excitement.

Nicholas shot him an evil look. "Seriously? I have a date tonight. And she is…" He cut a glance at the two boys watching them avidly. "Constructed like a solid outdoor restroom facility."

Jackson crinkled his brow in confusion and then almost choked with laughter at his brother's child-friendly version of *built like a brick shithouse*. It took him a few minutes to compose himself before he could answer.

"Well, I'm going to be busy tonight and I'd feel better if the boys were with someone I trust. You can just bring them back when you come on Monday for the cookout."

His brother laughed knowingly and slapped him on the back. "I was starting to get worried about you for a minute there, but I should have known you had plans for later. The player is back!"

Jackson grabbed him by the arm and pulled him into the hallway.

"Nick, I'm not talking about a date. Raina's here, remember?"

"So? You don't think she's trying to hook up with you, do you?"

Jackson narrowed his eyes. "Even if she was, so what? I know *you* aren't going to give me a lecture on morality. What are you always telling me?"

Nick pretended to think for a minute. "That I'm the better-looking brother and you'll never surpass me?"

"Something is wrong with you. Can you take the boys or not?"

"Sure, I'll take the kids. Just stay away from Raina. She was hitting on *me* the last time I saw her. She doesn't care where she gets it from as long as the guy is rich."

"Would you keep your voice down? She'll hear you."

Jackson glanced down the hall at the closed guest room door. He'd shown Raina to the room an hour ago and hadn't heard a peep from her since. She was probably sleeping, but still. They weren't far from her room and his brother wasn't exactly being quiet.

"Whatever. Stacey might not even mind if we just hang out at the arcade or something so the boys can play. Think it'll get me brownie points for being such a good uncle?" He wiggled his eyebrows suggestively.

"Well, it can't hurt."

"Come on, guys. Grab your stuff. We're going to the arcade," Nick called.

Jackson went into the boys' closet and pulled out a small backpack for Jase. He put his favorite pajamas in it, a handful of training pants and three sets of clothes, just in case he had an accident. "Jase, remember to use the potty at Uncle Nick's house. Okay, little man?"

Jase nodded solemnly at him without removing his thumb from his mouth.

"Yes, please do. Because Uncle Nick hates changing diapers." Nick sent Jackson a foul look before turning to help Chris put his stuff into a duffel bag.

Jackson hugged Jase and then Chris, running his hands over their tight curls affectionately. All his brothers and his parents took the boys overnight regularly so he knew they'd have a good time. It gave the boys a fun night out and it gave him a much needed break. It was a luxury that many single parents didn't have. He was so lucky to have his family nearby to help him and he appreciated them more than they knew.

"Okay little guys, let's roll."

Chris raced down the hallway while Jase followed quietly, clutching his Elmo backpack tightly to his chest.

Nicholas gave him a mock salute. "I'll leave you to do your good deed. Just remember what I said about Raina. Don't let her get her hooks into you. That girl is a vulture."

"HI."

Ridley watched as Jackson spun around. Her fingers tightened around the bag of laundry she'd taken from her backpack. She'd been about to come ask him if he minded her using his washing machine when she'd opened the door and overheard his conversation with his brother. Not that they'd been trying to be quiet.

The player is back!... She was hitting on me the last time I saw her. She doesn't care where she gets it from as long as the guy is rich.... That girl is a vulture.

Asshole.

In a way it was almost a relief to know that her initial assessment had been correct. In her experience, people weren't nice for no reason. Plenty of guys thought nailing a supermodel was something to brag about. But why would his brother be warning him away from her? Unless Jackson and her sister had some sort of history. Maybe they'd dated previously and his brother didn't approve? Well, if Jackson thought he was getting in her pants this weekend he was in for a rude surprise.

Or a swift kick in the balls.

"You said to make myself at home, so I thought I could throw a few things in the laundry, if you don't mind." It took everything inside her not to throw the bag at his head.

"Of course. Feel free to use whatever you need. It's not as ritzy as what you're used to, I'm sure. I've been here a year but I haven't really gotten everything organized yet."

"I don't need ritzy. Contrary to what most people think, models don't just show up for a few hours, get paid and then go party. You're holding weird positions for long periods of time and call times are at the butt-crack of dawn to get the best light."

Ridley stopped and took a deep breath. Correcting people's stereotypes about modeling wasn't something she normally bothered with, but after hearing his brother call her sister a vulture, she was already on edge.

You don't have to like this guy. You're just using him for his air-conditioning.

Jackson held up his hands in surrender. "Sorry, I didn't mean to imply you don't work hard. I've seen a few of your billboards lately. You're becoming a household name."

Ridley nodded, her hostility meter going down a few notches. "Thanks. It's what I've been working toward for years."

Even though they hadn't been as close lately, nothing could stop her pride at her sister's success. She'd been there in the early years when Raina had done ads for toothpaste and painkillers. She'd been disappointed along with her when she'd been turned down for casting call after casting call because she wasn't the "All-American" girl they were looking for. Code for "not blonde enough."

Women of color had always had a hard time in the modeling industry and Raina had been no exception. However, instead of accepting it, she'd done something unprecedented. While living in Washington, D.C., she'd started a style blog called "Legs" and modeled clothing for small fashion designers for free. Every week she'd featured an outfit by a different designer and then shown photos of herself wearing it on the streets and to trendy restaurants. Before long her blog had a cult following, and everyone wanted to know what she was wearing.

The modeling industry hadn't wanted her initially, so she'd gone out and created her own niche. People looked at Raina as just another model but the truth was she was an entrepreneur. An incredibly savvy one, at that.

He leaned against the wall and crossed his arms. "So, you canceled your latest shoot?"

"Yeah, I was in a car accident. I needed a break anyway." It was as good an explanation as any. Her shoulders slumped. She could hardly tell people she was in town hiding out. "People staring and taking pictures can get old, you know?"

"Really?"

When she raised her eyebrows he backed up a step. "Sorry, I just can't imagine having that kind of opportunity and turning it down. I wish someone would just offer me money for being pretty. I wouldn't have bothered with college!"

"So, I guess I shouldn't have gone to school either, huh? I guess all that time learning was wasted." She glared at him.

"No, of course not. I just meant—" He stopped and ran a hand through his hair. "Wow, can we start over? I've done nothing but put my foot in it today. Let's pretend we're just meeting. Hi, it's nice to meet you. I'm Jackson; my friends call me Jack or J. Or jackass, depending on who you ask." He smiled slowly, the type of grin that probably had women throwing their panties at him.

Ridley just sighed. "Nice to meet you, Jackson."

He gestured toward her. "And you are?"

"Seriously?"

"Come on, play along."

Ridley crossed her arms. "Okay. Hi, I'm Raina. You can call me Raina."

His lips twitched at the corners. "Okay, then. You know what? The locksmith probably won't call back for a while, so we might as well just hang out. We've been neighbors for months now but we've never had a chance to just sit and talk like this. I don't have much to snack on but I'm sure we can find something suitably unhealthy to eat while you tell me your story. The *real* one, not the tabloid version."

Ridley raised her chin. "Who says I have a story?"

"Everyone has a story. I'll tell you mine if you tell me yours," he teased.

"I don't think I need to know yours."

"Okay, suit yourself. I'm going to go get some work done then.

But if you change your mind, I'm ordering takeout around six." He turned and walked away.

Just before he turned the corner she called out, "Fine. I'll eat your takeout. After all, that's what vultures do, right?"

As he turned and stared at her, she grinned and walked back to the guest room.

The laundry could wait.

three

AN HOUR LATER, Jackson had made a sizable dent in his to-do list for the party the next day. The Alexander family had always held a get-together on Memorial Day weekend, but it used to be held at his parents' farm. It wasn't until after his wife died that his mother made the request to have it at Jackson's place.

It was her way of keeping him from withdrawing from the world, something he'd been all too happy to do after Cynthia passed. However, it took an iron will to resist his mother when she wanted something, so he'd been hosting for the past three years. This would be the first year in his new house.

It was also the first year he was actually looking forward to it.

An image of Raina sitting in her backyard, looking so lost and alone entered his mind. If he ever got locked out he'd have plenty of people to call. His parents, his brothers, and a whole slew of cousins. He couldn't imagine not having anyone to help him out. Having a big family wasn't something he'd ever given much thought to but after today... Well, he was suddenly really aware of how much easier his life was because of his family.

He groaned thinking of all the ways he'd put his foot in his mouth around her. Not only had she heard Nick call her a vulture, but then he'd implied that beautiful women didn't need to be smart.

It was no wonder she'd walked off.

He was so distracted that the shrill ring of his cell phone on the desk next to him set his teeth on edge. He grabbed the phone, cursing as the pile of invoices under the device scattered across the floor.

"Jackson Alexander."

"You are gonna love me for this one. I'm a genius. Tell me I'm a genius!"

"You're a genius, Mac. Now why the hell are you calling me? Aren't you supposed to be finding a group for the song we're working on?"

He stooped to pick up the papers off the floor, sure that his assistant was off task as usual. Some people thought he was crazy for keeping him around after the debacle with Alana but Jackson believed in loyalty. They'd been friends for years and Mac claimed nothing had happened between him and Alana. Jackson believed him.

The fact that he'd witnessed his friend pushing her away before they knew he was there helped considerably.

"That's why I'm calling. I found a group that's perfect. They're all gorgeous—well, most of them—and even better, they're local." Leave it to Mac to be more interested in the length of their legs than the quality of their voices.

"Can they at least sing? The last time I heard a group you found, only one member could even carry a tune."

Jackson winced at the memory of the pitiful group trying to sing *a cappella*. They had all looked like cover models, which was reason enough for Mac to be interested. Jackson couldn't hold it against him, though. Except for his obsession with beautiful women, Michael MacCrane was the hardest-working assistant Jackson had ever had and also a good friend.

He'd just learned not to trust the man's instincts when it came to young female singers.

"I'm telling you, Jack, these girls have voices like angels. But hey, you don't have to take my word for it. Girls, sing a few bars for the boss." There was a rustling sound as if Mac had put the phone down before he heard someone clear their throat.

It was just a simple rendition of the jazz tune, "Cry Me a River," but when they were done, Jackson pumped his fist in the air.

This was the break he had been waiting for.

———

RIDLEY ROLLED OVER AND YAWNED. Napping had seemed like a good idea at the time, but she was too anxious to sleep for more than a few minutes here and there, so now she was tired *and* groggy. She reached over to the nightstand where she'd left her cell phone charging.

Still no messages.

"Come on, Raina. I really need you to call back." She blew her hair out of her face and sighed. It was time to consider the possibility that Raina wasn't going to get in touch, but they'd never been mad at each other this long before.

Their relationship had been strained ever since she'd decided to look for their father. Their mother had been only too glad to tell them as girls what a good-for-nothing their father was, and how getting herself saddled with two kids was the worst mistake of her life. She'd adored their mother, but she hadn't been the easiest person to love, even when you were trying. She could understand why Raina didn't want to meet their other parent when the one they'd grown up with had made them so miserable.

But Ridley couldn't help hoping maybe their father was different. Maybe he *did* want them. Maybe she'd finally find the family she'd been wishing for her whole life. Not that all her wishing had done her any good.

If she had to be locked out, this was a pretty nice place to be, but she still wanted to get to her sister's house. Imposing on family was one thing—imposing on a perfect stranger was an entirely different matter altogether. Especially when the guy in question was sort of a jerk.

Now that he knew she'd overheard him and that his chances of getting her in bed were nonexistent, he was probably more than ready for her to leave. Having her here was sure to cramp his style when one of his girlfriends came over. Although if his brother was to be believed, he didn't have many girlfriends.

"There has to be something I can do." The waiting was going to drive her insane. She hated feeling helpless. She sat up and picked up her phone. A few taps later, the contact information for Agent Ian Graham was displayed on her screen. Her thumb hesitated over the number for a moment before she tapped it to initiate the call. It rang three times before she heard his gravelly voice.

"Agent Graham? It's Ridley Wells."

"Good to hear from you, Miss Wells. I've been trying to get in touch with you. Are you out of town?"

"Just for the weekend. Why?"

"I'm finishing up the accident report." He cleared his throat. "We've been trying to get a clearer picture of what your friend was doing in the days leading up to his death. You said he was a private investigator, right?"

"Yes. I hired him to do a search for my father."

"How much did he charge?"

Ridley frowned. "He charged by the hour. Usually about a hundred unless it required surveillance. So far, he hadn't needed to do that. He was mainly looking through paperwork, I think. I know he pulled my mom's credit history. He was trying to figure out exactly where she was living and who she had contact with around the time of my conception."

"Did he seem to be having money problems?"

"I didn't think so, but I'm not really sure. Why are you asking all these questions? What does this have to do with his car accident?"

"We're not sure. We noticed some unusual activity in the past month and thought you might be able to help us put the pieces together."

"I wouldn't know anything about his financial situation."

"You didn't wire him fifty thousand last week?"

"Fifty thousand? Uh, no. I don't have that kind of money," Ridley stated.

"Miss Wells, I don't want to alarm you but I'm sure you've figured out by now that the FBI isn't usually involved in cases like these."

"Please tell me what's going on."

"Mr. Finemore was spotted with a person of interest in one of my cases. Alberto Moreno. The FBI has been monitoring Mr. Moreno for years. He's suspected of arms dealing, racketeering, drug trafficking, you name it."

"Moreno? As in the Moreno crime family?" Ridley squeaked.

"Yes. I'm something of an expert on the Morenos, which is why I was asked to assist with Mr. Finemore's case. He met with Moreno the day before his death. Do you have any idea why?"

"Maybe he was doing investigative work for them?"

Agent Graham grunted. "If he was doing work for the Morenos it definitely wasn't legal. Look, I know Mr. Finemore was a friend of yours, but whatever he got himself into got him killed. You were the last person to see him alive. Somehow, you were also the first person at the scene of the accident."

He stopped speaking abruptly. Ridley had the distinct feeling that he hadn't meant to say that last part.

"What exactly are you implying, Agent Graham? You don't think I had anything to do with this, do you?"

"I didn't mean that. We just want to figure out what's going on before anyone else gets hurt. When will you be back in town?"

"I don't know. I'll call you back." Ridley hung up and immediately turned her phone off.

She dragged in a ragged breath, her heart beating so hard she couldn't hear anything else over the sound. It was tempting to pretend she'd never called Agent Graham. To go on ignoring the signs that had been there since the beginning.

Hadn't she thought it odd that an FBI agent would be involved in something as simple as a car accident? Now she could no longer ignore the obvious—she was in way over her head. Maybe she should have told Agent Graham that David had come to see her right before the accident. Not that she could see how that would make any difference.

Especially since he already suspected her of killing her friend.

If David had found evidence that Moreno was her father, he would have tried to verify it. But it was doubtful that he would have told Moreno directly of his suspicions. If she could stay off the grid for a while, there was a good chance that Moreno's people would never know what he really suspected. If she was lucky, they would never know that he might have a daughter. *Daughters*, she corrected. After all, this wasn't just about her.

It had been big news in Florida when the Morenos' only son had died. No wonder David had told her to lie low. If he'd suspected her father was a Moreno, then he wasn't just being paranoid when he'd told her he was on to something dangerous. He'd been trying to protect her.

Now he was dead, and if whoever killed him had followed her here, she'd led them right to her sister. If Moreno found her, it wouldn't be long before he found Raina, too.

She and her sister might be his only surviving children.

I have to get out of here.

After pulling her cell charger from the wall, she stuffed it in her backpack and made sure it was zipped securely. The thought of someone following her here, possibly hurting her sister or Jackson, made her sick to her stomach. It was a stupid idea to come here. All she'd done was bring trouble to her sister's doorstep. She was the one who'd wanted to find their father. This was her mess.

No one else deserved to be dragged into the maelstrom of her life.

The day hadn't been a total waste because at least she'd been able to rest for a bit and charge her phone. It seemed petty to leave without saying anything to Jackson, but it was probably easier this way. No explanations. No goodbyes.

Business as usual.

———

"THIS WAY, Raina! Give us that famous smile, sweetheart!"

"Come on, Legs. Just one shot."

Early Sunday morning, Raina Winters strutted past the horde of paparazzi camped out in front of the Fullerton Hotel, her security team surrounding her like a moving wall of muscle. Her agent had booked her on back-to-back appearances and photo shoots, so she didn't even have time to enjoy the picturesque hotel with its charming views of the Singapore River. The only thing she would see for the next two weeks unrelated to work was her hotel room, the back of her security chief's tee shirt, and the inside of her limo. But it would be worth it to get the first real vacation she'd had since she started modeling.

"Come on, Leggy! Give us a money shot."

The paparazzo who yelled out was one of the regulars who followed her from city to city. He was just as annoying as all the others, but at least he sold good shots of her. Unlike the greasy pig who'd deliberately gotten down low to take a crotch shot when she was exiting her limo after a night of partying last year. He'd made her look like she'd been completely wasted and showed her thong on purpose. Anyone would look like they were flashing their underwear if they had someone kneeling in front of them taking a picture!

"Just one, Sam," she murmured.

Samuel Gannon, her chief of security, turned back to her and nodded. He motioned for the other security guards to flank her, preventing the photographers from getting too close.

She turned to the side, lowered her chin, and flashed a wide smile. A blinding flurry of flashbulbs went off as the group scrambled to take shots before she whipped around and ducked into her limo. A second later Sam and two other security agents followed. The rest would trail them in a second limo. She only needed this much security when traveling and she couldn't deny that it was weird having so many people following her around.

In the beginning she'd tried to keep current on who was guarding her and would chat with them, ask about their families. As time went on and her need for additional security grew, it became too difficult to keep track. Sam had been with her since the beginning and she trusted his judgment.

That had to be good enough.

"This morning you have another shoot for..." Sam consulted the clipboard he held. "La Fleur. The skin-care company. Then this afternoon we have the layout for the energy drink."

"Vitamin supplement."

Sam smirked. "Whatever you want to call it."

She pulled her cell phone from her purse and turned it on. She'd been so exhausted the night before she'd shut it off before falling into bed. As it powered up, she looked out the window of the limo as they inched through the crowded streets of central Singapore. People lined the streets, their garments a kaleidoscope of colors. A bike passed by the limo so closely she wouldn't be surprised if he'd taken the paint off the door.

It was controlled chaos and she wished she could stop the limo and go wading in the sea of people. For once, she'd like to actually experience and enjoy a city while she was there. But she was booked solid for the next two days. Then she was off to the Bahamas for her first shoot with *Sports Illustrated.*

It was everything she'd been working toward for the last five years. The only thing she hadn't gotten yet was a major sponsorship deal. Her agent was working on a possible contract with a lingerie company, but she wouldn't agree unless she was going to be treated like a star.

If they weren't going to give her a pair of diamond-studded wings, then it wasn't worth her time.

The screen of her phone flashed and she swiped her thumb over the face to view her log of missed calls. Her sister Ridley had tried to reach her several more times. It was probably time she stopped avoiding her. This was the longest they'd ever gone without speaking since they'd had a crush on the same boy in high school.

"Oh crap."

Sam looked up from the printed schedule he was reviewing. "What? Is everything okay?"

"I'm not sure. My sister came to see me and I forgot to tell her I changed the security code."

"Oh, you mean the pathetically obvious security code that I made you change a month ago?" His deep laugh sounded more like the growl of an irritable bear. "Who uses their birthday?"

She gritted her teeth. "Whatever. The point is my sister is locked out. I'm so glad Jackson was home. At least I know she's safe with him."

Sam frowned. "What do we know about this guy?"

Raina rolled her eyes and pulled up Ridley's contact information so she could call her back.

"His boys come over and play in my yard all the time. He's a music producer, a single dad, and a real sweetheart. Any man who loves his momma that much is okay in my book. Ridley is probably safer with him than she would be staying at my house all alone. I was actually hoping to introduce them at some point, anyway. He's just the kind of guy my sister *needs* to be involved with, unlike the losers she normally picks. He's handsome, successful, and most importantly, rich."

She heaved a breath. "I'm really happy my sister came but man, this timing sucks. I've been trying to get in with *Sports Illustrated* forever. I can't miss this shoot."

"Why would you need to go home? Can't you just call your sister and give her the code?" Sam asked.

"I don't want her to be alone. I can barely understand her messages but she sounds like she's been crying. All I can hear is 'David's gone,' so it sounds like she broke up with her new boyfriend, who was more than a little weird in my opinion. I told her he sounded like a scam artist, but at least this one didn't last long—" She stopped suddenly, tracing her thumb over the screen of her phone. Ridley's number was still displayed.

"What?"

"Nothing, it's just... I *could* have not checked my messages this morning. That's possible, right?"

"Raina," Sam warned.

"What! I'm just saying this time change is huge. Killer. It's actually still Saturday evening back home. I could have been so tired that I shut my phone off last night and forgot to turn it back on this morning. Even if I remembered around lunchtime, well... It would be too late to call the East Coast then because it would be midnight there." Her lips curled up in a small smile.

"You have that look," Sam drawled. When she narrowed her

eyes at him, he clarified. "The look you get when you're about to do something you *know* you shouldn't. Which usually means I'll have a mess to clean up afterward."

"Don't worry, Sam. This is one mess that you won't have to deal with." Raina bit her lip. "Besides, I'm not actually going to do anything. It's more what I'm *not* going to do."

Sam didn't look mollified. "Are you going to ask your sister to join you in the Bahamas?"

"I am *not*." She grinned. "She's finally around the kind of guy she deserves to be with. I think she should stay exactly where she is."

———

THE ALARM on the wall of his study beeped. Jackson looked up. The system always sounded a warning when a door or window was opened. Something he considered a necessary precaution with two young children in the house.

He stood and strode to the window. Damn, he hadn't realized how late it had gotten. Some host he was. He'd mentioned ordering takeout to Raina, but it was already after seven o'clock. It would probably make more sense to take her into town and pick up something. Just then, he saw a blur of color at the edge of the yard. Raina was walking down his driveway with her backpack over her shoulder.

"Where is she going?" He watched as she looked down at something in her hand before turning left. She didn't look back.

Shit.

"Well, what did you expect?" He cursed under his breath and grabbed his keys off the edge of his desk.

Outside, he waited as his garage door opened with agonizing slowness. Once he was on the street, he gunned his engine.

Normally driving the convertible BMW was a pleasure. Today, he only cared that it was fast.

After he left his street he took a right onto Havensbrooke Drive and pressed his foot harder on the accelerator. Several of his neighbors raised a hand in greeting as he passed by, but he didn't slow down. As he approached the stoplight at the entrance to his community, he cursed. How could she have gotten so far ahead of him on foot? A horn honked behind him and he looked up to see that the light was green. He also saw a small figure turning right on the main road.

"Gotcha."

He pulled the wheel all the way to the right, cutting off the car that was about to make the turn. He ignored the chorus of honking horns behind him as he passed Raina and parked on the first side street he came to. He jumped out and jogged back to where she stood squinting at the small screen of her phone. When she heard him approach, she looked up absently.

"Excuse me, do you know where..." Her voice trailed off as she met his eyes.

"I'm sure I do but I'm not going to tell you. Why are you walking? Why didn't you just take one of your cars? Oh wait, if you're locked out you don't have your keys. Right. Where are you going anyway?"

She sighed and put her phone back in her pocket. "What does it matter?"

"Well, I was about to order dinner for myself and a guest until I realized said guest left without even saying goodbye."

She flushed slightly before squaring her shoulders. "Look, it's not going to happen."

"What's not going to happen?"

"Don't pretend. You know I overheard you talking to your brother. You've made your feelings pretty clear; you think all pretty girls are attention whores who are lucky enough to get paid for letting people take their picture."

He cringed at the word *whore* but didn't interrupt.

"And, you know what? That's fine because maybe I don't think much of pretty boys who talk about women as if we're all just vaginas with legs. Either way, I am not sleeping with you. So you can keep your fake sympathy. I'll just be on my way." She brushed past him and continued walking.

He jogged after her again.

"Please, wait. I know I've given you nothing but the worst possible impression of me today. But I guarantee you there are things about me that will surprise you."

"I highly doubt that." She pulled out her phone again, pointedly ignoring him.

"Hey! I'm a very nice person. I pay my taxes. I've never been arrested."

"Good for you." She didn't stop walking.

"You already know that I'm a musician," he added.

"Let me guess, you're kind of a big deal? Get over yourself."

Jackson scowled and sped up until he was walking next to her. "How can you think I'm this much of a jerk? Most single fathers don't have time to do jerky things."

Raina stopped walking so suddenly that her backpack swung off her shoulder and bumped against her thigh. "Wait, you're the guy..."

"What?" Jackson asked.

"Nothing." She swung her bag over her shoulder again but at least she'd stopped running away. "It's hard to believe you're the father of those adorable little boys. I used to tell people what a nice guy you were."

"Usually I am. Today, I am clearly not myself."

"Okay, well, whatever. I know I've said things I was ashamed of later, and Lord knows I put my foot in my mouth more than it's on the ground. That doesn't change anything. I seem to attract trouble and I don't want to bring that down on you or anyone else."

He shaded his eyes with his hand. "Are you in trouble, Raina?"

She looked away for a moment before her eyes met his again. "I don't know. I figure staying out of sight is a good idea though. Just in case."

He looked back at the road. There wasn't much traffic but they were definitely attracting attention. A blue sedan slowed down as it passed. Jackson lifted a hand in a friendly wave.

"Look, I don't know the situation, but the idea of you running off alone doesn't sit right with me. Hiding out at my place would be better than just taking off with no plan at all."

Raina closed her eyes, her exhaustion so palpable that he knew he'd won.

"Staying does have a certain appeal."

He turned back to his car, parked haphazardly at the curb behind them. "Let's go back. At the least you can sleep on it and then make a decision in the morning with a clear head."

After a moment, she turned toward the car. He opened the door for her and she sank into the luxurious leather interior. He closed the door gently and went around to the driver's side. Once he started the car, she turned her head toward him.

"Just so you know, you didn't win that argument. I'm just too tired to fight anymore."

He put the car in gear before glancing at her. "Believe me, beautiful, I know that. Let's save the fight for tomorrow."

"Okay." She leaned her head back and looked out the window.

The next time Jackson looked at her, she was sound asleep.

four

RIDLEY WOKE Sunday morning to a soft tapping sound.

It took her a moment to remember where she was. Gorgeous antique furniture. Silky-soft sheets. She definitely wasn't at home. The tapping sound started again. She turned her head toward the door.

"Raina? Are you awake?"

The deep voice coming through the door brought it all back. The accident. Agent Graham. Jackson. She pulled the pillow over her head and groaned.

"Raina?"

She threw the covers back. "Just a second!"

After a last-ditch attempt to tame the flyaway strands around her face, she went to the door and yanked it open. Jackson jumped back at the sudden movement.

"Good morning. I was coming to see if you were hungry. You crashed pretty hard last night." His eyes took in her sleep-creased face and wild hair.

I dare you to say something, thought Ridley.

"But if you aren't ready, that's fine. I can wait." He backed up a step.

She sighed. She must look truly feral if he was already backpedaling.

"No, I just need to brush my teeth and I'll be down. Thanks." She closed the door softly and grabbed her backpack. She carried it into the bathroom and pulled out her toothbrush. While she brushed her teeth, she inspected her face in the mirror. God, it was even worse than she thought. Not only did she still have creases from the pillow in her cheek but the eyelashes on her right side were stuck together, making her look like she was cross-eyed.

Sigh.

"A femme fatale you are not."

Ten minutes later, she crept down the staircase and stood in the middle of the biggest family room she'd ever seen. A huge wraparound sectional took up one wall and the other was dominated by a massive flat-screen television. Despite the bounty of electronics, the room still retained an airy comfort, probably because everything was a different shade of cream or gold.

There was a piano in the corner and she wandered over. To her surprise, instead of the usual book of classics, there were loose pages of sheet music. She picked one up. The lines and notes appeared to have been drawn in pencil.

"Raina?"

She whirled around, the sheet music drifting to the floor at her feet. Jackson stood in the doorway. He held a spatula in his hands.

"There you are. I'm in the kitchen."

Guiltily, she knelt and gathered the pages from the floor and placed them back on the piano. She wanted to ask about them but figured if she did, then he might decide to ask her questions, too. Lying sucked but it was a necessary evil just then, so it was probably better if they didn't have any deep conversations. So she walked through the family room and into the kitchen. Jackson stood at the range, stirring a mound of eggs in a skillet.

"Morning. Did you sleep well?"

Ridley watched him stirring the eggs for a moment before walking behind him to peer through the window into the back-yard. "Yeah, I think I may have actually passed out on the bed."

"Understandable. You like cheese on your eggs?"

She turned to see him holding a bag of shredded cheddar. At her nod, he spread a healthy layer on the eggs. Part of her wondered if she was still dreaming. A handsome man was cooking for her in a state-of-the-art, designer kitchen.

This was definitely *not* her life.

"So, I figure even if the locksmith doesn't call back today we can just take it easy. I have no plans other than cleaning the grill. You're welcome to hang out with me on the patio if you want." He handed her a plate and fork. They sat side by side at the breakfast bar.

"Sure. I'll help you." She took a tentative bite of her eggs. He must have noticed her expression because he grimaced.

"Sorry I'm not a better cook. Eggs are about all I can handle without poisoning anyone."

Ridley choked back a laugh. "No, they're good." After a couple of bites, she looked around. The house was perfectly quiet. "Are the kids coming down for breakfast?"

Jackson ducked his head. "Uh, no. Nick took them for the weekend. They won't be back until tomorrow."

"Oh, yes. I did overhear something about that yesterday." She pursed her lips and focused on her food.

"Uh, yeah. I wanted to apologize again for what you heard. Nick can be an ass but he's usually harmless."

Ridley snorted. "It's fine. I should know better than to eaves-drop by now. It never ends well."

They finished their food in comfortable silence. He rinsed his plate and put it in the dishwasher, so she did the same. He wiped off the counter with a damp rag and then clapped his hands.

"Okay, I'm going to grab my cleaning supplies and then I'll

meet you outside. It'll be nice to have company while I clean the grill. I always put it off until the last possible second because I hate doing it."

"I'll help you. I've cleaned a few grills in my time." She motioned toward the laundry room. "Do you mind if I throw a few things in the wash first? I was going to yesterday but..."

He nodded knowingly. "No problem. The detergents and stuff are in the cabinets overhead."

"Thanks."

She turned and walked back out to the family room and then took the stairs two at a time. By the time she got to her room, she was humming under her breath.

"You are so pathetic," she muttered. She shouldn't be so giddy at the prospect of spending more time with Jackson. He was just being nice; it wasn't like they were going on a date or something.

After throwing the entire contents of her backpack in the washing machine, Ridley stood looking at the clothes swirling around through the clear glass panel on the front. It was tempting to just stand there all day and let herself be hypnotized by the motion. Anything was better than thinking about the events of the past few days and the fact that these clothes were the only things she had to her name at the moment.

"Not that I have so much back in Florida, but still."

She'd been shaken after the accident but after a lot of prodding, a couple of bandages, and a few painkillers, she was released from the hospital. The first day after the accident, she thought it was the trauma of what she'd seen that had her imagining things. Books that weren't in the same place she'd left them. Doors left open that she *knew* she'd locked. Stupid stuff. It wasn't until she came home and found her apartment completely trashed that she'd been scared. And if her mother had taught her anything, it was how to move fast.

She'd withdrawn a bunch of cash from the ATM and then left a voice mail for her boss at the garden center. Once she'd gotten back home, she'd thrown a bunch of clothes into her hiking pack and ridden her bike to the bus station. It was almost funny to think of her rusty old ten-speed locked to the bike rack downtown. She wondered how long before someone cut it loose and disposed of it since there was no telling how long she'd be here. She'd told her boss that she needed a two-week vacation for a family emergency, but if things weren't cleared up by then she'd have to quit. As much as she loved her part-time job, she could always find another one later.

"I'm not even going to think about it. I'm just going to enjoy a relaxing afternoon." She would take Jackson's offer at face value— a nice guy offering friendly conversation. Nothing more, nothing less. For just a few hours, she would talk, laugh, and not worry about anything.

She walked back through the kitchen to the staircase she'd descended earlier, casting a longing look at the plush, cream-colored couch as she passed. This house was so beautiful, unlike anything she'd ever seen. How cozy it would be to snuggle into the deep cushions and read a book. Maybe after they were done cleaning up outside.

She went back to the guest room and checked her phone. She had one missed call. Maybe Raina had finally decided to stop ignoring her. But when she looked at the number she recognized it as her landlady.

"Mrs. Ashton called?"

Mrs. Ashton was a kindly older woman who rented out rooms in her large duplex to college students. She'd been willing to give Ridley a discount on the rent in exchange for her running errands such as picking up mail from her post-office box and getting basic groceries each week.

"I should have let her know I'd be gone. She probably needed something from the store." She immediately pressed the button to call her back.

She wasn't sure if she was going to stay in Virginia permanently but it was only fair to let Mrs. Ashton know that she would be gone for a while. She'd probably need to hire someone else to help her out while Ridley was gone.

"Hello?"

Ridley sat up straight at the weak voice coming over the line. "Mrs. Ashton? It's Ridley."

"Oh, thank goodness, child. Where have you been? I was so worried!"

"Worried? I just went out of town for the weekend."

"Oh, dear Lord. When we couldn't find you we thought you were in the building when it happened. I'm so glad you're all right."

A chill ran down Ridley's spine hearing the normally reserved Mrs. Ashton so excited. Even though she helped her with her groceries and random other things around the house, they'd never been particularly close. She'd learned more than once over the years that it just made it harder to move on in the end.

And she'd always had to move on.

"In the building when what happened?"

"There was a fire last night, Ridley. It seems to have started in your bedroom, although no one knows how that's possible. But all your things are gone. It's all gone."

"Oh my god," Ridley cried.

"The fire department was able to contain it so it didn't take any of the other rooms in the house. Thank goodness a passerby saw the smoke and called for help." She paused for a moment, seeming to collect herself. "I wish one of the other units was empty so I could give you one of those when you get back in town, but I just took on an exchange student. I'm fully booked."

"It's okay, Mrs. Ashton. I'm staying with family and I was

toying with the idea of relocating up here, anyway. I guess fate has made the decision for me..." Her legs trembled, so she sat on the edge of the bed.

"I'm so sorry, sweetheart."

Mrs. Ashton started talking again but she barely heard it. She hadn't thought she had much to her name, but what was the value of the old photographs of her mother whom she'd never see again? Or her half of the best-friends-forever necklace she and Raina had worn every day in junior high? What about the diaries she'd kept faithfully since high school, recording all her fears, dreams, and girlish wishes? She'd written in those journals until she'd learned the hard way that life wasn't a fairy tale and there were no handsome princes.

All of it, a lifetime of memories, just gone.

"I have to go. I'm so sorry you were worried about me. I'm just glad you're okay and no one was hurt in the fire. Thank you for everything." She hung up and sat staring at the wall in front of her.

It was only when a tear fell on the screen of her phone that she realized she was crying.

———

JACKSON STOOD in the doorway to the kitchen and watched as Raina opened the oven. After waiting for fifteen minutes, he'd come looking for her.

The quiet sobs coming through the guest-room door had affected him more than anything in a long time.

Raina closed the oven and turned. "Oh! You scared me. I didn't even hear you walk up."

Her long lashes were still spiky and wet from her tears. The effect was like a punch to the gut.

What was it about this girl?

Just the thought of her in pain was like a knife to the chest. He cleared his throat and backed up a step.

"Sorry, I didn't mean to scare you. When you didn't come outside, I figured you found something better to do."

Her face fell. "I'm so sorry. I totally forgot I was supposed to help with the grill."

"Sure, sure. You ditched me for something better. I get it." He heaved an exaggerated sigh. "Hey, I don't blame you. Cleaning gunk off a grill is hardly an irresistible proposition. But I was really hurt by that, just so you know. The only thing that will help is if you promise to share whatever that is that smells so good."

Her lips twitched. "You're crazy. I was going to share anyway. No guilt trip needed. I was just about to take it out of the oven."

"You really didn't have to cook. I was just going to order something." Jackson was truly in awe. She'd made an entire dish in less time than it took him to figure out where the plates were in his own kitchen.

"Well, I wanted to do something to make up for how rude I was yesterday. I shouldn't have just left like that."

"You don't have to apologize. I would have walked out, too."

"At least I know you aren't a vegetarian since your refrigerator is filled with nothing but raw meat. The freezer and pantry were only a little better, but I was able to find some frozen chicken breast and some canned vegetables."

"I haven't had time to shop lately, so we've only got the meat I'm marinating for the cookout tomorrow. I have to confess, we mainly eat microwave dinners. The only time we get home-cooked meals is when my mom comes. My mom's a feminist, so I'm pretty sure raising a son who can't cook is one of her lifelong disappointments."

His stomach grumbled loudly and they both laughed at the unexpected noise in the otherwise quiet kitchen. She slid her hand into an oven mitt and pulled open the oven. His mouth watered as a savory aroma immediately filled the room. She placed the dish carefully on the stovetop.

"Well, I can hear you're hungry, so let's dig in. I also made string beans with potatoes. I couldn't find anything else to make in the pantry." She started scooping food onto plates.

"I'm working on hiring someone to watch the boys and maybe cook a few times a week. None of the nannies I've interviewed have worked out so far." He held up his hands at the large servings she was dishing up. "I don't think I can eat all that!"

"Oh... actually this is mine." She turned back to her plate and giggled a little. It looked like it was heavier than she was. "I haven't had time to cook much lately, so I need a home-cooked meal myself." She settled down with her food and hummed as she bit off a piece of chicken.

They ate at the breakfast bar in the kitchen. He couldn't stop himself from staring as she got up to get a second helping.

"What! I'm not one of those girls who eat a salad and claim to be full. I'm *hungry*!"

"No, don't apologize. I appreciate a woman who can eat." He didn't add that he also appreciated the aftereffect of a healthy appetite, namely the soft curves stretching out her jeans and tee shirt. She already thought he was a pig. If she knew why he was really staring, she'd probably dump the casserole dish over his head.

"So, where were you coming from?"

Her hand paused before she speared another bite of food. "Florida. That's where I went to college."

"It's weird; I thought I read somewhere that you didn't go to college."

"Oh, I didn't finish." Raina looked away. "That's probably why. Anyway, I still have friends there. What about you? Have you always lived here?"

"Virginian, born and bred. My parents have a farm not too far from here. I went to college across the water in Norfolk. Dropped out before I finished, too. I was too busy playing the guitar to study anything useful."

She looked around. "Well, apparently you studied *something* useful."

"Not everyone thinks so. It was a long time before I started earning enough to make a living. Then I got my break about two years ago when a major country star liked one of my songs enough to record it."

Her eyes widened and he grinned, enjoying her shock. "Are you surprised? Let me guess, you assumed I was into R&B or hip-hop music, right?"

"Okay, you got me. Those were totally stereotypical assumptions to make. I hate when people assume they know me before I even open my mouth, so I'm a little ashamed that I'm guilty of doing it, too." She propped her head on her fist as she watched him. "So, what got you into country music?"

"My parents own a farm, remember? They're a little bit country and a little bit rock n' roll, as my dad would say. We heard country music around the house since I was a little kid. One of my uncles plays the guitar, and he taught me when I was about ten. I haven't stopped since. That first song turned into an album, then I got an offer to collaborate on another country star's album. The rest is history, I guess. Both of those albums did really well, so all my hard work finally paid off."

He stopped then and waited, holding her gaze. When she looked away, he knew she understood. He'd told her his story. Now it was her turn.

She sighed.

"My mom died a few years ago."

Jackson closed his eyes. "I am so sorry."

"Thanks. We weren't close and I regret that. That's when I first started searching for my biological father. I hired a private investigator to track him down. His name was David. He invited me to dinner to tell me what he found out. I didn't see any harm in going. He seemed nice enough." She stood and carried her plate over to the sink.

"Before long he was dropping by my place just to chat or bring Chinese. He liked jazz and was a well-respected businessman in the community. I thought I'd finally gotten lucky and met one of these nice guys I keep hearing so much about."

Jackson stood and put his hand on her shoulder. "You don't have to tell me anything you don't want to. I shouldn't have asked."

"No, it's okay. I should tell someone. I *need* to tell someone."

As he gazed down into her big, brown eyes, Jackson had a feeling he was going to be sorry he asked.

Mainly because the more he got to know her, the harder it was to leave her alone.

five

SHE BIT her lower lip as Jackson eyed her curiously. He was being so sweet to her even after she'd all but told him to kiss off. He'd done nothing but show her kindness and she'd responded with distrust and sarcasm. He didn't deserve that from her. Not after he'd been so nice.

I need all the nice I can get right about now.

"He was a real gentleman. He seemed a little flirty at times, but never made a move. I figured he was waiting until after he wrapped up my case before asking me out. But for the longest time he said he was hitting nothing but dead ends. Then last week, he came by my house one morning and told me he was on to something big. This was before the accident." She lowered her eyes.

"The accident?" Jackson asked gently.

He fell silent but kept his hand on her shoulder. Such a small sign of support, but it made it a little easier for her to talk knowing he was on her side. She'd spent the past two hours trying not to think about how her life had recently gone up in ashes.

Literally.

Maybe if she talked about it, she could get past the mind-numbing fear.

"He asked me to hold this for him." She pulled the pendant from beneath her shirt. "I thought it was a little odd. After all, if he was worried about it being stolen where he was going, why didn't he just leave it at home? But I was on my way to the bank anyway, so I decided to just put it in my safe-deposit box. I ended up on the road behind him. I saw when his car skidded and went through the guardrail." She swallowed, just the memory of it enough to steal her breath.

Jackson shook his head. "That must have been scary."

"I called the police and then tried to climb down to get to him. I didn't know how steep it was and I fell. When the police arrived, they helped pull me back up." Unconsciously, her hand fluttered to her wrist, where the bruises were still visible. "I could see him in the car. I kept asking the police to get him out, but they couldn't. The car was already on fire by then. We had to wait until fire and rescue arrived."

"I am so sorry."

Their eyes met and she couldn't look away. He raised a hand to her face and pushed a stray curl behind her ear. But he didn't step back after that. He seemed fascinated by her hair, rubbing the strands of a fat curl between his fingers.

"Raina—"

"My name is Ridley. Ridley Wells."

He released her, reluctantly. "Wait, what?"

"I just wanted to tell you, that is..." She twisted the bottom of her shirt in her fist. "Raina Winters isn't my real name. I changed it."

It was silly, actually. Almost borderline neurotic that it bothered her to hear him call her by her sister's name. *This doesn't absolve you*, she told herself. After all, she was still lying to him. But this evening with Jackson was one of the best she'd had in a long time. As stupid as it was, she wanted him to know her. The *real* her.

She stepped closer and placed her hand on his chest right over his heart. "I like you, Jackson. I just want you to know the real me."

"I want to know the real you, too. Ridley." He whispered it as if testing out the sound. "I like it. It fits you. Beautiful, strong, and as unique as you are."

"Thank you." She exhaled. Maybe she could just tell him the whole story? He actually seemed to understand.

"I'm glad you told me. Most of the women I meet are so fake. They just lie to get what they want but you are so different from what I expected."

Oh, wow. Ridley cringed. *So much for that.* She wasn't sure how to even respond to that. How was she ever going to explain what had happened? He'd probably just think she was a pathological liar and throw her out.

After a few moments of awkward silence he asked, "So, what happened after that?"

She pulled away and walked over to the window to look out into the night. It was dark, and she couldn't see much other than the shapes of the trees in the backyard.

"When I called the FBI agent on the case today, he told me that David was involved with some pretty sketchy people." She smiled weakly.

Jackson crouched down until she couldn't avoid his eyes. "Hey, hey. It's going to be okay."

"But it's not okay. That's why I ran yesterday." At Jackson's puzzled look, she continued, "I didn't tell them David was killed because of *my* case. He'd found a lead on my father. The FBI saw David meeting with a member of the Moreno crime family. What if that was his lead? What if Alberto Moreno is my father?" Her voice broke and she covered her mouth with her hand.

He pulled her against his chest and rubbed a hand up and down her back. It was a completely platonic move but it warmed her inside and out.

"We don't know that. It could be completely unrelated."

"But it makes sense. It explains why my mom didn't want him to find us and why she was so bitter. It even explains why we moved so much. She spent her entire life on the run from him and now because of me, he might know where we are."

She tried to hold herself rigid, not to lean too heavily into his unexpected embrace, but her willpower was no match for the warmth he offered. Her shoulders sagged and she leaned against him, boneless, as tears streamed down her cheeks.

"Do you mind if I ask my brother, Elliott, to look into it? He owns a security firm up in D.C. and has contacts within the FBI. He'll be able to find out what's going on. Okay?"

"Okay," she whispered. "I wish I knew what to do about this necklace. It must have been pretty valuable if David was worried about it being stolen."

"Do you want me to put it in my safe?"

"You have a safe?" At his nod, she reached up and unhooked the clasp at the back of her neck. "Thank you, Jackson. I'll have to get in contact with the FBI again and find out how to return it to his family."

"Not tonight you don't." He put the necklace in his pocket and ran his hands up and down her arms. "Tonight you just need to relax."

She wasn't used to men being so attentive unless they wanted something. But his hands never strayed from her arms and he didn't try to pull her any closer. As she turned to look up at him, Jackson's lips brushed over her hair. She wasn't entirely sure he'd meant to do it but the contact seared her straight down to her toes.

After the first rush of emotion passed, she covered her face with her hands, embarrassed to have gotten so needy in front of him. Jackson had the perfect life. Why would he want to hear all about her problems? He was gorgeous, successful, and seemed to know exactly what he wanted.

Which, of course, just made her feel even more pathetic in comparison.

"I'm just feeling sorry for myself. I feel like my life was finally starting to fall into place. But then this happened, so here I am. Hiding out."

"You're welcome to stay here as long as you need to. No one will think to look for you at my house, and you'll have plenty of time to figure out your next move. Stay with me."

"I don't want to impose."

"Do I look like I mind? It'll be fun." He wiggled his eyebrows suggestively.

"You are ridiculous." She pulled a paper towel from the holder on the counter and dabbed at her eyes. "I didn't mean to dump all this emotional crap on you."

"You're not dumping. I asked for your story, didn't I?"

"That was probably more than you bargained for. I'm sure you don't want to hear about my screwed-up life."

"I think you're being a little hard on yourself. Everyone makes mistakes, myself included."

Ridley scoffed. "You don't have to try to make me feel better."

"You think I'm just saying that?" Jackson tilted his head and regarded her through narrowed eyes. "My last girlfriend was only using me to get a record deal. Oh, and the last album I produced was such a flop that I'm pretty sure the only people who bought copies of it are my mom and dad."

Ridley stared at him, momentarily stunned. "I don't know what to say."

"You don't have to say anything. I just want you to know you're not the only one who screws up sometimes. No one is perfect. All we can do is go forward and try to do better." Jackson tipped her chin up until she met his eyes. "I'm just glad you're okay. I meant what I said. I'll cancel the locksmith. You're more than welcome to hide out here for as long as you want."

Ridley's eyes went wide, then she licked her lips nervously, unsettled by the warmth of his strong fingers touching her face. He went still as well, as if surprised by his own actions. Then he backed away and cleared his throat.

"Sorry. I don't want you to think I'm, you know, hitting on you. I'm sure you get more than enough of that."

Warmth spread through her at his words. "It's no problem," she whispered.

She wasn't normally the damsel-in-distress type but it had been so nice to be held. Comforted. If that was how he hit on her, she could do with a little more.

"Now, what do you say we just hang out and watch a movie? Neither one of us is going to think about anything heavy for the rest of the night." He grinned at her and she found herself smiling back.

"Okay, I can do that."

They cleaned the kitchen in amiable silence. Then Jackson turned to her and said, "Ready to go?" and held out a hand to her. She was startled into grasping it. He squeezed gently and pulled her after him into the living room.

She sat on the couch as he flipped through a stack of movies until he found the one he wanted. A warm, contented feeling settled over her and Ridley was tempted to allow herself to get swept up in the magic. To snuggle deep into the cushions of the couch and pretend this was her normal life and Jackson was her boyfriend.

Stop it, Ridley.

Jackson seemed like a nice guy and he'd done nothing but offer her help. But she'd learned the hard way over the years that no one did anything without eventually wanting something in return. It wouldn't do for her to get too attached to him or too accustomed to having his help. This was a temporary stop just like every other move in her life and when she moved on, she'd do it the same as always.

Alone.

———

"I CANNOT BELIEVE he just said that!" Raina was curled up on the opposite end of the couch giggling. *No, not Raina,* he reminded himself. Ridley.

Apparently Raina Winters was more than just a stage name. It was also a persona she used to hide her real personality. No one would believe the perfectly coiffed, man-eating Raina Winters was really a shy, sweet girl who giggled at slapstick comedy. Jackson picked up another piece of popcorn from the big bowl on the table next to him and threw it at her.

"I can't believe you've never seen a Will Ferrell movie before." Jackson shook his head in mock dismay and turned back to the TV.

While outwardly he was paying attention to the onscreen antics, in truth he only knew what was happening because he'd seen this particular comedy several times before. He'd spent most of the last hour staring at Ridley. Entranced by her smile. Captivated by her laugh.

And hard as a rock by her smooth bare legs brushing up against his.

Ridley turned and caught him looking. She grinned and kicked him playfully, her foot landing square in the middle of his stomach.

"Oooof. What was that for?" Jackson captured her foot, partially to keep her from knocking the wind out of him and partially to keep it from drifting any lower and giving her proof of just how much he *wasn't* paying attention to the movie.

"I don't know. I just wanted to say thanks. For suggesting this." She motioned toward the television where Will Ferrell's character read the news while wearing a ridiculously large fake mustache. "This has been, hands down, one of the crappiest weeks of my life. But somehow, I don't know, it doesn't seem as overwhelming anymore. A movie and some laughs with a friend are exactly what I needed."

A wicked part of him couldn't resist asking, "So, we're friends, huh?"

Her eyes widened slightly before a shy smile spread across her face. "I thought so..."

"I'm just kidding. Of course we're friends. As long as you aren't a Dallas fan."

"I never said I wasn't," she teased.

"La, la, la." He covered his ears and pretended he couldn't hear her.

Something inside him warmed as he watched her turn back to the movie and let out another giggle. Gone was the wary, distrustful girl he'd originally met. He doubted many people got to see the real Ridley with her bulletproof mental armor stripped off. Which was one more reason that his dick had to take a back seat.

She wasn't the kind of woman you slept with for a night.

She was the kind you watched stupid comedies with and told jokes to make her smile. The kind you held in your arms until she fell asleep. The kind who deserved a man who could love her with his whole heart, not the tattered remnants that currently took up space in his chest.

Since he knew he wasn't fit for any of the above, he was honored just to be her friend.

"You know what?"

She turned at the sound of his voice and raised her eyebrows. As she settled back on the pillows of the couch, her wild hair spilled over the edge, a riotous cascade of curls. She was so stunningly beautiful in that moment, he couldn't speak. When he finally found his voice again, he couldn't remember what he was going to say before, what excuse he was going to use to escape from the temptation of her laughter and her smile. So he just went with the truth.

"This is exactly what I needed, too."

———

RIDLEY SNUGGLED DEEPER into the cushions of the couch, watching as the flickering lights from the television played over Jackson's face. His mood had shifted toward the end of the movie and she wasn't sure what to make of it. They'd started off laughing like hyenas and throwing popcorn at each other before they'd gotten comfortable enough to put their legs up.

She should have kept her mouth closed. All her talk about how crappy her week had been had probably made him uncomfortable. But she'd wanted to express her gratitude for everything he'd done for her today. Not just letting her stay, but listening to her talk about David and hanging out with her so she didn't have to be alone.

She closed her eyes, helpless to resist the lure of rest after the hectic pace of traveling for the last few days. Returning to Virginia wasn't something she'd planned on doing yet. College was supposed to be her chance to escape her past, to branch out into a world where no one knew her. A chance to redefine herself as more than just "Raina's sister" or the girl with the bitter, chain-smoking mother who worked double shifts at the diner to keep them all fed. She'd had so many plans to make her mark on the world and be successful before she returned.

How telling that, for all her hope of being independent, the place she'd run to at the first sign of trouble was right back to her sister.

The final credits rolled and the screen went blank for a few seconds before the opening menu screen flashed. Ridley yawned so widely it felt like the sides of her face might crack. The clock on the wall to her left told her it was almost two in the morning. She thought of the soft, decadent bed upstairs in the guest room she was using and almost whimpered. It was way past time for her to go upstairs and get some sleep.

Instead she turned her head and looked at Jackson again.

He was such a puzzle. Men who looked like him weren't nice for no reason, yet he hadn't asked her for anything. He'd just been there when she had no one else. Why, she couldn't even begin to guess.

His features were relaxed in sleep, the long, sharp blade of his nose more prominent now that it didn't have to compete with his killer smile. His lashes rested against the tops of his cheekbones and she had to resist the urge to run a hand over his curly hair. It wasn't fair that he looked so beautiful and guileless in sleep when he carried such a lethal sexiness when fully awake.

"I would say 'penny for your thoughts' but I have a feeling *that* thought would cost more than I'm worth."

Ridley ripped her gaze from the curve of his lips up to his now wide-open eyes.

Oops.

"Hi. I was just…" She decided not to even address her blatant staring. "…wondering if I could borrow something to sleep in?"

"Sure, sure. Of course." He got up slowly, unfolding his long legs from the couch one at a time. "Follow me. Sorry I conked out at the end there. I guess I was more tired than I thought." He waved for her to follow him up the stairs and she did, keeping her eyes on her own feet so she couldn't ogle the way his jeans fit him as he walked.

She was in his room before she'd realized what she'd done. "Oh, I'll just wait out in the hall," she stammered.

"No. Stay." Those two simple words halted her in her tracks. He smiled a slow, sexy grin before pulling open the second drawer in his bureau. He rummaged for a while, pulling out shirts and then pushing them back in. "I'm trying to find one of my shorter ones so it won't swallow you up."

"Oh, I like them longer. It'll hang lower and cover my legs like a nightgown."

He stopped digging and glanced at her. Then his eyes dipped lower to take in her bare legs exposed by the mid-thigh, terry-cloth shorts she wore. "Right."

He held out a shirt and Ridley took it carefully, making sure their fingers didn't touch.

"Well, thanks again. Good night." She fled the room, racing down the darkened hallway, not stopping until she reached the door of the guest room. She turned the handle and opened the door, but before she entered she looked back.

She *had* to.

Jackson stood in the same position next to his dresser. The heat of his gaze burned over her entire body and she shivered as her nipples peaked against her shirt. She didn't know him well enough to interpret the look on his face but she could interpret her body's response.

God, she wanted him.

He'd been nothing but a gentleman all day, seeing to her every need, listening to her vent and keeping her company. He hadn't made any moves on her, hadn't done anything suggestive or said anything provocative. Was he just being a good host and making sure she made it to her room?

Or was he imagining what she would look like when she stripped off her clothes and went to bed wearing nothing but his shirt?

six

JACKSON WASN'T sure who moved first, but a second later he was down the hall and Ridley was in his arms. Her hair flowed over them as he held her against the wall. He buried his face in her neck and inhaled, his libido instantly going haywire at the warm, seductive scent of her skin. There were no words spoken between them, just the unspoken desires in their eyes.

I want you.

I know.

I want you, too.

When he finally anchored a hand in her hair and tilted her face up for his kiss, it was both a pain and a relief. Her lips opened under his with a breathy little moan. He would kick himself later for his angry assault on her mouth. There was no gentleness, no finesse. He held her captive against him as he took her mouth, capturing her tongue and sliding it against his own.

She was warm and soft in his arms, her breasts pressing against his chest as he held her against him. He was holding her too tightly but she didn't push away. She clung to him, her long legs snaking around his waist to hold him in the cradle of her thighs.

"Jackson," she pleaded.

"Hold on, baby. Just wait."

He groaned as she arched in his arms, rubbing her core against him. She was perfect, so soft and responsive. He worked her, angling so he could rub right against her sweet spot. Damn if she didn't catch his rhythm right away, rocking her hips up as he ground against her.

"Jackson. Please, please, please—" She broke off with a strangled cry when he slid her down so she was riding his thigh.

She went rigid in his arms before her head fell back against the wall. Her eyelids drifted down as she shuddered beneath him.

"Oh yeah, that's it," he whispered.

That look. Damn if she wasn't the most beautiful thing he'd ever seen with her head thrown back, ecstasy all over her face as her most intimate muscles clenched against his thigh.

He'd be seeing that look in his dreams.

"I'm sorry. I'm so sorry," he gasped, then took her mouth in another crushing kiss, kissing her deeply until he again had to pull away just to breathe.

He ripped his mouth from hers, the sight of her swollen lips almost making him dizzy.

"I told myself I wasn't going to do this. You need someone to lend a helping hand, not take advantage." He pressed his forehead against hers and took a deep breath.

It should have been better when he couldn't see the way she looked up at him, so soft and trusting. But even with his eyes closed, he could still see her face. The way she looked at him made him feel powerless. He could literally feel his self-control oozing out, drop by drop.

"Oh, that's right. You're supposed to stay away from me. I'm a vulture, remember?" She licked his bottom lip and he groaned.

When she kissed a trail from his jaw down to his neck, he

flinched and set her down. "That was my brother talking. I know better. But that doesn't make this a good idea."

"You really are a nice guy, aren't you?"

"Unfortunately, yes," he grumbled.

"Well, the fact that you don't seem any happier about it than I do..." She stood on tiptoe and wrapped her arms around his neck, brushing her body against his, inch by inch. "...makes me feel a little better. My ego anyway."

He stopped thinking the instant she plastered herself against him. It took a moment for him to direct enough blood to his brain to translate what she was saying.

"I'm definitely not happy about it, beautiful. I'm just trying not to be what you think I am."

She pulled back and looked him in the eye. "Jackson—"

He cut her off before she could continue. "I have a family picnic tomorrow, so there's going to be a lot of people around. But we always have tons of food and good music. You're welcome to join us. I want you to make yourself at home while you're here."

It was asking for trouble, but he couldn't stop himself from taking another kiss, bending her back over his arm until she was forced to cling to his shoulders to stay on her feet. Then, while she was still dazed, he turned and walked off.

There was a cold shower calling his name.

———

THE NEXT MORNING, Ridley threw her legs over the side of the bed and stood up. *Thank God.* Even though she'd been awake since the early hours, she'd been waiting for the sun to rise so she could move around the house. It was bad enough that she was a forced houseguest. She definitely didn't want to wake her host too early on a holiday.

She stretched and tugged the edges of Jackson's tee shirt

farther over her cotton shorts. A warm feeling spread through her as she remembered the look in his eyes last night when she'd asked to borrow something to wear. He had a way of looking at her that made her throat go dry.

The worst part was that she'd not only been restless and itchy after their hot little interlude, but because she'd been so keyed up, she'd heard every noise the house made. Every bump made her think someone was scaling the wall outside her window, every creak in the hallway sounded like footsteps. She'd had to turn on all the lights and wedge the chair from the dressing table under the handle of her door before she could even begin to relax.

Even after her makeshift security measures, she'd still spent most of the night staring at the intricate designs on the ceiling. Who would have thought you could create so many different patterns with plain white paint?

The thought of seeing Jackson after she'd all but molested him last night was just too embarrassing for words. Not that she didn't agree with him. Sleeping together would have been a huge mistake. She was only in town for a short time, and he didn't even know who she really was. But that didn't mean she liked being turned down. He'd just been so... *reasonable*. And yes, she was petty enough to hate him for it. She hoped he'd regretted it as soon as he got to his empty bed.

And she really, really, really hoped he'd had blue balls.

"It's just chemistry. It doesn't mean anything. Clearly I'm not irresistible since he walked away. Besides, I'm sure I'm not the first girl to borrow this shirt," she muttered before going to stand in front of the mirror over the antique dressing table. Her appearance made her wince.

Whoa, I look rough.

She immediately headed into the en suite bathroom. She may not be a supermodel, but she had enough female vanity not to want Jackson to see her with dark circles under her eyes and bedhead.

She took a long, leisurely shower, wishing the whole time she could take the five streams of water coming from the fancy showerhead with her when she left. After wrapping herself in one of the plush towels on the rack, she brushed her teeth and carefully untwisted her hair. It fell in long waves down her back. She was thankful she'd bundled her long hair up on her head to keep it from getting wet since she didn't have her hair-dryer.

"With any luck, Raina will call soon. Otherwise I'll look like a hot mess. I don't have my hair-dryer. I don't even have enough clothes."

Oh crap, the clothes.

She hung her head. She'd completely forgotten about the clothes she'd put in the wash yesterday. They'd been sitting for the better part of a day in the machine, so she'd no doubt have to rewash them before she could put them in the dryer.

"I guess getting up earlier has its uses." She dressed quickly, pulling on her shorts and the same tee shirt she'd slept in, before opening the door. She peered out into the hallway. A grin tugged at the edges of her mouth. It was more than a little ridiculous how she was creeping around. What would she have done even if Jackson was in the hallway? She squared her shoulders and walked to the staircase.

The early morning sun streamed through the expansive windows in the family room, bathing the beige furniture with buttery light. She couldn't suppress a sigh as she walked through the room and then through the kitchen to get to the laundry room. It was such a beautiful morning that she could almost forget why she was here. It was the kind of day that just begged for coffee outside on the patio with a bowl of fruit and a good book.

She pulled one of her shirts out of the washer and held it under her nose. It didn't smell moldy or anything and the clothes hadn't been sitting for *that* long. She shrugged her shoulders and pulled an armful out and then bent to throw them in the dryer.

"Well, good morning."

At the sound of the voice behind her Ridley stood up straight, bumping her head on the dryer. "Ouch!"

The clothes in her arms fell to the floor in a scattered heap. She held a hand to her forehead as she turned around.

One of the men she remembered from yesterday stood in the doorway to the laundry room. He looked just like Jackson so she had to assume this was Nick, the rude brother she'd overhead him talking to in the hallway. The two young boys she'd met in Raina's backyard stood directly behind him, watching her curiously.

"I wasn't expecting you to still be here." He looked down at her borrowed shirt and Ridley squirmed under his gaze. Despite the fact that she knew nothing had happened, it was still weird to have his brother see her wearing Jackson's shirt this early in the morning. She tugged the hem a little lower.

"Unfortunately, the locksmith hasn't called back yet. Your brother was kind enough to let me stay. And to loan me something to wear while my clothes are washing."

"How did you sleep?"

"Okay, I guess." Ridley blushed. The way he said it came across more like *where did you sleep?* She turned her attention to the two boys behind him.

"Did you guys have fun with your uncle?"

"Yes! We played games and ate ice cream. All night!" The oldest boy, *Chris*, if she remembered correctly, was practically quivering with glee as he said it.

The little one took his thumb out to say "Ice cream!" then immediately stuck it back in his mouth.

Nick smiled ruefully. "That was supposed to be our secret, remember?"

Ridley knelt down so she was more on their level. "That's okay. I won't tell. I like ice cream, too."

"Where's your mommy?" the little boy asked. Ridley looked up at Nicholas uncertainly. He looked a little stunned.

"Sorry, he's been really curious about that subject lately. Okay, Jase. Let's go find your dad." He tried to herd them back through the door. Jase didn't move, just stood watching her. Nicholas sighed.

"It's okay, really." She moved a little closer to Jase and looked him in the eyes. "I don't have a mommy anymore. She's gone."

"Our mom's gone, too. We've just got our dad," Chris said. He looked down at his sneakers, then peeked up at her shyly.

Ridley smiled at him. "But you've got a really awesome dad."

"You look like Miss Raina." Jase giggled and launched himself into her arms.

Nick looked at her curiously.

She grabbed Jase and pulled him into her lap. "That's because I am Miss Raina." She laughed weakly. "I guess I look a little different without my makeup on. Should I take that as an insult?"

Ridley couldn't resist squeezing his chubby little body. It filled her with a small pang to think that she might not ever get to have children of her own. When she was still young enough and stupid enough to believe in fate, she'd always assumed she'd meet the perfect guy eventually. They'd get married and have the kind of family she'd always longed for.

But all the friends she'd envied who'd gotten married after college had also gotten divorced just a few years later. Considering her track record with men, she wouldn't have fared any better if she'd actually married any of her boyfriends. The thought of putting her children through a nasty custody dispute made her feel ill.

"Okay guys." Nick's voice broke through her daydreaming. "Go on upstairs and put your stuff away. Make sure you wake up your father while you're at it." He rubbed his hands together in mock delight.

The boys whooped and raced for the stairs. Nick turned back to her. "Sorry about that. Jase has been curious about moms lately. It's hard to explain to a toddler why everyone else lives with both parents except for him, you know?"

Ridley waved away the apology. "It's fine. They're adorable. Besides, I understand. I grew up without my father and I'm still looking for him." She sighed and wiped a hand over her face. She definitely didn't want to think about her search for her father.

After a few moments, she looked up to find Nick staring at her. She glanced behind her and then back at him. "What? Did I say something wrong?"

"No, it's just that you really do look different without make-up." He stopped and held up his hands. "In a good way."

"Right. I'm sure vulture was meant as a compliment, too."

"No," he barked. At her strange look, he cleared his throat and then said in a more normal tone of voice, "It wasn't a compliment. But let's be real. You know *exactly* why I said it." Then he turned and walked out without another word.

"What was that about? These Alexander men are all crazy." An image of Jackson on the couch the previous night, his handsome face soft with sleep, crossed her mind. "Gorgeous, but crazy."

She got up off the floor and finished transferring her clothes from the washing machine to the dryer. Then she went back upstairs to call her sister again. She had to get out of this house. All the testosterone was clearly rattling her brain.

If Raina didn't answer soon, she'd be forced to resort to breaking and entering!

———

THAT AFTERNOON, Jackson glanced up the stairs, guilt twisting his stomach. It was past noon and Ridley still hadn't come down.

God, the memory of her.

He wished, in that moment, he'd gone upstairs before the movie ended. The memory of her tight little body against his was the last thing he needed right before a family picnic, but not kissing her last night would have taken more self-control than he had.

He closed his eyes and tried to think of something else before he got another erection. He ran through baseball stats, the track listing for the last album he'd produced, and was halfway through mentally reciting the states in alphabetical order before he felt calm enough to open his eyes.

He walked back to the kitchen and stared blankly out the window into the backyard where his brothers were setting up the last of the picnic tables.

He'd done the right thing in walking away, but damn if it hadn't been one of the hardest things he'd ever done. Seducing her last night would have been a mistake. He didn't want her to come to his bed because she was scared and feeling vulnerable. He wanted her to come to him because she wanted him just as much as he wanted her.

He just hoped she hadn't interpreted his "make yourself at home" last night as "make yourself scarce." He really wanted her to come down and join the party. After everything she'd been through, she needed to relax and get her mind off things.

"Hey, what are you doing in here?" Nick stepped in from the patio, pulling the sliding glass doors closed behind him. "Everyone's starting to arrive."

Irritated that he was just standing in the middle of his kitchen mooning like a teenage boy, Jackson turned to dig in the refrigerator. A second later he handed his brother a platter of sliced tomatoes, lettuce, and cheese.

"I'm just getting the last of the food together."

Nick arched a brow. "Right. The fact that you're inside has nothing to do with the beautiful girl upstairs in your bedroom."

He didn't look at his brother as he yanked the ketchup, mustard, and relish bottles from the refrigerator and set them out on the table.

"Of course she's beautiful. She's a model, so she's hardly going to be ugly, right? And she's not in my bedroom—get your mind out of the gutter."

He slammed the last bottle on the table harder than he'd intended and the wood responded with a loud CRACK.

"Can't you just put her in a hotel?" Nick grumbled.

Jackson looked back at the stairs again. "Look, I already called a locksmith, but you and I both know that no one is coming out on a holiday. In the meantime, Ridley is staying here with us where she's safe."

"Ridley?" Nick asked.

"Yeah, it's her real name. Anyway, she's a nice girl and there's no reason to push her off to a hotel where she'll be by herself."

Before his brother could question him further, namely about why Jackson felt it was his responsibility to keep her safe, the sliding door opened again and Matt came barreling inside.

"Whoa, watch it!" Nick juggled the tray in his hands, trying to keep the tomatoes from sliding off the edge as Matt clipped his shoulder in his haste to get by.

"Sorry, man. I just need to get out of here." Matt's cheeks were bright red beneath his normally dusky skin color. He'd either gotten an instant sunburn or was really pissed.

"What happened?" Jackson crossed his arms. Matt didn't say anything.

Jackson looked at his brother and motioned toward the door.

Without a word, Nicholas carried the tray outside to the backyard and closed the door behind him. He was glad his brother wasn't the type to take offense. They were all great friends but he knew how Matt was. He'd have a much better chance of finding out what was bothering him if they didn't have an audience.

"You look pissed off. You were in a decent enough mood when you got here, so what's happened in the last hour that has you looking like you're ready to spit nails?"

"It's nothing. I think I should go. I don't want to ruin your party for everyone else."

"Let me guess, Trent and Mara just arrived, right? Man, you have got to let it go. She's a grown woman. She's had boyfriends before and you haven't been this crazy."

"He's going to ask her to marry him. He just told me." Matt growled and then in a sudden move turned and punched a hole in the wall next to him.

The sliding glass door opened again. Trent and Mara stood on the patio gaping at them. Nicholas walked up behind them and peered over Mara's shoulder.

"Damn! Cleanup on aisle four," he joked.

Matt stalked into the living room and Jackson ran his hands over his hair roughly. How had a simple family cookout turned into a soap opera?

seven

"WHAT DO you mean you won't give me the code?"

Ridley bit her lip and hoped no one downstairs could hear her. Not that they needed any more evidence of the crazy town her life had become.

"Exactly what I said. I am not giving you the code," Raina pronounced. "I am so sorry about what happened to David. I didn't like the idea of him poking around in our past, but I wouldn't have wished him dead, especially not in a fiery car crash. But if the police think it wasn't an accident, then that means he was mixed up with some pretty shady people. And if they're looking for you, the first place they'll look is my house."

"I told you, I never told David about you."

"I know, but if he had any investigative skills at all, he would have figured out that you were a twin. It wouldn't have taken much for him to figure out who I am. And if he figured it out, then someone else could have, too."

She paused and took a breath. "Plus, if the FBI really does think you're involved in David's accident, you need to stay hidden. They can't arrest you if they can't find you. At least at Jackson's house, I know you're safe."

Ridley mentally counted backward from ten. "Raina. I cannot just stay at some guy's house who I don't even know. What am I supposed to tell Jackson?"

"All I want you to do is stay safe until I can get home. Don't worry about Jackson. He owes me a favor. I'll talk to him."

"No! You can't do that!" Ridley bit her lip.

There was silence on the other end of the line.

"Okay, what is going on here?" Raina asked. "Why wouldn't I talk to Jackson?"

Ridley groaned and flopped down on the bed. She wasn't sure what kind of outcome she'd been envisioning, but she'd never expected for Raina to want to call Jackson and explain everything. Now she had to come clean and, considering how many times she'd chastised her sister for lying, Raina was never going to let her hear the end of it.

"Because he thinks you're here. When he saw me outside, he thought it was you. And I didn't tell him otherwise."

"Whoa, whoa, whoa! You're pretending to be me?"

Ridley gritted her teeth at the howls of laughter coming through the phone. "This isn't funny, Ray. I didn't know what else to do! I needed a place to stay and I figured I could get in contact with you and get the money to get out of here without anyone ever being the wiser."

"I know, I know. Miss Honesty telling a lie. It's probably killing you having to pretend to be me."

"I hate lying to him," Ridley whispered. All she could think of was Jackson's face when he'd held her last night. So open. So trusting.

"You really like him, don't you?" Raina asked. For once, she didn't sound like she was poking fun.

Ridley stood, her mind made up. "That's it. I'm telling him the truth. He deserves that much. Hopefully he won't throw me out."

"No, don't do that! I know you feel bad, but as soon as you tell him, he's part of this. He's harboring a criminal. Is that what you want?"

"That's not fair, Raina. Of course I don't want that. I never wanted any of this."

"I know you hate keeping secrets but he won't be able to resist looking you up and asking questions. We can't afford that right now. I'm sure the police have no proof against you, but I'd still rather no one knows where you are. The shoot is wrapping up in less than a week. Once I'm home, we can figure out a long-term plan. You're going to stay with me, right?"

Ridley shrugged, then remembered that her sister couldn't see her. "I haven't thought that far ahead. But I'll probably stay for a while. Until I figure out what to do, anyway."

"Are you okay, Ridley? Really? He's being nice to you, isn't he? I'll kick his ass if he hasn't been."

"Raina! Of course he's been nice. He even stayed up to watch a movie with me so I wouldn't be alone. He's been great. I just feel bad that I'm taking up all his time. He probably has a girlfriend he's neglecting because he feels obligated to stay here with me."

"I don't think he has a girlfriend. Or at least I've never seen any evidence of one. Come to think of it, I've never seen his ex-wife either." She was quiet for a moment. "So, you guys stayed up late last night? Just watching a movie?"

"Yeah, it was some comedy with Will Ferrell. He fell asleep toward the end of the movie. I think he's been pretty stressed out lately, too."

"Uh huh. It sounds like you two got pretty close last night."

Ridley would have crossed her arms if she wasn't holding the phone. "Don't start, Raina. Nothing happened. It was just two friends watching a movie."

"Friends, huh? Friends with benefits?"

"I'm hanging up now," Ridley warned.

"Oh, calm down. I'm just kidding. Not that it would hurt you any to seduce a handsome, successful man. You could do worse, you know?"

"I'm not here to steal his virtue," Ridley said. "I'm just trying to stay out of the way until you get back."

"Okay but I still think a little romance would do you good. Jackson is exactly the kind of guy I want for you. A real man, not like the guys you've been with who only want to use you."

"Hey, if we're going to start debating judgment skills, then I am not the one with the worst track record," Ridley argued.

"Let's see, there was the guy who just wanted you to cook for him. Was that John? Yeah, it was John. There was the guy who wanted you to write his term papers for him. I don't even remember his name. Then there was Nate, the surfer dude who was high all the time."

"Yeah, well who hasn't picked losers when they were in college? You dated that guy who liked women's underwear, remember?"

"Oh yeah, that was a shining moment, but my current boyfriend owns half the commercial real estate on the East Coast, so at least I've improved. I just want the same for you."

"I know you do. But Jackson and I are just friends. Especially since he thinks I'm you."

"Well, that should make it easier to seduce him, not harder."

"Raina!"

"Okay, okay, I can take a hint. But I still think you should sleep with him. I saw him with his shirt off once. He is really built. Seeing him naked would *totally* make you feel better."

"Sure. I'll get right on that, sis."

"You're joking but I'm not. Well, if you change your mind, do it quickly because I'll be back in about a week." She paused. "I've really missed you, Ri."

Touched, Ridley sucked in a breath, blinking back a sudden rush of tears. "I've missed you, too. Now, hurry up and get home!"

After they hung up she put her phone back on the nightstand. She'd lived apart from her sister ever since graduating from high school, but up until she met David, they'd talked on the phone every day. Raina would be back in a week. She'd already been here almost two days, so what were a few more? But for some reason it felt like forever.

She was suddenly really homesick and for her, home wasn't a place.

It was Raina.

———

NICHOLAS ALEXANDER HATED to be wrong. Almost as much as he hated Chinese food and clip-on ties. But since he'd learned over the years that even *his* radar could be faulty at times, he decided to bring in the experts. As he walked down the driveway to his car, he pulled out his cell phone and hit the third speed dial. While everyone was distracted inside, it was the perfect time to do a little sleuthing.

"You rang, little brother?" The wry voice coming through his cell phone was about two octaves deeper than his. His older brother, Elliott, was the kind of man that lesser men feared. And not just because he was bigger than most everyone else.

"I'm glad you haven't left yet. I need you to look into someone for me. A woman." Nick glanced behind him to make sure he was still alone. Most of the partygoers had already arrived but it would be just his luck for Jackson or worse, their mother, to somehow overhear.

"It's always a woman with you, isn't it?" The dry laugh coming over the line was a surprise. Elliott wasn't the happy-happy, joy-joy type and treated most conversations as if they were life or death. Nick was actually surprised his brother wasn't grilling him for details on the "subject" yet.

"So, you want to know if your new flavor of the month has any skeletons in the closet? Namely, any irate husbands who'll come after you with a baseball bat?"

"Hey! That was *one* time," Nick countered. "And he wasn't her husband. At least I don't think he was."

"He was," Elliott replied firmly.

"Oh, damn. I actually didn't know that." Nick made a mental note to start having Elliott check out his future bedmates. He liked to have fun but he wasn't trying to break up anybody's home. His parents had managed to raise him better than that.

"Anyway, it's not for me. It's for Jackson."

As he expected, that statement got his brother's attention. "Subject's name, age, and birthplace."

"She's a model, so most of her information is already out there. Her name is Raina Winters."

"Leggy?" Elliott sounded surprised.

"Yeah, they call her 'Legs.' You know who she is?"

Elliott grunted. "I'm pretty sure every straight man in the western hemisphere knows who she is. She's frickin' hot."

Nick tugged at the collar of his shirt. He closed his eyes tightly against images of those famously long legs wrapped around his neck while their owner bucked and moaned beneath him. They'd only spent one night together, but it had changed everything. He'd told her things he'd never told a woman, experienced things he thought weren't possible. He'd lost himself in her.

Then the next morning she'd just walked away.

Focus, Nick!

"Well, she claims to be locked out of her house. Jackson seems to have bought her story and he's letting her stay with him. She's been there since yesterday."

"You think she's lying about being locked out?"

"I don't know, but if she is I'd rather find out now before she wraps Jackson any further around her little finger. She told Jackson her real name is Ridley. That should help."

His fingers clenched into a fist. When she'd needed a place to stay, she'd turned to Jackson. She'd confided her real name to Jackson.

Not to Nick.

Their night together clearly hadn't meant as much to her as it had to him. Not that he didn't already know that. Her refusal to see or talk to him since had pretty much driven that point home.

As angry as it made him, he couldn't fault his brother for helping her. What was he supposed to say? *I know she's your neighbor and you knew her first, but I claim dibs?*

Even though she doesn't want me.

Just the thought of telling his little brother about her soul-crushing rejection made him feel about two inches tall.

"Anyway, can you check her financials and see if she's having money problems?"

After Eli's grunt of assent, he ended the call and closed his eyes. He couldn't make his brother stay away from her, but that didn't mean he wasn't keeping his eyes open. There was nothing to indicate that Raina would use Jackson to get back at him, but he would be prepared just in case.

If she was still the lying bitch he remembered, his brother didn't stand a chance.

———

"I KNOW THIS IS HARD, but you have to get a grip," Jackson said.

"I'm sorry about your wall, man. I'll pay for the damage." Matt stared at something on the ground and kicked at it, looking so miserable that Ridley was suddenly embarrassed to be there.

She had stopped in the middle of the staircase after coming down to see what all the commotion was. Of course, her impeccable sense of timing put her right in the middle of a private conversation. At least the guys were facing away from her.

"Come on, Matt. Talk to me. What's really the deal here? Your sister is getting married, not moving to a foreign country." Jackson crossed his arms. "You've always been so overprotective of her."

"She's his family." Ridley froze when they both looked at her. "I'm so sorry. I really didn't mean to overhear. It's just, I don't know. I get it." She walked down the staircase until she stood next to Matt.

"I'd feel the same way if my sister was getting married. It's always been just the two of us against the world. When she gets married, suddenly someone else is her next of kin. I'd be happy for her, of course. But I'd be sad, too. It would feel like someone was taking her away from me."

"You're right. I've always been the one who took care of her and now it's like..." Matt crossed his arms and glared at the floor.

"Like someone's taking your place?" she suggested gently.

"I'm being an ass."

"You're being human. You're only an ass if you don't go apologize so that your sister can stop worrying about you."

"You're right." He looked at Jackson. "I meant what I said about your wall. I'll fix it tomorrow." He punched him in the arm and then walked out.

Jackson watched him go and then turned back to her. He stared for so long Ridley squirmed under his scrutiny. Was he annoyed she'd butted into his conversation?

"I didn't mean to intrude."

"You didn't. I'm just amazed. It's not easy to convince Matt to see reason. I feel like I'm watching one of those nature shows when the guy talks to the angry crocodile and manages to tame it. How did you know what to say to him?"

"I'm no crocodile whisperer. Like I said, I get it. I love my sister but we're very different and I know what it's like to be the one who's left behind."

Jackson went still, a dark look passing over his features.

"I understand loss, too. Believe me," he whispered.

When he looked up at her, Ridley swallowed. Hard. There was something in his eyes that reflected what she saw in the mirror every day. Sadness. Loneliness.

Longing.

It was almost too intense to witness, so she looked away, breaking the spell.

"Still, I apologize. I should have just walked out when I realized you guys were having a private conversation. I've been told I'm too nosy."

A tendril of warmth curled through her as their eyes met.

"I'm glad you didn't. You managed to get him to admit something that I've been trying to force out of him since college. I owe you one."

"I think saving me from death by grass stain more than makes up for it."

They laughed together, the earlier tension in the room dissipating. Jackson was quiet for a moment, then clapped his hands together.

"I was actually on my way upstairs to get you. Come join the party. I want you to meet the rest of the gang."

He led her from the family room, through the kitchen, and out the glass doors to the patio. Ridley stopped short when she saw all the people milling around the backyard.

"Whoa! This is a lot of people. I thought you were just having a family barbecue?"

"My family does this every year and I swear every year my

family gets bigger and bigger. You invite a few people who invite a few people. You know how it is."

"Not really." Ridley stepped out onto the patio behind him and they were immediately surrounded.

She hung back, in awe of his easy confidence as he hugged a few people and slapped a couple of the guys on the back. He seemed oblivious to the way the women looked at him with hungry stares and flirtatious smiles. Jackson reached back and grabbed her hand, pulling her to his side. Her heart sped up.

It doesn't mean anything, he's just being nice so you don't get lost in the crowd, she thought. Still, she couldn't deny the feel of his large hand around hers was a thrill.

Several of the girls looked at Ridley critically before dismissing her and turning back to Jackson. Apparently they didn't find her to be a threat.

It took all her willpower not to throw her arms around him and say, "He's mine. Back off, biyatches!" just to see the looks on their faces. She doubted Jackson would share the humor though, so she refrained.

Jackson pulled her closer until she stood right under his arm. "Ridley, I want to introduce my oldest brother, Bennett."

A ruggedly handsome man with light brown skin shook her hand vigorously. "Nice to meet you, Ridley. I hope you're feeling better."

She blushed furiously as everyone looked at her speculatively. "I am, much better." She glanced up at Jackson. He seemed to understand her discomfort because he quickly turned to someone else.

"And these are the other members of our usual group, Trent Townsend and Mara Simmons. Mara is Matt's twin sister."

He addressed Mara directly. "You should have seen her talking to Matt earlier. He actually listened to her. It was amazing."

Embarrassed at the praise, Ridley shook hands with them both, surprised when Mara pulled her into a quick hug.

"Thanks for talking Matt down. He just came back from overseas and he hasn't been himself lately. I don't think he's adjusting to civilian life so well."

Mara looked over at Trent who hugged her close to his side and kissed the tip of her nose.

Ridley swallowed back a sudden stab of envy. With just one look, she could sense the bond between them. She'd always wondered what it would be like to have that kind of connection with someone.

"Well, let's get something to eat. I went a little overboard on the grill." Jackson tugged her toward the long picnic tables set up in the middle of the lawn.

The two boys she remembered from earlier that morning ran up. The smallest one didn't wait to be picked up, just latched on to Jackson's pant leg and started climbing like he was scaling a wall. "Daddy, we want ice cream!"

Jackson scooped him up and held him cuddled in the crook of his arm. "Not yet, little man. Let's get some food first."

Ridley's heart slammed against her chest. It shouldn't be so hot that he was such a devoted father. She busied herself by picking up a paper plate and filling it with potato chips. He'd kissed her last night, but that didn't mean he was single. For all she knew his ex-wife or girlfriend could be at the party, too. Jackson wasn't the kind of man any sane woman would let get away, especially if they had a family.

She pushed down a pang of regret and focused on the food. The last time she'd liked a guy he'd ended up dead, so it was probably better if she kept her thoughts off romance. Her time was going to be occupied in the near future with just trying to stay out of harm's way.

She put a hot dog on a bun and bit into it angrily.

"So, your real name is actually Ridley?" Matt appeared on her left and she jumped. "I'm surprised you didn't just use your real name. It's so distinctive. Although I can understand not liking it. The only people who call me Matthew are my mother and people who want to get punched in the face. And don't even get Mara started on her name."

"What? Mara is perfect. Short, feminine, and easy to pronounce."

"It's actually *Marina*. My parents love to sail." Matt rolled his eyes. "So, why do you look like *you* want to punch a wall now?" Matt grabbed a paper plate. "Or like you want to punch Jackson. What did he do?"

She choked down the last piece of her food. "Nothing. So, how old are Jackson's kids?" She didn't look at him as she asked, just put another hot dog on her plate and picked up the ketchup bottle.

Matt raised an eyebrow when she squeezed too hard and ketchup squirted all over the table. "What's up with all this love in the air? I need to watch my back before I get hit with an arrow."

"What? I didn't say... I was just wondering."

Matt looked at her from the corner of his eye. "You were just wondering where their mother is? Normally I'd make you work for it, but I like you. So, I'll just tell you straight out that you might not want to go there. Jackson is a great guy but ever since his wife died, he hasn't been the same."

Ridley looked back at Jackson and the two kids clinging to him. "Oh, no. I had no idea. When they said they didn't have a mom, I assumed it was due to divorce or something. Was it recent?"

"About three years ago. Jase had just been born. I don't even think the boys remember her. Jackson doesn't like talking about it, so he usually lets people assume he's divorced. I'm only telling you this so you'll understand why I'm warning you. You seem like a nice girl and I'd hate to see you get your heart broken."

Jackson looked up then and their eyes met.

I understand loss, too. Believe me.

"Don't worry about me. Jackson is just being nice since we're neighbors. My heart is in no danger."

But even as she said it she knew it was a lie.

eight

JACKSON BOBBED his head to the beat of the music, pretending that he was having a good time. His other brother, Elliott, had finally shown up and taken over his usual party position as makeshift DJ. He'd hooked his laptop computer up to a pair of monster-size speakers and put on a huge pair of earphones. Antisocial as a rule, he preferred presiding over the music so he didn't have to dance or talk to anyone. Or rather, deal with people who walked up and tried to talk to him.

Luckily Jackson had been able to grab him before he'd gotten busy to ask him to find out a little more about Ridley's friend, David. If anyone could get to the bottom of a mystery, it was Elliott.

Bennett was on the other side of the yard keeping an eye on the boys while they played. Nicholas was near them, flirting with a pretty blonde in a miniskirt. The girls were dancing, the guys were watching, and there was plenty of food. On all accounts, it was a successful party.

Other than the fact that he couldn't keep his eyes off his temporary houseguest.

"As the host of this party, you should probably smile every

once in a while. Act like you're having fun." Mara appeared at his left elbow, looking like a Sofía Vergara clone in her crisp, white shorts and tank top.

"I am having fun. Especially now that you're here." He winked at her. Flirting with Mara was a time-honored tradition in their group, partially because she was naturally playful, and partially because it pissed off Matt so much. He frowned as he thought of the fist-sized hole in his living room wall.

As if she sensed the direction of his thoughts, Mara frowned, too. "I'm worried about Matt. Will you talk to him?"

"Of course. Ridley was able to calm him earlier, so I think he's okay now. But hopefully I can get him to talk to me before he puts his fist through anything else."

She nodded quickly and then surprised him by throwing her arms around his neck. He had to switch his beer to his left hand to keep from dropping it. When she pulled back, her eyes were slightly shiny.

Please God, don't start crying.

"Sorry. I'm fine. Don't get that panicked look." She swiped under her eyes. "It's just been a hard transition with him coming back from Iraq. Then there's the thing with Trent." She flushed slightly and averted her eyes.

All joking aside, he'd never taken flirting with Mara seriously, so he couldn't deny that the idea of her and Trent as a couple was just... *weird.* As beautiful as she was, it would feel too much like hitting on his own sister if he'd had one. Plus, if he was honest, she really wasn't his type. Cynthia had been quiet, more into playing the piano and singing to the boys than socializing. As wild and outgoing as he appeared to his friends, he connected better with quiet, introverted women.

Women like Ridley.

"Jackson, there you are," a voice called out.

He turned and then groaned.

What the hell is she doing here?

Alana, inappropriately dressed as usual in some sort of clingy, white silk dress, picked her way across the lawn on her needle-thin heels.

Mara turned as well and then glared at him. "Please tell me you're not still seeing her?"

Alana reached them before he could answer. Her gaze settled on Mara. "Oh hello, Mona. It's been ages."

Mara didn't even bother responding, just turned and walked off.

"What are you doing here, Alana?"

He didn't bother with pleasantries. If her past behavior was anything to go on, she only showed up when she wanted something. It was just a matter of getting her to admit what it was.

"I remembered you used to have your little party every year for Memorial Day. I just took a chance and decided to swing by." She glanced around, a look of disgust passing over her face when she took in the tables lined with picnic food. "I don't know *why* you don't get this catered."

"You remembering the date doesn't explain why you're here. We broke up a year ago."

"We broke up ten months ago. I think we were a little rash," Alana purred. She smoothed a non-existent wrinkle out of her dress. It wasn't like her to be fidgety or self-conscious, so the movement was telling.

"You slept with my assistant."

It was strange how saying it out loud wasn't as difficult as it had been just a few months ago. She seemed alarmed at his blunt statement but covered it quickly with a cajoling expression.

"I did not sleep with him. That was a misunderstanding." She tried to reach for his arm but he stepped back.

"I don't think I misunderstood you bent over his desk. Not

that it matters because I'm seeing someone else now." The lie jumped, unbidden, from his mouth.

Shit.

"You are? Who? It's that Mona girl, isn't it? She always had a thing for you." Alana crossed her arms.

"It's not Mara. It's no one you know."

He really wasn't trying to hurt her feelings but maybe thinking he had a girlfriend would finally convince her that it was over between them. Nothing else he'd tried had gotten the point across.

"Look, I'm sorry for the way things ended between us but I've moved on and I suggest you do the same." Happy that for once he had the last word, he turned to walk away and then stopped dead in his tracks.

Ridley stood right behind him watching the exchange with wide eyes.

———

"OH, great. She has a lot of nerve showing up here." Matt looked over her shoulder and frowned. Ridley turned and peered in the same direction. There were so many people there that she couldn't be sure what he was looking at.

Until her eyes zeroed in on Jackson and Mara talking to a beautiful woman in a short, white dress.

"Who is that?" She hated to ask, hated that she wanted to know so badly. The woman was tall and thin with long, curly brown hair. Her light brown skin looked airbrushed, almost as if she'd photoshopped herself before leaving the house. Just then, she tossed her long hair over her shoulder and smiled at Jackson.

Ridley hated her on sight.

Mara turned and walked away from them, her shoulders

drawn up and her lips twisted into a snarl. Matt chuckled and tossed his empty beer bottle in one of the recycling bins nearby.

"That is Jackson's bitchy ex-girlfriend. Looks like she's already pissed Mara off. Typical."

Jackson crossed his arms, his body language communicating that he definitely didn't want to be there. Miss Photoshop clearly didn't get the message because she kept moving closer and closer, leaning toward him as she spoke even as he leaned away. Ridley clenched her fists.

Without thinking about what she was doing, she found herself moving in their direction.

"I'm sorry for the way things ended between us but I've moved on and I suggest you do the same." Jackson turned as she walked up. Her mouth went dry.

The bravado that had compelled her to march over there didn't extend to knowing what to say.

"Hey. I was wondering where you'd gone off to."

The other woman looked her up and down but didn't extend her hand. "I'm Alana. I don't think I've met you before."

"Nice to meet you. I'm Ridley."

Jackson put an arm around her and anchored her to his side. "Hey, baby. I didn't mean to abandon you." He nuzzled her hair and snaked an arm around her back to settle possessively on her waist.

She looked at him in shock, then quickly covered her reaction with a bright smile. Her pulse raced as she curled against Jackson's chest. It shouldn't give her such satisfaction to see the other woman's eyes narrow at the affectionate gesture.

If he wanted her to play along to get rid of a clingy ex-girlfriend, she could do that. It was no big deal, despite the fact that her libido was suddenly wide awake and doing the samba. She'd have to be dead not to react to the flex and play of Jackson's muscles under the thin, short-sleeved shirt he wore.

Especially when he was holding her so tightly she was plastered against those muscles.

"No, I was fine," she managed to get out, hoping her voice didn't betray just how turned on she actually was. Did he have to smell like that, all warm and slightly sweet?

"I was just hanging out with Matt and watching the boys play. The thing is, I hate to be a party pooper but I think I'm going to go upstairs and lie down for a bit."

She figured it was as good an excuse as any. It was one thing to play lovers for a few minutes to fool his ex, but she couldn't be this close to Jackson for too long without melting into a puddle. No doubt, they were already attracting attention. She turned and met Nick's frosty gaze. She smiled at him, but he didn't smile back.

What is his deal?

"You live here?" Alana asked suspiciously. "Who are you, one of his little cousins?"

Ridley would have laughed in any other circumstance. She was used to the criticism. When people found out who her sister was, their first question was usually *why don't you look like that?* She was immune to rudeness at this point and she certainly wasn't going to take offense when the criticism came from a woman who looked like she had bird feathers or something equally ridiculous stuck to her eyelashes.

"Yes, I live here."

The ironic thing was she didn't even have to lie. She currently *was* living here, and unless her sister changed her mind about letting her stay in her house alone, she'd be here until Raina came back.

Jackson's hand tightened around her waist before he turned to look at her, his gratitude clear by the way the stress lines around his eyes relaxed a little. In that moment, Ridley experienced a fierce surge of protectiveness.

Cat fights weren't her style and she'd never been the type to engage in verbal spats over a man. If a man wanted to be with her, then he needed to tell other women he was taken.

Period.

But in this case, not only was Jackson not her boyfriend but she could clearly read the SOS the poor man was sending out. This girl looked like the type who wouldn't take no for an answer, and as his friend, she was more than happy to help him get this she-cat-in-heat off his back.

"Like I said, I'm going upstairs to rest. Are you coming?" she asked.

Jackson nodded slowly as if he couldn't believe what she was saying. Alana watched them with slitted eyes, her mouth falling open slightly as Ridley threaded her fingers through Jackson's. Just as they were walking off, Ridley turned back.

"And if Jackson and I are cousins, then I'm pretty sure we're both going to hell."

———

DID *she really just say that?*

Jackson was fully aware that he was playing with fire. He couldn't articulate what had made him do it. It was one thing to tell Alana he was dating someone else, but to draft Ridley into playing the part without permission was just asking to get slapped. He was lucky she'd gone along with it at all.

He certainly hadn't expected to hear her stick up for him in that honey-sweet voice of hers. Not only had she gotten him away from Alana, but she'd slyly insinuated they were sneaking off to have sex. Or at least that was how he'd interpreted it. He wasn't sure if she'd meant it to sound that way or if his dick had taken over his hearing.

Either way, he wasn't going to resist if she wanted to drag him upstairs. Even if it really was just to sleep.

"Sorry, I probably shouldn't have said that. She just pissed me off. One of your *cousins*. Really? Who hugs their cousin like that?" Ridley shook her head. "I won't ask why you were attracted to her. She's very pretty. Other than the crazy things stuck to her eyelashes and the pound of makeup she's wearing."

"No comment. But I'm willing to admit that most of my relationships are pretty shallow. My friends pushed me hard to get back into the dating scene after…"

"After your wife died. It's okay, Matt told me. I'm really sorry." She squeezed his hand as she said it.

His wife was usually a subject he didn't discuss with anyone. Part of him was angry that Matt had told her, but the other part was glad. Jackson couldn't figure out why, but for some reason he didn't mind talking about it with Ridley. She seemed like she really was sorry for his pain and not just saying it to score points like most of the women who eventually found out.

"Thanks. It was a hard time and after a while I started dating just to shut everyone else up. I'm sure you can imagine the kind of women they were setting me up with."

"Hey, I'm not judging. My own sister apparently thinks I'm a prude and need to sleep with a 'real man' like you."

Jackson choked, letting go of her hand to thump himself on the chest. "What?"

"I know. Crazy, right?" Ridley continued, seemingly oblivious to the fact that he was now completely aroused.

He put his hands in his pockets and tried to hitch his pants higher to cover his erection. "She actually said that?"

"Pretty much. She knows you're exactly my type, so she thinks I should use this time to seduce you. Of course, I told her I'd get right on that." She laughed and covered her face with her hands. "Wow, that's even more embarrassing than the first time I said it!"

"Jesus, Ridley." Jackson held a hand to his heart, which was now pounding so hard he worried it might jump out of his chest and land on the grass. "If I actually thought you meant that, you wouldn't be safe anywhere."

"Jackson..." she pleaded. "Don't make fun of me." She peeked at him from between her fingers.

"I'm not making fun of you, trust me." He stepped closer and pulled her hands down, holding them firmly in his. She watched with wide eyes as he dipped his head, her lips parting as he moved in.

There were a million reasons this was a bad idea. In fact, he'd listed them mentally just last night. However, he suddenly couldn't come up with even one. As he zeroed in on her mouth, all he could see was that her bottom lip was slightly fuller than the top. He was going to *bite* that plump lip.

Just then Matt walked up. "Hey. Look who just arrived."

It took Jackson a few moments before he could tear his gaze away from Ridley. She squeezed her eyes shut and let out a soft sigh, her breath wafting across his cheek. There were so many thoughts running through his head, all of them screaming at him to pick her up, throw her over his shoulder, and take her in the house. Then they could "get right on it" as she'd jokingly put it.

Only he wouldn't be playing around.

"Jackson? Uh, should I give you two a minute?" He met Matt's amused eyes and then followed his finger to where he pointed across the grass. What he saw cooled him down instantly. He took a deep breath and stepped back from Ridley.

"We'll *definitely* pick up this conversation later." Then he turned to the older couple walking in their direction.

"Mom! Dad! Over here." He waved his arm to attract their attention.

Alana, who'd been hovering off to the side watching them, huffed out a breath and scurried in the opposite direction, her short dress riding up as she trotted away.

"Well, what got her so excited? Not that I'm not happy she's finally gone," Ridley said.

He reflexively pulled her against his side again. Not that he wanted to fool his parents. His mother had eyes like a hawk and fooling her was something he hadn't attempted since he was a teenager. No, he realized he wanted Ridley to meet his parents just because he liked her.

"She never got along with my mother. She's probably afraid to face her. My mom is a bit intimidating sometimes."

Before she could answer, his parents approached. His father immediately pulled him into a hearty hug. "There's my boy!"

Jackson laughed and hugged him back, his father's joy contagious. Mark Alexander had a way of making every gathering a party and treated everyone he met like family.

Between volunteer work mentoring at their church and taking on more summer workers than he needed just so the local boys could have productive work, he was always helping others in some way. When Jackson was younger, it was hard for him to understand why his father gave so much of his time and energy to others. In some cases, he'd felt like people took advantage of his father's welcoming nature.

Now that he was older and hopefully wiser, he saw his father's actions for what they truly were.

Kindness.

He hugged his mother and gently kissed her cheek, then stood still so she could fuss over him as she liked to do. After several exclamations over how thin he was and how he needed to take better care of himself, he was finally able to get a word in edgewise.

"Mom and Dad, I'd like you to meet Ridley Wells. Ridley is my neighbor and lives the next street over. Ridley, these are my parents, Mark and Julia Alexander."

Ridley glanced up at him and smiled softly, looking relieved when he didn't mention anything about the accident. He hated that she still seemed ashamed about it. His parents wouldn't fault her for her circumstances. If anything, his mother would probably bundle her up and coo over her just like she did her own children.

"Hello, Ridley. I'm so glad you decided to join us today." His mother hugged her briefly and she shook hands with his father.

"Jackson was really nice to invite me. I just wish I'd had time to prepare something."

His mother's eyes lit up. "That's all right, honey. Do you like potato salad? Mine is on the end of the buffet in the red-and-white bowl."

"I'll be sure to try it. My potato salad was never anything special, but I make really good seafood salad. It's one of my sister's favorites."

Jackson was amazed. The one time he'd introduced Alana to his parents, they'd spent the entire evening making awkward conversation. Ridley, however, seemed to have no problem chatting with them. When he tuned back into the conversation, his father was trying to convince her to make him a shrimp salad.

"Dad! She's not here to work. You're going to scare her away."

His father winked at him and nodded in Ridley's direction. Jackson shook his head slowly, hoping his father understood that they were just friends. The idea of being just friends with a beautiful woman was foreign to his dad—well, to pretty much every guy he knew. But after the way they'd connected last night, they definitely weren't strangers, yet they weren't going to be lovers, either. He owed her better than that.

"Oh, honey. What happened to you?"

When Ridley went rigid at his side, he knew his mother had caught sight of the bruises she'd tried to cover with her long-sleeved shirt.

"Oh, it's nothing. I was in an a...accident," she stammered.

"That looks really bad!" Julia held Ridley's wrist and pulled her sleeve back to examine the marks on her wrist.

"Mom, don't—" He shook his head at her.

Julia's eyes went wide and then she looked back at Ridley, who pulled the sleeves of her shirt all the way down. Then she gave him a short nod as if to say "We'll talk about this later." Jackson had no doubt his mother would want the whole story as soon as she could get him alone.

"Well, I hope we'll be seeing more of you. Such a pretty girl!" She pulled Ridley into a tight hug, rocking her back and forth. When she finally released her, she smoothed a gentle hand over her hair.

Ridley blushed. "Thank you."

"Well, excuse us, kids, but it's time for me to say hello to the rest of the family." Julia turned to Jackson. "Oh, and I found a nanny for you, Jackson. Remember Miss Bessie from church?"

"Miss Bessie? She used to baby-sit *me*. And I'm pretty sure she was really old even then."

His mother narrowed her eyes.

"Not that it matters," he added quickly. "Thank you for the recommendation, Mom."

"Of course. I want my babies to be well taken care of. Speaking of which, I got new bunk beds for the boys. Why don't you drop them off on Sunday so they can spend a few days with me? I'm due for some grandma time with my little rascals." She glanced at Ridley with a sly smile. "You can bring Ridley with you. We'd love to see you for Sunday dinner."

Jackson smiled knowingly. "Right. Thanks, Mom. I'll take you up on that." He bent over so his mother could kiss his cheek again before his parents crossed to the table where Elliott stood, bobbing his head to the music.

"Your mom is something else. Was I imagining that or is she matchmaking?" Ridley asked.

"It means she liked you. She's probably hoping I use the kid-free time to wine and dine you." He winked at her.

When Elliott saw their mother, he immediately cut the music and handed her a microphone.

"When she said she needed to say hi to the rest of the family I didn't think she meant a speech." Ridley turned to him with wide eyes.

"Welcome to life with the Alexanders."

nine

"HELLO, family! Thank you for coming to the annual Alexander Memorial Day barbecue!"

Ridley felt like she was in a sitcom as she watched Mrs. Alexander tap her microphone a few times before beaming her bright smile at the guests assembled.

Her blood pressure was still high from almost kissing Jackson. As embarrassing as it had been, she was glad Matt had come to warn them. They'd been right outside where anyone could see them. What if his *parents* had walked up while they were tonguing each other down?

"We used to meet at the family home, the Alexander-Bennett Co-op, affectionately known around our parts as the 'ABC Farm.' A few years ago I asked Jackson to start hosting, mainly so he couldn't avoid us."

There was a resounding cheer from the crowd before Elliott held up a hand to quiet them. Ridley glanced around. It was an eclectic group of people, some older, some younger and every shade of skin possible.

"I see a few new faces this year, which really warms my heart.

Our party always includes family *and* friends because in the Alexander family, if we love you, then you're one of us. My sons have friends who have been hanging around since college and just because I didn't birth you doesn't mean you aren't mine." She waved to Trent, Matt, and Mara, who were standing near the front.

"Now, many of you know the story of how the Alexander family barbecue started, but for those who don't, I'll share it again. It was, oh, a million years ago," she said, eliciting a soft titter from the crowd, "that I met a handsome young man named Mark Alexander." She looked over at her husband, who stood with his arm around Bennett's shoulders.

"We lived on neighboring farms our entire lives and I even played with his younger sister, Maria. But since he was a little older than I was, I never really took notice of him until the summer my parents took me to the Alexanders' farm for a party. When Maria introduced me to her older brother, who was home after recently graduating from college, well... Let's just say my teenage heart went pitter-pat."

Ridley leaned back against Jackson's chest, completely wrapped up in the story. She could just see the scene his mother described—a young woman meeting the love of her life for the first time on a hot summer day.

"I thought he was quite handsome and sophisticated. That didn't last long, however, because he said something stupid, as young men often do, and we hated each other for the rest of the summer!"

Ridley laughed along with everyone else as Mark held up his hands, then bowed theatrically.

Jackson pulled her closer to whisper in her ear. "He always acts embarrassed, but secretly I think he loves it when she tells this story."

"I bet he does." Ridley sighed. "It's obvious how much they

love each other. I've only just met them and I can feel it." They turned their attention back up front as Julia cleared her throat.

"Anyway, after many failed attempts on Mark's part to get back into my good graces, tragedy struck. My dear parents died in a car crash, leaving me as the sole owner of the Bennett farm."

She stopped and looked up, one hand over her heart. Silence descended over the group, everyone equally affected by the grief in Julia's voice. When she looked back at the crowd, tears shimmered in her eyes.

"I was so lost, but faith is what carried me through. That and the gracious love of the Alexander family. Mark, especially, was by my side through that heartbreaking time and taught me that family is about so much more than a blood bond. Family is about the heart."

Ridley sighed as Julia blew a kiss to her husband. She wiped her eyes quickly, embarrassed to be so moved by the story. It was exactly the kind of thing she'd always hoped to find with someone. A genuine love, deep and true, that could carry you through the tragedies and the joys of life.

She'd started to believe it didn't exist.

"Ever since then, we've continued the tradition and hosted our own summer party as a reminder to cherish the ones you love and the time you have together. This year coming up will be our thirtieth wedding anniversary."

She stopped as everyone broke into applause. Ridley clapped along with everyone else. She couldn't even imagine spending thirty years with someone. They'd been together longer than she'd been alive.

"And the most important thing I've learned from these thirty years is to take each day as it comes and cherish it."

"I asked her that one day," Jackson whispered in her ear.

"What? You asked her about being married?"

"No, I asked her how she knew my dad was the one. She's

always said you're with the right person when no matter how bad things get, you'd still rather be with them than anywhere else. She always says that no matter how long she and my dad are together, she still wants more time with him. She wants one more day. Every day."

His arm tightened around her waist and Ridley stopped breathing. For a long moment they stood staring at each other until his mother's voice came over the sound system again, breaking the spell.

Ridley whipped back around and faced front. Jackson's arm squeezed her tightly before he let her go. She moved away slightly, ignoring the rapid beating of her heart.

"Enjoy the rest of the party, everyone, and make sure you take a plate home. Don't you leave us with all this food! On second thought, leave some of those ribs for Jackson—he's getting too skinny." On that note, Mrs. Alexander pushed the microphone back to Elliott and bustled over to the picnic tables.

Jackson groaned. "Oh, the joys of having a big family."

"It's nice! She's worried about her baby boy."

"Do I look like a baby to you?"

She giggled when he flexed his muscles. "Okay, okay. You are definitely not a baby."

"All right, I guess I should stop showing off. Come on, I want you to meet some of my cousins. They live over in West Haven."

———

A FEW HOURS LATER, Jackson was forced to admit there wasn't anything else he could clean up or move around in the backyard. His parents had taken care of packing up the leftover food and Matt had stayed to help him corral all the recycling and trash containers into the garage.

There was simply nothing left for him to do. Except go in the house and face Ridley.

You're an ass, you know that?

He cringed. Introducing her to his cousins and then leaving her to fend for herself had seemed like a good idea at the time. She was just so beautiful and fit in far too well with his family and friends. The last thing he wanted was for them to start something they couldn't finish.

He'd been *this* close to kissing her in the middle of the yard before his parents had shown up and he had no doubt it would have been as hot as he thought it'd be. But as hot as the fire sparked between them, it would be a temporary thing at best. She deserved better than that.

"I'm going to take off." Matt appeared at his left elbow holding one of the plastic containers of food that Julia had divvied up for everyone to take home. "Hopefully Mara and Trent will already be asleep by the time I get there."

Jackson clapped him on the shoulder. "Are you going to be okay? Seriously?"

Matt shrugged. "Yeah. It's weird. For months all you can think about is coming home but when you get here, you realize everyone else hasn't been sitting on their hands while you've been gone. Things change and you just have to deal with it. I'll be fine."

"Getting your own place would help."

"Funny you should say that. Nick has decided to take care of that for me. He's taking me out to look for condos this week. You know how he is. According to him, I just need to get laid and not having my own place is blocking my swag."

"That sounds like something Nick would say."

They both shook their heads. Jackson had gotten a reputation over the last year as a player, but it was nothing compared to Nick's. His brother took debauchery to another level and treated it like a career.

"Where's Ridley?" Matt asked.

Jackson nodded toward the house. "I noticed her go in a while ago. I think the boys wanted to show her some of their games. I should probably go rescue her. I'm sure they're tired and cranky by now and need to go to bed."

"Can I tell you something? Without you getting mad?" Matt shuffled his feet.

"We've been friends too long for you to hold back on me now."

Matt stared at him for a moment, then said, "Ridley's great and I think she's perfect for you. So get off your ass and do something about it before I do."

Then he turned and walked off.

"Good night to you too, old friend!" he called out after Matt's retreating back. The only reply Matt gave was raising his hand and pointing his middle finger to the sky.

Jackson was still smiling when he walked into the house. A light glowed faintly in the kitchen. The rest of the house was dark.

"Ridley?"

The counter was wiped clean and all the party platters had been stacked neatly next to the sink. He walked back out to the family room and up the stairs. Ridley was no doubt exhausted and had probably gone to bed already. Not that he could blame her. He was used to listening to Chris's chatter but someone who wasn't would feel like their head was spinning after an hour or so.

"Come on, boys. It's time for bed." There was no reply. He hadn't really been expecting one.

Despite the fact that bedtime came around the same time every night, it was always a fight to get them to brush their teeth, put on their pajamas, and stop asking for water and bathroom breaks. It was usually a good hour before he was able to get them settled down and in the bed. As he approached the boys' bedroom door, he heard the soft murmur of voices.

He pushed the door open and to his delight found both boys

clustered around Ridley on floor pillows as she read from one of their favorite books.

"But I was never to see Peter Pan again. Now I tell his story to my children and they will tell it to their children, and so it will go on—for all children grow up. Except one."

As she finished the last page of the book, she hugged them to her before waving them over to their beds. Jackson watched, astonished, as they scrambled beneath their covers and waited patiently for Ridley to tuck them in.

Who are these angels and what have they done with my real children? Jackson thought.

Normally he would give the boys hugs and kisses good night, but he was afraid to break the spell. He backed out of the room and waited in the hall for Ridley to come out. She appeared a moment later, pulling the door closed behind her.

"Hey. Is everyone gone?"

He nodded and leaned his head back against the wall. The day was starting to catch up with him and he was suddenly exhausted.

"So, did you guys finish cleaning up outside?"

"We did. Matt helped me put everything back. Sorry for just leaving you on your own at the end there."

"I hardly expected you to stick to me all night. Besides, I got a chance to chat with your brother, Bennett. Did you know he's been cultivating new strains of disease-resistant crops?"

"No, I had no idea. He's always so quiet." His oldest brother was usually reserved around people he'd just met, but it wasn't hard to believe that he'd opened up to Ridley.

She seemed to have that effect on people.

"He said he's working on a new corn hybrid right now. I only work with flowers, but it was so interesting to hear about how technology is changing the farming industry." Ridley tucked her hands in her pockets and leaned against the wall next to him.

"I really appreciate you putting the boys to bed. You didn't have to do that. I know they're a handful. Jase is usually up five or six times wanting water or something. Anything to keep him from having to go to bed. Luckily Chris sleeps just like I do—like a corpse."

"It was no problem. They're wonderful. Boisterous and happy just as they should be." A wistful look passed over her face as she glanced back at the closed bedroom door.

"You really love kids," Jackson said. He didn't phrase it as a question. "I noticed it when we first met and even more so today. And the boys adore you."

"I adore them, too. Children represent the best of us. My mom had to work late a lot of the time, so my sister and I were usually on our own. We used to take turns 'mothering' each other. It's sad, but we were just imitating the bedtime rituals we saw on television. Our own mother wasn't the most maternal person."

"Sorry. That's rough. I know how hard it is to be a single parent, but I'm trying to make sure my kids never feel it."

"Now that I'm older, I'm trying to understand that it wasn't personal. She got pregnant accidentally and we never had a lot of money. So, I think under the circumstances she was doing the best she could even if it wasn't anywhere near good enough."

Jackson looked over at her. "It still sucks."

Ridley laughed out loud before covering her mouth with her hand and glancing at the boys' door. "Oh, Jackson. You have such a way with words."

Just then the boys' door opened and Jase came out into the hallway. "RiRi, I want kisses." He raced over and threw his arms around Ridley's legs. She scooped him up and kissed him soundly on the cheek before depositing him back on the floor. He then grabbed Jackson around the legs and hugged him, too.

Jase pointed at Jackson. "You put Daddy night-night with kisses, too?"

"I don't think your daddy needs help going to sleep, baby."

"You'd be wrong about that," Jackson muttered.

Their eyes held for a moment before she blushed and looked away. She held out her hand to Jase. "Come on, back to bed." He grasped her hand and allowed her to lead him back to the room.

A moment later she emerged again, pulling the door shut behind her. "You weren't kidding about Chris. He's already snoring!"

"I wish I could say I don't know where the snoring comes from, but unfortunately he inherited that from me, too."

He couldn't help staring at her. After a day in the sun, her light brown skin was tanned a shade darker. She looked golden and glowing with health, especially since she'd loosened her ponytail so her long curls spilled around her shoulders.

"What?" Her hand came up to her face. "You're staring."

"I am. You're beautiful."

"Jackson? I mean I know we were pretending to be together before but—" She stopped, seemingly at a loss for words.

"It wasn't much of an act on my part. I like you, Ridley," he admitted softly. "Way more than I should."

"I like you, too. More than just about anyone else I've met. What's wrong with two people liking each other?" she asked.

She stepped close enough that her scent enveloped him, a soft fragrance which reminded him of wildflowers. He tried to keep his hands out of the equation, sure that if he touched her again there was nothing in the world that would convince him to let her go. But when she stood on tiptoe and ran her hands over his hair, he gave up.

He grabbed her by the bottom and squeezed. Then she was kissing him and his thoughts scattered. There was just the soft, sweet press of her lips against his and the darkly addictive taste of her in his mouth. She moaned softly and the sound raced through him like a shiver. God, those sounds she made went straight to his dick every time.

Her soft curls brushed against his nose and the effect was like a sucker punch to the gut, lust tightening his muscles in an iron-clad grip. It took everything in him not to carry her to his bed. But in that moment, as he held her cuddled against him, he knew he needed to stop things now. Because she liked him. She *trusted* him.

And he was the last thing she needed.

He let out a breath. "There's so much you don't know about me. You deserve someone who's ready to love you. I can't be that guy."

He put her down carefully and stepped back. She licked her lips and he groaned. She wasn't even trying to make this easy for him.

If she was anyone else, maybe he could say to hell with it and just do what he was dying to do. Kiss her, thread his hands through all that wild hair, and own her mouth. Fantasies of pressing her against the wall and of her wrapping her long legs around his waist raced through his mind. There was no doubt in his mind that they'd burn each other up, no doubt that the embers crackling between them would ignite into a raging inferno if he took her to bed.

But she wasn't someone else, and he liked her too much to toy with her. So he had to do the only thing he could.

Walk away.

———

"TELL me you and Jackson have never... you know?"

Ridley sat on the edge of the bed in the guest room clutching her cell phone to her ear like a lifeline. All her senses were still reeling from that kiss. If she stood up straight she just might pass out again.

Damn, the man could kiss.

Even though Jackson had walked away, she couldn't deny the thrill she got from pushing him so close to the edge. Until she remembered that he thought she was her sister. Was he responding to her, or was this just leftover lust for Raina? She had to know.

"Huh? Who is this?"

"Raina, it's me. Who did you think it was?"

"Oh, hey, sis. Since when do you stay up past ten thirty?"

Ridley lay down and crossed her legs on top of the fluffy comforter. "I'm not as boring as you seem to think. Now answer the question. Have you and Jackson ever dated? Because I'm catching some vibes that he kind of likes you. Which is a little weird, to be honest. Since, you know, I'm not you."

"Relax. Jackson and I are just friends. We're probably better described as acquaintances. His boys come over and play in my yard and we talk about the weather. The usual neighborly talk, I guess."

"Oh. Well, good."

"Why?" Raina drawled. "Did he do something?"

"No." Ridley mentally crossed her fingers. "I just wanted to make sure. This whole thing is stressful enough. The last thing I need is to find out that he's one of your boyfriends."

"He's a nice guy and always invites me over when he's having a party. I've never gone, but I have to say that family parties like it's 1999. They have some kind of shindig for every holiday. Even the ones that no one has ever heard of, like 'Grandparent's Day' and 'Save a Hedgehog Day'. It's weird."

"I think it's nice. A family that actually enjoys spending time together is kind of refreshing."

"Well, whatever. That much family time is enough to give me

an itch. I'm glad you're enjoying yourself, though. Once I'm back, we can figure out what kind of mess you're in."

"Hopefully, the police will have more information about what's going on soon. So far, all I know is that David found out something about our father that got him killed. The FBI saw him talking to a guy who's a member of a well-known crime family. So, it turns out you were right."

"I didn't want to be," Raina whispered.

"I know. I'm sorry about the way I reacted before. You were just trying to warn me, and I bit your head off. Said terrible things. And the whole time you were right. Some things are better left in the past."

"I'm sorry, too. I shouldn't have been so judgmental. Just because I don't want to meet our father doesn't mean I should expect you to feel the same way. After all this is over, I'll have Sam look into it for you. He's got crazy connections."

It was a tempting offer, but it felt a little like poking the lid on Pandora's box. What if Sam found proof Moreno was their father? Did she really want to know? Could she live with that knowledge the rest of her life, or was it better just to wonder?

Or what if what he found was even worse?

"Thanks, Raina. But I think maybe I'm finally ready to let this one go."

The thought made her inexplicably sad. Raina must have sensed it because she was quiet for a minute, then said brightly, "Anyway, I'll be back this weekend. If this shoot was anything other than *Sports Illustrated*, you know I'd come home immediately, right?"

"I know. I don't want you to miss this, either. I've been here this long, so I can hang out for a few more days. I don't suppose it'll make much difference at this point."

But as she hung up with her sister she wondered if the next few days wouldn't be the hardest she'd ever been through.

Ridley got up from the bed and wandered over to the window. She pushed it up and stuck her head out into the warm, humid night air. Her room faced the back of the house so all she could see were trees and the backs of other houses. Raina's house should be a few houses down on the right. There was a light shining through the trees right where her sister's house should be.

Was that a light on?

Ridley leaned farther, stretching as far as she could over the windowsill. Just then the light went off. She shook her head. That must be one of Raina's neighbors. She'd probably misjudged the distance. Then she remembered the phone call from Mrs. Ashton. If someone was willing to burn down her apartment, what would stop them from trying to do the same to her sister's house?

Nothing, she thought with a shiver. She backed up and closed the window, making sure the locks were in place.

Absolutely nothing.

ten

"NO! NO, PLEASE! LEAVE ME ALONE!"

Jackson bolted straight up in bed, his heart racing. The clock on his bedside table blinked 2:02 a.m. He was surprised he'd fallen asleep at all. After leaving Ridley standing alone in the hallway, he'd been too riled up, okay, too damn aroused, to relax.

He'd paced the floor for a while. He'd taken a cold shower. He'd done push-ups until he was too exhausted to continue. None of it had made a damn bit of difference.

Normally he'd go downstairs and watch a movie or something but he didn't want to take the chance of running into Ridley. He wasn't a saint, and if confronted with her sweet little body again while his blood was still high, he couldn't guarantee he'd be honorable enough to walk away this time. She'd end up bent over the couch with her little shorts around her ankles as he took her from behind.

And *damn* if that wasn't a mental image. He swore as he hardened again beneath the sheets.

Then he heard a soft moan.

"I don't know anything! Just leave me alone." There was silence, then the soft sound of crying.

"What the hell? Ridley?" He threw off his covers and sprinted through his open door and down the hall. He'd deliberately given her a room that was as far away from his as possible so she could have her privacy. Now he was cursing the decision as a million scenarios raced through his mind. What if the people she was running from had followed her here? Broken into the house?

He crashed through the door and then blinked in the bright light. Ridley lay on the top of the bed, thrashing back and forth. Every light in the room was blazing, including the lights in the adjoining bathroom. He approached the bed carefully. He'd always heard you shouldn't wake people in the midst of a night-mare, but for the life of him he couldn't remember what you *should* do. Surely he wasn't supposed to just leave her in terror?

"Just let me go," she sobbed.

"Forget this." Jackson climbed on the bed next to her and pulled her into his arms. She immediately clung to his bare chest and pressed her wet cheeks against his skin.

"Shhh, it's okay. Ridley, you're safe," he whispered to her and stroked a hand up and down her back. After a few minutes, she calmed. When he looked down, her eyes were open but wild and though she was looking directly at him, he couldn't tell if she really knew he was there.

Finally her eyes focused and she whispered, "Jackson?"

"I'm here. Ridley, I'm right here."

She squeezed her eyes shut again and tears slid down her cheeks. "I woke you. I'm so sorry. It was just a dream. A stupid dream."

He held her tighter. It seemed completely inadequate, but in that moment it was all he had. He couldn't fight the demons for her, but he could hold her and let her know she wasn't alone, at least. He knew what it was like to feel utterly isolated.

As if you were standing in the midst of a storm with nothing to anchor you.

"You want to tell me what it was about?"

Ridley was quiet for a moment, then a shiver wracked her slender frame. "They tried to burn down my apartment."

"What?" Jackson pulled back slightly so he could see her face.

"I keep a small apartment in Florida. My landlady called yesterday. There was a fire the day after I left. Then before bed, I thought I saw something outside the window. I'm scared, Jackson. What if the people who killed David are looking for me? What if they're trying to kill me, too?" Her eyes welled with tears again.

"Shhh, now. You don't know that for sure. Either way, they don't know where you are, and they're not going to find out if I have anything to do about it. It's okay, Ridley. You're safe here." He made soft noises as he rubbed her back.

She took several shaky breaths, then finally exhaled the long, rattling sigh of the truly exhausted. After a few minutes, her breathing finally slowed to a normal rate. He looked down at the top of her head, a profound sense of peace washing over him.

"You don't have to stay. I'm okay now. I know you don't want to be here."

"That's not true. I wasn't asleep, anyway. I was trying to decide whether I should take another cold shower or not."

She blushed and lowered her eyes. "Well, that's your own fault."

"I know, baby girl." He kissed the top of her head.

Her fingers danced gently over the tattoo on his chest. "I've never been into tattoos, but this fits you."

He looked down at the design he'd gotten in his first year of college. "I was called 'Treble' because I was a music major. I was always humming bars and scribbling pieces of songs on napkins. Eventually it became less like 'treble' and more like 'trouble.' I have no idea why, of course." He wiggled his eyebrows at her.

Relief swept through him when she smiled in response, looking more like herself.

"What about you?" He tilted his head in her direction. "Tell me something about you. Something no one knows."

She sighed and laid her head on his chest. "I love to garden."

"Really?"

"Yeah. What? You can't imagine me gardening? I don't mind getting a little dirty."

"I just bet you don't."

She smacked his chest playfully. "I guess I walked right into that one, didn't I?"

He squeezed her. "I'm just teasing you."

"I've been saving to start my own landscape-design business. I had the perfect location picked out and everything. Who knows how long before I can go back, though? I feel like my whole life is on hold."

He stopped rubbing her back and turned them so they were laying side by side, facing each other.

"If you're passionate about this, then don't let anything hold you back. You can start a business here. I'll be your first client. You've seen what my yard looks like. I need all the help I can get."

"You know I'd love to help you but this is exactly why I wanted to open a business in Florida. My sister has offered to help me so many times, but I want to do it on my own. To the people there, I'm just Ridley. No one could say I was successful due to who I know."

"When I was first starting out and needed the money to buy professional equipment, Nick was the first in line to help me out. If he hadn't done that, I wouldn't be where I am now. Everyone needs help in the beginning. There's no shame in that. That's what people who care about you do. They help you."

"And you want to help me? Because you care about me?"

"Yeah, I do. You deserve to get everything you want."

"But I can't have what I want," she whispered.

"What do you—" Jackson broke off with a strangled sound

when the soft hand that had been resting against his chest reached down and gripped him through the soft cotton of his sweatpants. *"Whoa."* He gulped when she turned her face and kissed his chest. "What are you doing?"

She tugged on the waistband of his sweatpants gently.

"Getting what I want."

———

TO THINK that she'd gone so long without knowing how crazy passion could make you and how hot and hungry you could feel when that passion was denied.

Even at their best, none of her previous boyfriends had come anywhere near the way Jackson made her feel with just two stolen kisses.

And they didn't have abs like these.

She traced each one and then followed the same path with her tongue.

He reared up off the bed. "I thought we agreed that this was a bad idea."

She looked up at him innocently. "You agreed. I didn't."

"Ridley," he warned.

"I have a proposition for you," she whispered against his beautifully taut lower abdomen.

"Christ." He shuddered as she bit him gently. "Yes. Whatever you want, I say yes."

"One night. You said you aren't ready to love and that's okay. Let's just get it out of our systems, and tomorrow it'll be like it never happened. Like a dream."

What if she walked away from Jackson without indulging and then never met anyone else she had this connection with? What if she never understood what her girlfriends in college had whispered about, the kind of lust that made you forget your own name and do things that embarrassed you the next morning?

For once she would take her sister's advice and worry about the consequences later.

"If you don't agree, just tell me you don't want me and I'll stop."

"That would be impossible," he mumbled.

Trailing her fingers around his neck, she stroked the sensitive skin behind his ears. His eyes slid closed against the sensual pressure she was exerting. She shifted her attention to the bunched muscles in his neck and giggled softly at his moans when she stopped touching him.

Once his eyes opened again, she reached up and pulled the band from her hair. She gently combed the thick strands around her face before pushing Jackson to lie on his back.

"I was trying to be the good guy here."

"Don't be," she whispered. She licked her lips slowly and Jackson cursed softly. "So, we're in agreement?"

"Hell yeah. I've got a lot to work out of my system where you're concerned." His hands came up and found her breasts through the tee shirt she'd borrowed. "*Damn*, girl. My shirt never looked this good on me."

"It'll look even better once I take it off." She yanked it over her head and let it drift to the floor next to the bed.

The thin cotton panties she wore couldn't conceal the wet heat between her legs as she leaned over him, tendrils of her hair trailing over his chest and stomach.

Despite her protests, he flipped her onto her back and covered her body with his before she could move. He grabbed her hands and held them over her head. Ridley tried to free herself, but found she had no strength to struggle. The force of his arms holding her down was strangely thrilling and she savored the feeling of his thick body pressing her into the mattress.

Jackson would never hurt her and her trust in him made her feel safe despite her captivity.

Then he licked a path from her neck down to her shoulder. She squirmed beneath him as he gently laved a nipple before kissing each of her ribs. He licked into the dip of her belly button and then glanced up at her before moving lower.

"If you only knew the things I want to do to you," he breathed against her thigh.

Is he? Oh, yes he is, she thought breathlessly, right before he bit her lower belly.

She cried out when he licked her through the soft silk at her core, the heat of his tongue penetrating through the fabric.

"Open for me, baby girl. That's it." He growled his approval when her legs fell open and then he moved forward, his whole body crowding into the space between them. He kissed her like he was kissing her mouth, like he couldn't get enough. He held her thighs open, not letting her close them.

"Jackson." She shuddered beneath him as he tongued the material until it clung to her skin. He looked up at her, his eyes even darker, glazed over with lust.

Then he hooked a finger in her panties and edged them to the side. He held her gaze as he leaned back down, his mouth meeting her skin to skin for the first time.

"Oh my god." She grabbed the sheets, twisting them until her fingers felt like they'd break. Perspiration broke out over her skin as he did something with his teeth that sent her flying. Colors exploded behind her eyelids as she came under his mouth, her flesh contracting against his lips.

She clamped a hand over her mouth as sensations raced over every inch of her skin. He kept at it, licking deeper until she felt herself climbing again.

"Jackson, please!"

Her cries seemed to incite him, drive him harder as he pulled her between his lips over and over. She pushed backward with her hands, instinctively trying to escape from the overwhelming sensations, but he wouldn't let her. Her breaths came faster and faster as he gripped her thighs and forced her to take it. Forced her to take the pleasure until she came for him again.

Tears slid down her cheeks as she shivered under him. The wave of ecstasy finally crested and she was left panting in its wake. Once she was aware of herself again, she looked down to see him watching her. She turned her face against her arm, suddenly embarrassed.

"Don't get shy on me now," he teased. He gently pried the tangled sheet from her fists and then yanked it from the bed.

She let out a startled laugh. "Sorry about that. I didn't rip it, did I?"

He gave her a slow, sexy smile.

"Not yet."

JACKSON COULD BARELY HEAR his own thoughts over the sound of his blood rushing. Ridley lay sprawled on the bed, her lush naked breasts taunting him as he tried to remember what he needed to do. He'd just had the thought but lost it every time he looked at her.

"I have to cover you up. I can't think when you look like that."

He put her shirt back on before he wrapped her in the sheet. As crazy as she made him, he knew he needed to take her back to his bed. They were too close to his sons' room and he didn't have any protection with him.

He picked her up and cradled her against his chest. He paused at the door to the guest room and listened before he stepped out into the hall. It was quiet, so he carried her down the hall to his room. After he settled her on his bed, he walked back to the door and locked it.

When he turned around and looked at her, she bit her lip and pulled the sheet up higher.

"Oh, you won't be needing that again for a few hours."

"Hours?" she squeaked.

He grinned and pulled open the top drawer of his dresser. There was an entire box of condoms in the corner.

Shit, how long have these been in here?

He flipped it over to check the expiration date and almost cheered. He pulled out a strip of six and carried it to the night table next to the bed. Ridley watched him with wide eyes.

"Don't worry; I've got more if we need them."

Her eyebrows shot up. "Oh, I see. Someone's pretty confident." Her eyes held a hint of a challenge as she kneeled on the bed in front of him.

"Shouldn't I be? Or perhaps I haven't convinced you I'm worth your time yet?"

He climbed on the bed next to her and buried his face in her neck. The skin there was so delicate and soft and she smelled so damn good. His soft bites drew a strangled cry from her throat.

"I can't wait to be inside you." He put both hands under her shoulders and pulled her against him for a deep, punishing kiss, his hips rocking his erection against her core. "If I only get one night, I have to know what it feels like. Just the thought of you squeezing me so hard while you're screaming my name—"

"Jackson." She moaned beneath him, her hands tightening on his shoulders so hard that her nails bit into his skin.

"Hold on, baby."

It took a little maneuvering to remove his sweatpants without being separated from her soft body for too long. He reached over to the nightstand and pulled a packet off the strip. He ripped the foil open and was just about to roll the condom on when she propped herself up on one elbow and placed a hand on his arm to stop him.

"Wait, I just want..." She pushed him onto his back. "...to taste you, too."

He stopped breathing at the first touch of her moist lips against his shaft.

"Oh, shit." His fingers fisted in her long locks when she suddenly took the tip into her mouth and swirled her tongue over the head. Her long lashes settled against her cheeks as she lapped at him, her little pink tongue curling around the base before she worked her way back up. When she finally pulled back to trace the tip of her finger around the tip, her full lips looked slightly swollen.

Just the sight made him feel like a caveman.

He was a patient man but there was only so much he could take, and if she didn't stop teasing him, it would be over before it began. He wanted their first time together to be amazing. And this time there would be no interruptions.

He pushed her back on the bed, unable to think of anything other than getting inside her. He rolled the protection down over his shaft and lay in the cradle of her thighs. She sighed as their naked flesh met and clung.

"You feel so good," she whispered. She wrapped her long legs around his waist.

He rocked his hips, sliding inside her in one thick thrust.

He threw his head back, the tight grip of her body almost too much. He pulled out and then thrust again, grinding himself into the soft heat between her legs. She sighed and arched up against him. The movement pushed her breasts against his chest.

He sucked in his breath at the sight of her perfect, toffee-colored breasts. Her dusky nipples looked like Hershey's Kisses against the caramel of her skin.

"So pretty and perfect. And so responsive." Her unique aroma wrapped around him as he pressed his face between her breasts. He wanted to roll himself in the sweet scent until it clung to his skin.

He teased the tip of one nipple with his finger before he took it into his mouth and sucked it deep. She cried out as he rolled it between his lips, drawing the tip between his teeth lightly. He played with it as he moved inside her, his thrusts coming faster and harder until they ended up diagonal on the mattress with her head hanging over the edge.

"Oh, you're going to make me come again," she panted, her words almost incoherent as he rode her with long, thick thrusts that had her full breasts bouncing against his mouth.

Moisture flooded her core and he groaned. She was so wet, so hot.

"Come for me." He turned his face and muttered the words against her open mouth. He had to see her face when she came. He *needed* it. "Come for me again. Let me see how much you want it."

Then her back bowed and her inner muscles clamped down around him. Her eyes flew open and he saw it, the moment she lost control of herself.

"Oh God, I can't," she wailed before her hands tightened in his hair.

They both cried out at the exquisite sensation as he pistoned back and forth through her rapidly clenching muscles. As her inner walls trembled around him, he couldn't hold back any more and just let go.

Moments later, as he lay panting in the cradle of her arms, he looked at her in amazement. He'd expected it to be good. He'd even expected it to be better than anything he'd ever felt before.

What he hadn't expected was not wanting it to ever end.

eleven

WHIRRRRRRRR.

Ridley flopped over in bed, pulling the pillow over her head. She was so cozy and warm. She could just stay in this bed forever, especially since she'd just been dreaming about the best sex of her life.

A second later, her eyes popped open as the events of the previous night rushed back. The heated talk in the hall. Going to bed alone. Waking up from her nightmare in Jackson's arms. She turned and looked at the space next to her.

Empty.

Ohmygodohmygodohmygod.

The man had done things to her body that she'd only read about in books. He'd touched her in places and licked her in places that she couldn't even think about without blushing.

She dropped her head back down on the pillow as heat rushed from her head to her toes.

If she'd wanted to know what all her girlfriends had whispered about in college, what had made them do the crazy things they did for their boyfriends, she'd definitely gotten her wish. A man who could make you feel like that at night could get away with pretty much anything in the daylight.

What had she been thinking? Had she really believed that they could have sex and then pretend like it hadn't happened?

WHIRRRRRRRR.

Ridley pushed the pillow off her head violently and it fell over the side of the bed. "Ugh. What is that noise?"

The morning sunlight coming through the sheer white curtains in her room was almost blinding. She blinked against the light and groped the night table until her hand hit her cell phone. She lifted her head just enough to see the time.

"It's only seven thirty. Who's making this much noise at seven thirty?" Her head dropped down to the bare mattress and she took a deep breath.

WHIRRRRRRRR.

"That's it." She sat up and pushed the heavy comforter and silky-soft sheets back. It almost pained her to do it. Jackson had carried her back to her room in the middle of the night and she'd been in the most restful sleep ever since then.

Before being awakened at the unseemly hour of seven thirty a.m., that is.

She marched down the stairs, still wearing Jackson's shirt and her terry-cloth shorts. Her bare feet barely made any noise on the carpeted stairs. Once she reached the bottom she looked both ways. Nothing seemed amiss. The family room looked undisturbed. The only thing that was different was the can of unopened paint next to the front door.

"Who's painting at this hour?"

WHIRRRRRRRR.

She jumped, the noise so much louder now that she was downstairs. It had come from behind her, so she spun on her heel and went into the formal living room. It was done all in white with accents of Wedgwood blue. It didn't look like Jackson's style at all, but now that she saw how snooty his ex-girlfriend was, she had to wonder if this room reflected *her* taste.

She bent to look out the window. Matt was kneeling in the front yard next to something that looked like a big piece of white cardboard. A cloud of white dust flew around him. A second later, the noise started again.

WHIRRRRRRRR.

Ridley shook her head. She'd heard Matt when he said he would fix the hole in the wall, but she hadn't thought he'd come over at the butt-crack of dawn to do it. Just when she was about to pull the window up and tell him what she thought of his timing, he stood and pulled his shirt up to wipe his face, exposing a perfect six-pack.

"Wow."

"I'll let him know you think so."

Ridley turned slowly to face Jackson. "Oh, um, hi. I came downstairs to see what was making so much noise."

Not to ogle your best friend's insanely ripped abs.

Neither of them said anything for a moment and Ridley could only stare at him greedily. He looked just as good wearing slacks and a dress shirt as he had the previous night in nothing but sweatpants. And without sweatpants.

It doesn't count, remember?

She was the one who'd come up with the stupid idea to keep their sex-a-thon to just one night, but she was already wishing she'd kept her big mouth shut. How was she supposed to pretend she didn't know what he looked like under his clothes? That his skin was smooth and warm and felt like wet silk under her tongue. She shivered and crossed her arms.

Just then the door opened and Matt stepped in carrying a piece of the white cardboard. Jackson rushed over to help him.

"I needed to replace more than I thought," Matt said. When he saw Ridley, he raised his chin in greeting. "Morning. Sorry for all the noise. I didn't even think about it since Jackson sleeps like the dead."

"Well, I won't deny I was ready to give you a piece of my mind when that sawing noise woke me up. What were you doing, anyway?"

Jackson pointed to the cardboard Matt had propped against the wall. "Since he punched out a section of the wall, he had to cut another piece of drywall to replace it. Then we'll spackle and sand it. After that, we'll paint over it so it all matches."

"Oh. I was wondering if you were redecorating or something."

"Well, it was a forced redecoration." He smirked at Matt.

"I'll get out of the way. I'm sure you guys have a lot of work to do." She walked back to the stairs.

"Hey, wait." Jackson jogged over to stand next to her. Since she was on the second stair, she was able to look him right in the eye. The perfect height so that she couldn't avoid his whisky-brown gaze.

Geez.

"I wanted to make sure you were okay after last night." He stepped closer until he brushed up against her. "I wish I could have kept you in my bed all night."

Pleasure spread through her at his words. "I understand. I wouldn't want the boys to come running in and see me there. Plus, we did say just one night."

His eyes searched hers. "Yeah, just one night." Then he looked away and cleared his throat. "Anyway, I hate to do this but I need a favor."

"Of course. Whatever you need."

"The baby-sitter my mom recommended is coming over this morning. Her name is Bessie Johnson. The thing is, I have an early meeting with a director about my group's first music video that I don't want to miss. If it was anyone else, I would cancel, but it's not like I really need to meet her since I've known her for years. Would you mind letting her in?"

"Of course. After everything you've done for me, I'd love to be able to return the favor."

He let out a breath. "Oh, good. I hate to ask but I really don't want to cancel on this director. He's our first choice and hard to pin down. So, ok. Um, Chris is old enough to pour cereal; they just need help with the milk. Once Miss Bessie arrives, she can take it from there."

Ridley put her hands on his shoulders. "It's going to be fine. Breathe!"

"It's been kind of stressful. The boys' grandmother used to watch them four days out of the week and then my mom would take them on Fridays. But now that Cynthia's mom has moved away, I'm really struggling. It's harder than I thought to find a childcare provider that you trust."

"Of course it is. After all, this isn't something you can afford to get wrong. I totally understand."

"Thank you. Hey, you should come with me sometime. I'm working on something a little different and I'd love to get your take on it. I'm trying to branch out into pop music and I've found this girl group I think could be the next big thing."

"I would love to see what you do." Ridley hadn't given much thought to how music was produced previously. Like most people, her impressions were mainly what she'd seen on television and in movies.

"Tomorrow, then. I'll show you around the studio and maybe you can even watch the group record a session."

"Okay. Now, go! You don't want to be late. We'll be fine here." She pushed him toward the door.

"Thank you, Ridley. I'll owe you one."

Their eyes met and she gulped. Jackson might not want to

start making her promises because if he owed her one, she had a pretty good idea of how to collect.

———

"JACK? Have you heard a word I've said?"

Jackson turned to his left and raised his eyebrows at his assistant's scowl. "What?"

He'd arrived at the office just in time for the video conference with the director they'd been eyeing to do the group's first video. He was known for dance videos, which was exactly what they wanted. If they were going to make an entry into the pop world, they needed a club-worthy hit. Too bad he hadn't been able to keep his mind on anything the guy said.

Mac crossed his arms. "You never told me what you thought of his idea. As a matter of fact, I'd bet you don't even remember the guy's pitch. You keep spacing out on me. What's the deal?"

"Sorry, I'm really distracted today. I've just got some stuff going on at home."

Just one night. It doesn't count.

Right.

Any chance he'd had of being a gentleman and not seducing her had died an instant death the moment he'd climbed into bed with her. Ridley had been like a dream. It had been just as hot as he'd thought it would be and twice as memorable.

He had a feeling the night that didn't count was going to cost him more than just a few hours of lost productivity. If he couldn't get a handle on his crazy emotions, it might cost him his sanity.

"Jackson?" This time Mac was watching him with open amusement. He wondered how long his friend had been calling him this time.

"Huh?"

"I said is everything all right with the kids?"

"Oh yeah, yeah, they're fine. I just have a guest this week."

"Oh right. Your hot neighbor. Matt already has a betting pool going on how long before you nail this one." Mac chuckled.

The thought that his friends were thinking anything sexual about Ridley was enough to make his blood boil. Any man actually. *No one* should see her the way he'd seen her last night or think about the things she could do with that lush mouth.

"It's not like that. So keep her name out of your filthy mouth," Jackson growled.

"Whoa! Take it easy, man." Mac backed up a few steps and then cleared his throat. "Damn, Matt was right. You've really got it bad."

Jackson flexed his fists. "I'm serious, Mac. She's my neighbor and I'm just trying to help her out. Don't turn it into something dirty."

Mac tried, unsuccessfully, to hide his smile. "Okay, okay. Sorry. No disrespect intended."

Jackson walked into his office and closed the door. He dropped down into his desk chair and looked around his crowded workspace. He hadn't gotten much of anything done all day.

His inability to concentrate was part of the problem. Ridley was sneaking into his thoughts wherever he was, no matter how inappropriate. He ignored the inner voice that called him a coward. Ridley affected him more than any woman he had ever met. A man had the right to be a little freaked out.

But now he was being forced to admit that close proximity wasn't the only reason he was fascinated with her. Ridley was nowhere near him, yet he couldn't seem to think of anything else.

He had to get a handle on his feelings or he wasn't going to be getting any work done. The way he saw it, he had two choices. He could abide by the rules of their one-night deal or he could spend some time with her and let his fascination run its course.

The more he thought about it, the more sense it made. Of

course he was entranced by Ridley. She was beautiful, and what red-blooded man wouldn't be affected by a gorgeous woman who offered him a night of hot, no-strings sex? But if he spent more time with her, he'd start to see her flaws. It would at least take some of the fascination away. Then he could get back to work—no harm, no foul.

Either way, he wasn't going to hide his attraction to her any longer. She was a grown woman and he would leave the decision in her hands. They'd agreed on one night, but if she gave him even the slightest indication that she'd welcome a little quality time before she left town again, he was more than ready to deliver.

He swiveled in his chair and pulled up his e-mail. When he saw there was a note from Elliott, he smiled.

He opened the message and then double-clicked on the attachment. The top page was a blown up copy of a Florida driver's license. *David Randall Finemore.*

"Elliott, you always come through for me."

He'd just wanted to find out a little about the guy, but it looked like Eli had done a full-scale background check. He scrolled through the file. There were several more photographs. They were candid shots, most taken from far away.

Surveillance photos.

The first one was of two men sitting at an outdoor restaurant. Upon closer inspection, he could see that one of the men was David.

David Finemore meeting Alberto Moreno.

He recognized his brother's handwriting scrawled across the image. He'd also written the date the photo was taken.

"This was taken over a year ago."

Hadn't Ridley said she'd only just met the guy? He scrolled through the rest of the photos quickly. Most were just of David, but Moreno appeared in a few other shots. Some of them were dated even further back than the first one. His brow furrowed as he came to the last picture. Whoever had been following the guy had been thorough.

He flipped through the rest of his mail. There wasn't anything else that couldn't wait. He hurriedly signed his approval on a few bills and then put them in his outbox for Mac to pick up. He might as well finish up early so they could go out to dinner. He could show Ridley what Elliott had found and see how she felt about an encore of the previous night's festivities. The sooner he got his fascination with Ridley out of his system, the sooner he could get back to normal.

This was a business decision, even if it felt better than anything he had done for a while.

———

RIDLEY PULLED an Adirondack chair into a shady part of the lawn. She glanced back at the house before settling down with a paperback book she'd found in the family room. Miss Bessie had arrived at precisely 9:29 a.m. and had seemed more than a little surprised to see her.

When he'd introduced her to his parents, he hadn't mentioned where she was staying, so of course his mother's friend wouldn't expect a woman to open the door.

Talk about awkward.

After her initial fumbling introduction, she'd spent the next few hours puttering around in her room. Things seemed to be going well other than a few loud crashes and what sounded like a full-scale tantrum. She'd finally come down to investigate, only to find the boys eating sandwiches at the kitchen table, ominously quiet.

She'd made herself a quick turkey and cheese sandwich before deciding to eat outside. Right before she'd left, she'd heard Miss Bessie telling Jase to take his thumb out of his mouth.

She hadn't sucked her thumb, but she'd been a quiet, introverted child much like Jase. It hadn't been easy growing up around adults who constantly told her to "speak up" or "just smile, honey!" With any luck, the trio would get along once they got to know each other. She hoped so, anyway. Otherwise Jackson would be searching for yet another nanny.

After reading several pages, she put the book aside. Perhaps a murder mystery hadn't been the best choice. Not when she was smack in the middle of her own unsolved murder case. How could she relax as if she was on vacation when someone she thought of as a friend was dead, probably because of her? She thought of the jeweled necklace she'd given Jackson to put in his safe.

It was a good thing she'd been on her way to the bank that day. Otherwise, if she'd put the necklace in her jewelry box with the rest of her jewelry, it would have been stolen when her apartment was broken into. She'd have to ask Agent Graham to contact David's next of kin so she could return it. Clearly, it had been important to him.

"Oh, hi! Sorry, I didn't think anyone would be back here."

Ridley looked up to see a young woman with smooth brown skin and short curls, followed by two young boys.

"Hi. Were you looking for Jackson?"

"No, we were just taking a shortcut over to the next street. Sorry to disturb you."

"Can we play with Chris, Mom? Please?" One of the boys jumped up and down next to his mother excitedly.

"The boys are just finishing lunch. Maybe they'd like to play outside. I'll go check." Ridley held up a finger and sat up. Before she could get out of the chair, the back door of the house burst open and she heard a high-pitched shriek.

"Get it away, get it away, get it away! Eeeeeeeeek!!"

Miss Bessie came barreling down the back steps, shaking

frenetically and throwing her head back and forth. "Oh sweet Lord Jesus, it's a spider. Get it off!"

A giggle came from behind Ridley and she turned to see the two boys being shushed by their mother. Ridley tried valiantly to stifle her own smile as she hurried toward the older woman. She was trembling so furiously Ridley worried she'd hurt herself.

"Wait, I'll get it off. Just... wait." She put her arms on the woman's trembling shoulders until she stopped throwing her head around. A quick visual inspection proved that there was nothing on her. "See, it's already gone. You're fine."

"He picked it up." The older woman shuddered, revulsion all over her face. "He brought it to me on his hand. I thought he was showing me a toy."

The back door opened again and Chris and Jase came outside. Jase took his thumb out of his mouth to say, "Spider! I had a spider!"

Miss Bessie shuddered again. "I can't stand spiders. I can't believe that sweet little baby was touching that nasty thing."

Ridley walked over to Jase slowly. "Where's the spider now, Jase? Is he gone?"

Jase nodded solemnly. "I lost him."

"It's okay. Maybe he went home."

"Oh, look! There it is!" Chris pointed at Miss Bessie's shoulder. She immediately started dancing around again. Chris erupted into giggles. "I'm just joking. It's gone."

"Chris! That's not nice." Ridley shook her head and turned back to the older woman.

"Some of the neighborhood children are playing outside. I can keep an eye on the boys if that's all right with you."

Miss Bessie exhaled, her shoulders drooping visibly. "Only if you don't mind. I would appreciate that. I wanted to start cooking early, anyway." She gave a defeated smile before turning and walking back in the house.

Jase tugged the edge of Ridley's shirt until she looked down. "She no like my spider." He sounded so crestfallen that it was hard to keep a straight face.

"You like spiders?" she asked. He nodded.

"He likes all bugs," Chris interjected.

Oh boy. Ridley was starting to understand why Jackson was having such a hard time keeping a nanny. If there was anything that most women couldn't tolerate, it was creepy crawlies. Luckily, gardening had forced her to get over her aversion early. You couldn't work with flowers without encountering insects.

She knelt next to Jase. "Lots of people are scared of spiders. That's why she ran away. Is there anything you're afraid of?"

"Um, the thunder," Jase mumbled around his thumb.

"I don't like thunder, either. I'd much rather it stays outside. That's how most people feel about spiders. Let's keep the spiders outside so Miss Bessie isn't scared, okay? Maybe later we can play in the dirt some so you can see where the bugs live."

Jase's eyes rounded and then he grinned. "Okay."

"Okay. Let's go have some fun."

Chris let out a happy screech before running and jumping over the three steps leading from the patio to the yard.

The sound was reminiscent of summers past and the freedom of entire days devoted to nothing but adventure, friends, and fun. There had been many summers she and Raina had wandered their neighborhood while their mother was at work. They'd ridden their bikes all day, searched for hidden pirate treasure, skipped rope, and drawn lines on the sidewalk in front of their building for hopscotch. They'd done everything together and every day had been an adventure.

The world had seemed wide open back then.

"I didn't get a chance to introduce myself. I'm Katie Mason. We live three houses down." The other woman had wandered closer to where Ridley stood watching the children chase each other around the yard.

"I'm Ridley. I actually don't even live here. Not really, anyway. I'm just visiting."

Katie nodded, a knowing smile on her face. "Your presence here is dashing the hopes of many of the women in the neighborhood. Jackson is considered quite a catch around here. A single, handsome man living in a big place like this all alone tends to attract attention. He's probably been hit on by all the single women at some point. Probably by some of the married ones, too."

"I don't think anyone needs to lose any sleep over my being here. I'll be gone in a week or so."

"I hope you'll stay for a while. I'm excited to see some new faces in town," Katie said. "A lot of the wives here are a little older. I don't get Botox or play tennis, so there's just not much common ground. I thought about getting a job to keep me busy while Don's at work, but that didn't go over too well."

"Don is your husband?" Ridley ventured. A shadow crossed the other woman's face before she squared her shoulders.

"Yeah. We've been married almost seven years." She didn't look too happy about it, though. She sighed and then said, "He's not home much, so the kids and I are usually on our own. That's why I was trying to find a part-time job before the kids go back to school. But I've technically been unemployed since getting married, so it's harder than I thought."

"Unemployed? That makes it sound like you haven't been doing anything. I don't even have children and I find that insulting. You've been raising kids."

"I'm used to it, believe me."

Ridley shook her head in disbelief. "If you were watching someone else's children, you'd be considered self-employed. An entrepreneur with your own business. So why is it any different just because you're watching your own? That doesn't seem fair."

"Well, the fact that I don't have any current skills isn't helping, I suppose. But the only experience I have is being a wife and mother. There doesn't seem to be much demand for that lately."

Ridley looked back at the house.

"Oh, I think you'd be surprised. What would you say if I told you there might be a job available where all you had to do was watch two kids close in age to your own and cook dinner a few nights a week? Would you be interested?"

"I'd say I think you're making that up. Of course I'd be interested!" Katie said.

"Let's get together tomorrow and I'll let you know what I find out. In the meantime, let's see if we can keep the kids occupied by letting them play in the dirt a little."

Katie pushed up her sleeves. "Just another day in the life of a suburban mom."

twelve

"I'M HOME," Jackson called out. "Chris? Jase?"

He dropped his bag by the door. It had been a long day, but a good one. After his breakup with Alana, his career had suffered. He'd been too distracted to be creative, which was the only reason he'd put out the substandard album that would haunt him for his entire career.

Not that he paid much attention to the media, but when terms like "has-been" start to be bandied around, even he had to notice. He had started to question if he'd lost the one thing that had made him so successful.

His enthusiasm.

Now that he was back in his creative groove, he was writing songs again. Once Divine recorded the single he'd just written for them, they could shoot their first video and start planning the album's release. He would finally be able to prove the naysayers wrong.

"Where is everyone?"

He wasn't used to being able to share this kind of stuff with anyone but had found himself rushing to get home so he could tell Ridley. She'd understand how important it was to him. How much it meant to finally be back on track. He stood still, listening. Nothing.

Something was different in the house. He scrutinized the room, trying to figure out if Ridley had changed something, perhaps put something back in a different place from where he usually kept it. Nothing seemed out of place.

The small bowl where he kept his keys was the only thing on the entry table since Jase had broken the few knickknacks he'd been stupid enough to place there. *What's different in here?* He turned in circles for a full minute before he figured it out.

It was clean.

The maid service usually cleaned on the weekends, but with the boys in the house it didn't stay clean for long. It was almost weird to see it so organized. He walked into the family room and stopped in his tracks. Chris and Jase sat on the couch as still as statues. There wasn't a smudge of dirt or a grass stain on either of them.

"Hey guys, what are you doing sitting in here? I thought you'd be outside playing."

He walked farther into the room and then stopped and sniffed. *What the hell is that smell?* There was a pungent odor wafting from the kitchen that made his nose itch. Stifling a sneeze, he edged his way into the kitchen, his eyes widening at the massive pile of pots and pans lining the counter. Smack in the middle of the chaos was an elderly woman stirring a large pot.

Miss Bessie.

Backing up before she saw him, he turned and retraced his steps to the family room. The room was so clean it sparkled. The house hadn't looked this good since he'd bought it. His sons were still in the same position as before, like melancholy figurines with their identical downcast expressions.

"So, it looks like Miss Bessie is working on dinner for us." His words didn't trigger a response as both boys continued to stare at their sneakers. "And she did a great job cleaning up."

Two pairs of eyes turned chilly glares in his direction.

"She didn't clean up—*we* did. The only reason we finished before you came home was because Ridley helped us dust. You can't reach much when you're as short as we are." Chris jumped up and put his hands on his hips, affecting an indignant pose. "And she made us change clothes! She said we shouldn't wear playclothes to the dinner table."

Jackson resisted the urge to laugh. All his baby-sitters growing up had been like Miss Bessie, which was probably why his mother had recommended her. She was always saying the boys were too spoiled and could use a little "down South" discipline. He was aware he indulged them too much at times, but it was hard not to. He wanted to give them everything he'd enjoyed growing up. Especially a father who was there for them.

"Oh, Jackson! I didn't even know you were home!" Miss Bessie bustled into the room and gave him a hearty hug. "We've missed you at Sunday service. You're just as skinny as your momma said!"

"Yes, ma'am. How have you been?"

"Oh, I've been just fine. Come on over here and sit."

"Thank you for coming on such short notice." Jackson followed her into the dining room and sat in the chair she indicated at the head of the table.

He motioned for the boys to sit down as well. They climbed into the chairs, looking at him uncertainly. They never ate in the formal dining room, but he could only hope they didn't mention it in front of Miss Bessie. He was no doubt violating some parenting rule by not teaching his boys proper table manners before elementary school.

"Your momma keeps telling me you're not eating right, so I

made you a pot roast. This'll put some meat on your bones for sure."

He groaned as she set a full plate in front of him. He wanted to set a good example for the boys, but he had to draw the line somewhere and Miss Bessie's roast just looked... questionable. It smelled even worse. He really didn't want to hurt her feelings, especially with the way she smiled at him, obviously proud of the meal.

"Where's Ridley? I mean, Miss Raina?"

Chris leaned over and whispered loudly, "She told us her real name is Ridley. She has two names. Like Spiderman! His real name is Peter Parker, except no one knows it's him."

"That's right. It's too bad she can't climb buildings and shoot that cool stuff from her hands. Did she go upstairs?"

Chris shrugged.

Jackson almost hoped she didn't come down. There was no reason she should have to suffer through the meal also. He hadn't even taken a bite yet and he already felt light-headed.

Well, at least she said it was beef. How bad could it be?

He picked up his fork, speared a small piece, and swiped it through the heavy gravy on the plate.

"Jackson Alexander! Did you say grace?" Miss Bessie's face was the picture of shocked outrage.

The boys giggled as he dropped the fork.

"No, ma'am. Sorry. I was just... really hungry." He closed his eyes and prayed for strength. He opened them again to see Miss Bessie hurriedly gathering up her belongings.

"You can't stay?" He tried not to sound too optimistic.

If this first meal was any indication of her cooking skill, he feared to think of what they had to endure in the future. Images of sharing dinner with Ridley over the weekend brought a smile to his face. Even though he didn't want her to have to suffer through the meal, he couldn't help wishing she was sitting across from him, making faces. He knew she'd get the humor in the situation.

"Actually, I hate to do this to you, but I won't be able to work for you this summer after all. I'm so sorry, but keeping up with two active little boys is more taxing than I thought. I think I'm getting too old for this."

She was inching toward the door, smiling apologetically. "Your boys are really very..." she grimaced. "...sweet."

Jackson bit his lip to keep from laughing. He knew his boys were a handful, especially for an older person who couldn't chase after them to keep them out of trouble.

"It's no problem. I understand—" His reply was interrupted by the sound of the front door swinging shut behind her as she rushed out.

Okay then.

"Is she gone?" Chris whispered.

Jackson laughed out loud. "Yes, she's gone. I guess we can go back to our caveman ways now."

Truthfully, he was glad he didn't have to hurt her feelings by firing her. However, he had to admit his situation was getting desperate. He needed to devote his attention to producing Divine. He was so close to getting back on top.

If he got this close and failed, he wasn't sure he'd have it in him to try again.

He looked up to see Chris and Jase watching him. Chris poked the meat on his plate with the tip of his fork, dispiritedly. Jackson dropped his own fork.

"Who wants pizza?"

———

AFTER TEN MINUTES of searching without finding her, Jackson started to wonder if Ridley was angry with him. He'd expected things to be awkward the next day but he hadn't expected her to avoid him completely. She hadn't seemed mad that morning, though she could have just been distracted by Matt.

He scowled. She'd *definitely* been distracted by Matt.

Just the thought of it made him feel, well, he wasn't exactly sure. Matt was a good guy and they'd seemed to get along well at the party. Should he really be surprised if Ridley liked him? The whole point of their one-night rule was to get it out of their systems so they could move on. It was really none of his business if she liked someone else. The thought certainly shouldn't make him want to punch his friend in the face.

Hell.

"Ridley? Are you in here?" He stuck his head in the guest room after a quick knock. The door was partially open, so he could only hope he wasn't catching her napping or *God forbid*, undressing. His hormones were already in overdrive around her. Another glimpse of her naked would probably send him so far into Neanderthal territory that he'd just club her over the head and drag her to his bedroom.

Luckily the room was empty.

He didn't find her in the boys' room or outside in the backyard. He wanted to thank her for helping the boys clean the house. Even before Chris had told him, he'd known they'd had help. He could always tell when the boys cleaned up; anything higher than four feet was left untouched. His suspicions were confirmed when he saw her with the dust rag and can of furniture polish in her hand as he entered his office.

Funny how the last place you look is always where you find what you're looking for.

"Hey, there you are."

She looked up and grinned. "Jackson! You're home."

His breath caught. The thought that she might have missed him was such an unexpected pleasure. He wanted her to miss him.

and enjoy being with him. He wanted things he had no right to want.

She raised her hand in greeting and accidentally knocked over one of the books on the edge of the desk. A puff of dust billowed up. She sneezed delicately and wrinkled her nose at the layers of dirt on the table.

Jackson was almost embarrassed at the state of his office. He never let the maids come up here because he didn't like anyone else in his space. It didn't surprise him that having Ridley in his office didn't bother him. Everything about her calmed him.

"I was wondering where you were." He felt like an idiot. Did his hands have to sweat like a teenager's every time she was around? He wiped his palms on his slacks.

"I was trying to finish this before you came up here." She put the furniture polish on the table and turned to face him. "I would have come to dinner but I thought maybe you guys needed some family time alone."

Jackson looked at her nervously wringing her hands and felt better instantly. Apparently he wasn't the only one who was uneasy. Which meant that maybe she wouldn't be averse to ditching their one-night policy in exchange for an as-many-times-as-they-could-do-it policy?

"Oh, be honest. You just didn't want to eat that monstrosity she was creating in the kitchen." Their eyes met and they both burst into laughter.

"I didn't want to say anything, but whatever she was cooking did smell awful. Did you actually eat it?"

Her eyes widened, the apparent horror of the thought causing her to reach out for him. The feel of her hand gripping his arm sent tingles of electricity through him. He cleared his throat and tried to remember her question.

"No, she left before we ate, so I didn't feel obligated to choke it down to avoid hurt feelings. I did taste enough of it to declare it unfit for consumption. Maybe she left out an ingredient. Either way, I don't think what she left out was the problem, but what she left in."

"The boys didn't seem to like her so much. I guess she was a little strict."

"Well, it's not a problem anymore because she quit. I am officially desperate."

Ridley didn't look surprised. "Yeah, I figured that was coming when Jase brought her a spider. She was so afraid she ran out of the house into the backyard, shaking like she was having a seizure."

"Not again. I thought we'd broken him of that. He knows he's not supposed to bring insects in the house."

"I think it was already in the house. He just wanted to, um, *share* his discovery with her. Then, after she finally calmed down, Chris pretended to see the spider on her shoulder and that set her off again. I felt so guilty laughing but I couldn't help it. Anyway, I explained to Jase that most people are scared of bugs but I'm not sure how much help that will be in the future. But I did meet someone today who might be able to help you with your childcare problem if you're willing to be a little open-minded."

"I'm willing to be *very* open-minded at this point." He offered her his arm. "Come on, I was going to take the boys out for pizza anyway. You can tell me the whole story while we're surrounded by screaming kids."

Ridley dropped her cleaning rag on top of the desk and slid her arm through his.

"How could a girl resist an invitation like that?"

———

"SO, did you get to meet your video director?"

Jackson had taken them to the boys' favorite pizza arcade,

Bingos. Although they were eating greasy pizza in hard plastic booths and were surrounded by what seemed like hundreds of screaming children, she and Jackson were in a world all their own.

She hadn't been sure what to make of things after that morning. He'd been friendly but he hadn't mentioned wanting to do it again. She'd honestly thought that one night together would assuage the fascination she'd felt for him since they met, but images of their night together had been tormenting her all day.

Jackson, on the other hand, seemed perfectly fine. Perhaps one night had been enough for him.

"I did, but I'm not sure if we're going to hire him. We're trying to do something different with this group. I really want to get it right."

"I'm sure you will."

He looked out the plate glass window next to them at the parking lot. A harried-looking mother was trying to pull a screaming toddler over to a minivan.

"I don't know. I've been distracted lately. I actually forgot about a label party I'm supposed to attend Thursday night. I told everyone I'd be there a few weeks ago and then promptly forgot all about it." He glanced at her suddenly, a gleam in his eye. "Hey, do you want to go to an insanely boring industry launch party with me?"

Is he asking me out?

"I'd love to. It'll give me an excuse to go shopping."

She prodded the pizza on her plate, trying not to let her excitement slip into her voice. Maybe this was his way of getting closer to her? A thrill went through her at the idea of an evening out with him.

"Good. Although I have to warn you, they're probably not what you're expecting. It's a lot of self-important people trying to impress each other and a lot of old guys showing off their trophy wives. But hopefully the music will be worth it."

"It'll just be nice to get out of the house. I'm starting to get a little bit of cabin fever. Oh, speaking of getting out of the house, I met one of your neighbors today. Katie Mason. Married to a guy named Donald?"

Jackson's brow crinkled. "Yeah, the Masons. Chris plays with their son, Matthew, sometimes. They tend to keep to themselves. I think he's some kind of surgeon."

"Well, Katie was outside when Miss Bessie came running out of the house. We spent some time talking and she said something that made me think about your situation."

"My situation?" he repeated.

"Looking for a nanny. From what you've told me, it sounds like what you want is so simple, but yet you haven't been able to find anyone."

"I've found people. Just not the right ones." He shook his head ruefully.

"Exactly. Well, Katie has been looking for a job and hasn't been able to find one because, according to her, she's only qualified to be a wife and mother and there isn't much demand for that these days. Well, that made me think of you. That's basically what you need. You can just hire a wife and mom."

"I'm pretty sure that's illegal."

"Jackson!" She swatted his arm. "You know what I mean. Katie has two boys of her own, so she clearly has experience with children, and the boys are already friendly with her kids. She wants to do a summer camp for them."

"Really?"

"Yeah. She was great with the kids today and I had a good time, too. Jase was beside himself when we dug up spots for the flowers I want to plant."

Jackson glanced behind them where Chris was playing Skee-Ball and Jase was jumping into a vat of colorful balls.

"So, what do you think?"

"I think it's a great idea. I've known the Masons for a while, practically since I moved in. They were one of the few families that actually came over to welcome me to the neighborhood. She baked this apple turnover thing that was amazing. I had no idea she would be interested in watching other children. Why don't you invite her over tomorrow?"

Ridley clapped her hands. "Great. This is so exciting! I can't wait to tell Katie. We talked a lot today and she's a lot of fun. She gave me some great ideas for my column, too."

"Your column?"

Ridley hugged herself, so overcome with excitement she could almost burst. "I've decided to do a column about gardening on the "Legs" blog. It was really rewarding to teach the kids about plants and their life cycles. They get so excited about things."

It was something that Raina had been trying to convince her to do for years. She'd always said no because she didn't want people thinking she was using her sister's success. But Jackson had given her a new perspective on things. A column would give her a chance to try out some of her new design ideas and reach more people than she could on her own.

"That's great, Ridley!"

"What you said about accepting help really changed my way of thinking. It doesn't matter if people only read my column in the beginning because of the fashion side. They'll keep reading it because they like it."

Jackson leaned across the booth and tugged on a lock of her hair. Warmth arrowed straight down to her core. What would it be like to have him look at her like that all the time? To have the right to lean across the table and kiss him right now? She looked down at the table and clenched her fists in her lap.

"Speaking of news, I have some for you, too. About your friend David."

Ridley looked up, her earlier excitement draining away. "About David? What about him?"

"Remember I told you I was going to ask my brother Eli to look into things?" At her nod, he continued, "Well, he got copies of part of David's FBI file. He didn't get the whole thing, so he's still going to do his own background check, but he got some of the surveillance photos of him meeting with the Morenos. They go back for more than a year."

"Oh my god." Ridley suddenly felt sick.

"No, this is a good thing." Jackson grabbed her hands.

"How is it good? I thought he was nice and just got caught up in something by accident. If he's been meeting up with them for that long, then that means he was some kind of criminal!"

"It also means whatever he was doing with the Morenos had nothing to do with you. You didn't know him that long, right?"

Ridley let out a slow breath. "You're right. I didn't even think about that. I only met him a few months ago. So, that means he didn't suspect Moreno of being my father. He probably never had any leads at all. It was just a lie so he could keep charging me."

"Probably. But either way, you can relax a little now. It's too bad that you can't get your money back, but at least it's over with."

"You're right. And hopefully my column will do well. It's something I can do anywhere, you know? It'll be easy for me to keep it up even after I go back."

The thought didn't sound nearly as appealing as it had just a week ago. Technically, she didn't really even need to be in hiding anymore. She could just enjoy a little vacation time with her sister and then go back to her life. She was surprised to find that the idea didn't make her as happy as it should, as happy as it would have just a few days ago.

"Go back?"

"Yeah. When I go back to Florida."

"Right." A flash of something crossed his face as he looked at her. "We should probably go. I have a lot of stuff I need to work on tonight." He nodded curtly and left the booth, calling out to the kids.

Ridley folded her arms around herself again, this time to stop herself from trembling.

She'd always thought it was a nice change when she moved on. It was like wiping the slate clean of all her screw-ups and starting over. But this time she didn't think she'd be moving on to something better.

This time, walking away seemed more like a cop-out than a fresh start.

thirteen

JACKSON STOOD over the chair and watched Ridley's chest rise and fall as she slept. He had come downstairs with every intention of apologizing for his attitude since they'd left the pizza place.

His carefully thought-out speech had deserted him when he came across her sprawled in one of the armchairs in the family room, her head thrown back against the armrest, her hair wild around her shoulders. She was beautiful even when she was sleeping.

He'd been such an ass. She'd tried to make conversation on the way home but he'd barely spoken two words to her in reply. She'd finally given up and gone upstairs alone when they reached the house. He picked up the remote and turned the television off. After he'd put the boys to bed, he'd gone into his own room and shut the door. She must have come down sometime after that.

It had taken him by surprise when she'd mentioned going back to Florida so casually. As if she couldn't wait to leave. Just the idea of her not being around anymore made him feel panicky. She owned a house here, so surely she'd come back sometime, right? The idea of not seeing her every day just seemed crazy.

Unfathomable.

"What are you doing to me?" He trailed a finger over her cheek and she shifted in her sleep.

"Jackson?" She turned over in the chair and would have fallen out if he wasn't there to catch her. Her arms twined around his neck as he lifted her into his.

"What are you doing?" she mumbled sleepily.

"I have no idea." He carried her upstairs to his room and laid her gently amidst the rumpled linens.

In the dim light coming through the window, he could just make out her face. She blinked at him a few times before her eyes turned soft, slumberous.

"Come here," she whispered.

He didn't waste any time. He dropped down on the bed next to her and pulled her into his arms. Her head fell back as his lips found her throat. She let out a soft "ah" as he nipped his way down the soft skin of her neck. He gently pulled her cotton tee shirt over her head and groaned as he saw she hadn't been wearing a bra.

"I thought—" She broke off with a moan when he nuzzled his face between her breasts.

The scent of her skin was driving him crazy.

"I thought you were mad at me."

He tugged at her jeans and watched, mesmerized, as she moved next to him on the bed and arched her back so she could pull them off. The seductive thrust of her hips made his throat go dry.

"I wasn't mad at you. I was mad at myself."

She laughed, a low, throaty sound, as he captured her leg and pulled her closer. A few kicks later, her jeans were on the floor next to the bed. Her eyes held his as she arched her back again, this time to slide her panties off. She sat up and flung them at his head like a slingshot.

"*Christ.* Come over here."

She straddled him and he anchored a hand in her hair and pulled her down for his kiss. He loved her taste, the way she melted against him, the sounds she made. Nothing had ever been this good.

"What do you say we forget the one-night thing?"

Ridley whimpered and bit his bottom lip. "Forget it? You mean not do this anymore? I don't like that plan."

"No. I mean forget it and just do whatever we want."

She nipped along his jawline and then pressed her tongue against his pulse. "Whatever we want, hmm?"

He laughed and flipped them over. She squealed as her back hit the bed.

"Mmm hmm. I know exactly what I want to do first."

Her eyes fluttered closed as he returned to his position between her breasts, nuzzling and licking his way down to her belly button.

"You do?" she whispered.

"Mmm, can you guess?" He nipped at her hipbone.

"Oh my, I think... I can't think."

Her legs fell open as he lowered his head between her thighs. The scent of her was like a drug, filling his nostrils, wrapping around him and through him until he was consumed by it.

She cried out at the first lash of his tongue. The sound echoed in his ears as he lapped at her, already lost in her taste. He pulled one of the pillows from the head of the bed to him so he could prop her higher.

"What are you doing?" she asked breathlessly.

"Just getting comfortable, baby girl. I'm not done with you yet."

He was nowhere near done, but that didn't mean he couldn't enjoy a few detours. Propping her hips up also gave him a unique view of her breasts. He leaned over and laved each of her nipples until they pebbled against his tongue. She gripped his hair and held him against her, moaning when he pulled away.

Her moans turned to soft sighs when he settled between her thighs. Another long lick of her core had her arching off the bed.

"Jackson, stop teasing me."

He laughed softly and gripped her thighs, pulling her closer. The position pushed her against his mouth and he growled his approval. He drew the lips of her sex between his teeth lightly until she cried out.

"Oh. Oh!" She clamped her hand over her mouth to muffle her cries as she came.

He moved with her, keeping his mouth on her as she clenched against his tongue, trying to prolong her pleasure. Finally she dropped down against the bed and sighed.

He turned her gently on her stomach until her perfectly round ass was beneath him. *Hell yeah.* Now he could play.

She shivered as he caressed the soft skin of her back, pressing his thumbs gently next to the indentation of her spine. She arched under his fingers like a cat. He followed the same path with his tongue until she trembled.

He reached over to the nightstand and grabbed another condom. At the rate they were going he would need a new box by tomorrow. He glanced over at Ridley. She was up on her arms, watching him.

"Hurry up." She wiggled her ass in his direction.

"Damn. I'm on my way." He ripped the package open carefully and rolled the condom on.

He moved behind her, enjoying the view. She looked over her shoulder and winked. He teased her with the tip of his shaft and her mouth fell open on a soft sigh. She pushed back and took him deep. They both cried out.

He twisted the long fall of her hair around his fist and pulled gently as he rocked back and forth, taking her deeper with every thrust. Before long he was powering forward as she pushed back, their hips coming together with savage intensity. It was unlike anything he'd ever experienced. Being inside her was about more than just desire. Every inch of him felt alive when he was with her and he wanted nothing more than to please her in a way that no other man could.

"Jackson. Jackson." Her head fell forward as she panted his name and her fingers twisted in the sheets again. He was overcome with a sense of supreme masculine satisfaction. She might have a life in Florida that he wasn't a part of, but he was willing to bet she didn't have *this*. Maybe he couldn't keep her here, but he'd be damned if he wouldn't give her something worth remembering.

He closed his eyes as she tightened around him, crying out his name again. The way she called his name made him feel almost primal. He cupped her breasts, leaning over her back and biting her shoulder gently as he sank even deeper.

"Oh, damn. I'm coming." Tremors raced through him as he clutched her against him. He closed his eyes and let out a long groan as the last spasm left his body.

He pulled out gently and they fell back against the sheets in a tangle of sweaty limbs.

"Wow." Ridley turned her head to look at him. "I like our new plan."

He chuckled and pulled her closer for a quick kiss. "I like it, too. Stay with me awhile?"

"Okay," she whispered.

"Be right back." He went to the bathroom and disposed of the condom. On the way back, he peered out into the hallway to make sure the boys' bedroom door was still closed.

She was watching him curiously when he got back into bed.

"I just wanted to make sure we didn't wake them."

A shy smile spread across her face before she pressed her face into the pillow. "I was loud. I couldn't help it."

He smirked. "I don't want you to help it." He slid under the covers and moved over until he was in the center of the bed.

"By the way," he whispered. He waited until she looked over at him sleepily. "I'm sorry."

She grinned and snuggled up against him.

"You are so forgiven."

———

WEDNESDAY AFTERNOON, Ridley sat on the edge of the bed staring at her cell phone. Jackson had asked Katie to meet them at the park so the boys could play while they talked things over. From the screeching and loud sounds below her room, the kids were already excited.

If she was going to make her call, this was the best time to do it. Otherwise, she'd get caught up and lose track of time and if she put it off any longer she'd end up taking the easy way out by buying something new. But in the end her pragmatic nature won out and she decided to just get it over with.

Due to the time difference, it was doubtful that Raina would actually answer. She could just leave a message and then deal with the teasing later.

Hearing her sister say *I told you so* wasn't something she was looking forward to.

"Hey, Ri! How are things back home?" Raina answered the phone as if she were still on East Coast time instead of it being early morning the way she knew it was in Singapore.

"Oh, hey. I'm so sorry to wake you. I didn't think you'd actually answer."

There was a soft whooshing sound in the background and Ridley wondered if their connection was really that bad or if she was just hearing things.

"It's not early here. I'm in the Bahamas now. We're in the same time zone you are."

She'd completely forgotten that her sister never stayed in the same place for long. Although she supposed she could have at least pretended to pay attention when they'd last spoken and Raina had told her where she was going next.

"Well, the thing is, I have a favor to ask. And I don't want you to worry that I'll be upset if you say no." She took a deep breath. "It's just that Jackson has asked me to go to this industry party, but I don't have anything to wear. I was going to buy something but I thought why do that when I know you've got tons of dressy stuff at your house."

There was silence before Raina said, "Jackson asked you out?"

Ridley struggled to keep her voice neutral as she replied, "No, he didn't ask me out. It's for work. It's some party his label is throwing for a new jazz singer. You know how much I love jazz." *Stop babbling, Ridley.*

"Oh my god, you slept with him, didn't you? You dirty slut!" Raina crowed.

Even from another country, no one could embarrass her quite like her sister.

"Raina! It's not like that. I mean, yes we did, but it's not like I just jumped on the man." *Okay, I kind of did, but whatever.* "I really like him," she surprised herself by saying.

"I can tell. I'm happy for you, Ri." Raina did sound happy for her. She was quiet for a moment before she said, "The code is Mom's name spelled backward. So just type out the letters N-A-O-J on the keypad. You still remember where the spare key is, right?"

"I still have it from the day I originally tried to get in." She started mentally preparing a list of what she'd need. It didn't make sense to keep going over there, so she might as well just pack up a suitcase and bring it back.

"You know, I wanted you to avoid my house but if you're going to do this, at least dress up a little."

Ridley stopped adding items to her mental list long enough to say, "Huh?"

"You know what I mean. Just dress up a little, wear some makeup for once." Ridley wrinkled her nose at the phone. "Anyone watching will just assume that I'm home from my latest travels. No one thinks anything of my strange comings and goings at this point. I'm actually away from home more than I'm there."

"You think I should dress as you? Why? I don't have to hide anymore, remember? Whatever David was doing for the Morenos had nothing to do with me."

"I'd still rather you stay invisible until Sam checks things out, but I want you to dress up for my sake. There's usually paparazzi lurking around the house and of course they'll assume it's me coming home from a shoot. I don't want to be the next 'What NOT to Wear' headline, so please dress up a little. Oh and don't take Jackson with you."

"Why not? I can do it faster with help. You're being awfully difficult about this."

"I'm not! It's just that he's too well known and I'm sure he doesn't want to be linked to me in the media. Is there anyone else you can get to take you?"

Ridley thought back to the day of the cookout. While it had been overwhelming to meet so many people at once, she was glad she'd gone now.

"Yeah, I think I know a few people who wouldn't mind helping out."

———

"SO, what's it like to have a sister? As much as I love Matt, there are just certain things I can't talk to him about. What's her name?"

Ridley waited patiently for Mara to finish applying yet another layer of lip gloss before answering. Mara had been more than happy to come over and "glamify" her after she'd gotten off work. She'd given the excuse that she was trying out ideas for her next blog column. Mara, it turned out, was a fan of the "Legs" blog and more than willing to help out.

They'd been immersed in the guest room for the past thirty minutes while Ridley tried on and rejected each of the outfits Mara had brought with her. After Mara had finally just pulled one of the tops over her head forcefully, they were now working on makeup. She'd never known there could be so many pots of crap used just to paint a face.

"It's, uh, Rina." She mentally crossed her heart. It wasn't actually lying, right? Just omitting a letter.

"Is she a model, too?"

"No, she's my complete opposite, actually. We've always been best friends despite being so different. But it's not easy when your sister is smarter, more confident, and more popular than you are. It's living with constant comparison and feeling like you never measure up."

"Do you feel like *she* treats you that way?" Mara asked, her voice raising a couple of octaves. She looked like she was insulted on Ridley's behalf.

"No, no. She's my biggest fan. She's *always* defended me. The same way Matt has always defended you."

Mara blew out a breath. "He *has* always defended me. Maybe that's part of the problem. I never stood up for myself, so now he doesn't believe I can stand on my own two feet. I wonder if I've been as much of the problem as he has by leaning on him too much."

"Matt just needs time. He's been protecting you from guys your whole life and now he's supposed to pretend he doesn't care one of his friends has seen you naked?"

Mara cringed. "Ugh. You're right. I didn't really think about how much harder it would be that I was dating someone he knows so well. I'm sure he remembers every bad thing Trent's ever done and feels like he needs to warn me."

"Since he can't, he ends up putting his fist through walls," Ridley added.

"I asked Jackson to talk to him," Mara muttered. Then she turned Ridley to the mirror gently. "What do you think?"

Ridley leaned forward and inspected her newly long lashes; flawless skin; and rosy, slicked lips. "Wow. I look so... shiny." She couldn't imagine wearing makeup just to hang around the house but Raina always had. She hadn't even worn this much makeup when she went to prom.

"Thanks so much for your help, Mara. I'll give your stuff back as soon as I get more clothes from the house. I just didn't want to go out looking like a bum. If I do, there'll be a tabloid picture of me tomorrow claiming I just left rehab."

Mara rubbed her hands together. "No problem. I had fun. I'm channeling my mom for this project. She placed as high as first runner-up in the Miss Columbia pageant back in the seventies. This was before she met my dad and came with him to the U.S. She still talks about how close she was to that damn crown. She was always so disappointed that I didn't want to do the pageant thing."

Mara picked up a silk headband and then held it against the loose top Ridley was wearing. After staring at it for a minute, she apparently changed her mind and tossed it back on the dressing table.

"I don't blame you. The thought of all those people staring makes me want to throw up."

"But isn't that what it's like to model?"

Oops.

"Um, kind of. Luckily, I don't do a lot of runway work."

"I guess it's different if it's just you and the photographer, huh? Although, I could get over it if I had legs like yours."

Ridley raised an eyebrow. "Considering how Trent looks at you, I'd say you're doing just fine. I only wish someone would look at me like that."

"Well, you can stop wishing. Someone *does* look at you like that." Mara stared at her until Ridley laughed.

"*Stop*. It's not like that. Jackson and I are, well, we're nothing actually. He's amazing and I like him a lot but I don't have any illusions about where this is going. He doesn't want a long-term thing and I'm just passing through, anyway."

"You don't really think someone followed you here, do you?" Mara asked. Ridley had told her a little about the accident. There was something about Mara that made her extremely easy to talk to. Which was dangerous, in more ways than one.

"I don't think so. The police are investigating, so the best thing I can do is stay out of the way and try to move on with my life. I'm sure that's the real reason Jackson asked me to this event. I think he just wanted to take my mind off things."

"Uh huh. Well, I'm glad he did because this gives you the perfect excuse to flaunt it in front of him a little. I've got five that says he swallows his tongue when he sees you wearing your glamour gear." Mara held out her hand.

"It's not like he hasn't seen me dressed up before, so I doubt he'll be blown away. I'm sure he'll do what every other guy does. Stare at the boobs, stare at the legs, and then once the blood goes back to his brain, he'll be over it. No big deal."

The other woman kept her hand out until Ridley shook it reluctantly. "This is ridiculous, but it's your money."

Mara dug around in the black tote bag she'd brought and pulled out a pair of slinky black sandals. "He's not going to know what hit him."

———

IT TOOK several trips for her, Mara, and Matt to haul all the stuff she'd brought up to her room. She'd made a good call by asking for Raina's help. It would have been ridiculous to go out and buy dressy clothes, shoes, and handbags when Raina practically had a department store in her closet.

I hope Raina really doesn't mind that I took all this stuff. Rather than waste time sorting through it all she'd figured it was easier to take a bunch with her. She could decide what she wanted to wear later.

Raina won't mind you borrowing it. Especially since it's for a cause she supports.

Ridley snorted, remembering her sister's words. No, Raina definitely wouldn't have any problem with her taking so much if it meant she was seducing Jackson. This was what her scheming sister had been hoping for the entire time!

"Okay, I think that's the last of it." Matt bounded down the stairs. "I thought Mara had a lot of crap. Girls are crazy. How many pairs of shoes does one person need?"

"Well, I figured it was better to bring a bunch. You know, just in case."

"In case of what? A shoe emergency?" Matt stepped back when she swiped at him. "Okay, okay. I know better than to question female logic. Oh, I meant to ask if we need to go back to clean up those muddy footprints? Those are really nice hardwood floors you've got over there. I'd hate to see those get ruined."

Ridley's head shot up. "Muddy footprints? I didn't see anything when we came in."

"Not by the front door. They're in the laundry room by the door leading from the garage. I figured you must have tracked them in the last time you went."

Her heart sped up slightly. How could there be muddy footprints in the house? The last time she was there, she'd been at the back door and she hadn't even gotten in the house. She took a deep breath. There was no sense in panicking. Maybe Raina had left them before her trip. Or maybe her bodyguard, Sam, had tracked them in. She looked up to see Matt watching her with concern.

"Are you okay? We can go back and clean them up if you want."

"No! It's fine. The wood in there is... uh, specially treated. It'll be fine. We don't need to go back."

"Okay. If you're sure. Well, if you don't need anything else, I have to meet Nick. He's taking me to look at condos."

"I'm pretty sure I've got it all." She leaned out the open front door and waved at Mara. "Thanks again. I'll call you tomorrow."

She watched as they walked across the lawn and then stopped next to a car pulling in. Nick got out and exchanged a handshake with Matt before continuing toward the house.

Great. Just what I need right now.

Nick had hated her practically on sight. The last thing she needed was to see him while she was still all dolled up in her "Raina-wear." He'd probably make fun of her or, better yet, accuse her of trying to seduce his brother. Although she had no defense against that claim if he did. She was definitely trying to seduce his brother. An evil grin pulled the edges of her lips as he walked up.

"So you're *dating* my brother now? And you're what? Moving in?" Nick charged up the steps and grabbed her by the arm.

"Hey, what are you doing?" Ridley tried to yank her arm from his grip, but he tightened his hold until it almost hurt.

"I'm taking you in the house. You and I are going to have a talk."

fourteen

NICK HAD TRIED to stay out of it, he really had. He was on guard and Elliott was still searching for information. He'd thought they could be alert enough on Jackson's behalf.

But when he'd driven up to his brother's house and heard that Jackson was taking Raina on a date, the control he thought he'd mastered snapped.

He grabbed her by the arm, ignoring her gasp of outrage. She was a master at playing it up, pretending to feel things she really didn't. No one knew that better than he did, yet he still relaxed his grip a bit as he dragged her across the threshold and into the house.

"I knew you were a bitch, but I didn't think even *you* were that cold."

He advanced on her, walking forward until she was backed up against the wall. She was tall for a woman but she still had to look up to meet his eyes. He stilled, surprised at the sheen of tears in her eyes. Raina didn't cry. Ever. The impact was almost enough to make him back down.

Almost, but not quite.

"Nick, what are you talking about? I don't know what I did to make you hate me so much."

He laughed cruelly. "You don't know what you did?" He swore and then braced a hand on the wall above her head. "You don't remember? Is that the game we're going to play? We had the most amazing night, the hottest, wettest sex in every position we could bend ourselves into, and you don't remember?"

He clenched his fists, on the verge of turning and running out. He'd never raised a hand to a woman in his life and never would, but damn if he didn't want to just *shake* her until her teeth rattled. Or spank her. No, no spanking. Her soft curves beneath the palm of his hand would be more his undoing than hers.

"Nick, wait. You don't understand—"

Still on edge from the visual image of her bent over, he slapped the wall above her head, the loud sound making her jump. He didn't want to hear her excuses or whatever lies she'd prepared to explain what she was up to. She was using his brother to punish him and it had to stop.

"I know what you're trying to do. You screwed with my head and I let you. But leave Jackson alone. I mean it."

She gazed at him with wide, watchful eyes. The innocent look was just an act; he knew that but he couldn't stop himself from reacting to it. His body saw her hurting and it strained to do whatever necessary to protect her.

Even though his mind knew that Raina needed protection about as much as a baby piranha.

"Stop fucking with my brother's head." He leaned down until they were nose to nose and whispered, "We both know he's not the one you really want."

His eyes dropped to her lips and he thought, *To hell with it.*

Then he dragged her against him and covered her mouth with his.

JACKSON SIGNED his approval on the video treatment Mac had handed him just that morning and slid it back into its envelope. They'd finally come up with an original concept for the video and now that he'd approved the budget, the project could proceed.

He'd taken work home with him, instead of staying at the office so he could enjoy a little more time with the boys.

And with Ridley.

More and more when he thought of family, his thoughts included her. If he didn't see her for too long, he missed her. If she needed something, he wanted to help her get it. For someone who was determined not to sign up for commitment, he was teetering dangerously close to falling for her.

He could see it coming for him and was powerless to stop it.

Raised voices floated up the stairs. The loudest one sounded like his brother, Nick. He got up and walked to the top of the stairs. Ridley stood against the wall and *holy hell*, she looked amazing. When she'd told him about her undercover mission to get clothes from her house, he'd asked her to bring Matt along as well. Elliott already had bodyguards assigned to watch his house, but he still wanted someone he knew personally to go with her. Plus, Matt had a pickup so they could get everything she needed in one trip.

Just then, Nick hit the wall with his fist.

"I know what you're trying to do. You screwed with my head and I let you. But leave Jackson alone. I mean it. Stop fucking with my brother's head."

Ridley looked afraid and Jackson's fists clenched at his side. He knew Nick was just trying to protect him, but this was taking things too far. He wouldn't let his woman be threatened in their own home. He opened his mouth to yell out a warning.

Then Nick leaned down and kissed Ridley.

Kissed Ridley.

"What the hell is going on here?" Jackson barked.

Nick jumped back and ran his fingers roughly through his hair. "Jack, I can explain. I should have just told you from the beginning."

Ridley stayed in her position by the wall, her hands over her mouth. When she looked up at him, two tears slid down her cheeks.

Jackson hadn't moved from his position at the head of the stairs. He descended the stairs slowly, taking each step individually.

One. Two. Three. Four.

He counted the steps, holding the numbers in his head. Anything was better than the image of Ridley pressed against the wall, fear in her eyes. While his own brother...

He looked at Ridley directly. "Can you go in the family room for a minute, please? I need to talk to my brother alone."

She nodded mutely, her hands still over her mouth. She edged past them, giving Nick a wary look as she passed. As soon as she was out of striking range, Jackson flew across the room and tackled Nick.

"What the hell?" Nick held up his arms to ward off the blows but more than a few connected because Jackson felt the satisfying crunch as his knuckles hit bone.

Ridley screamed in the background but he barely heard her. All he could see was Nick, pushing himself against Ridley. Touching her. Kissing her.

He growled and threw another punch at his brother's head.

"Jack, stop!" Nick wasn't even trying to fight back at this point, just trying to protect his face from the raining blows.

The front door banged against the wall and the next thing he knew, he was being hauled backward. Matt grabbed Jackson and pulled his arms behind him. He managed to get an arm free and lunged forward again, dragging Matt with him.

Nick reared back and fell into the entryway table. It fell to the floor with a resounding crash. Ridley jumped back as pieces of the wood went flying.

"Are you okay?" Jackson asked her. Everything in him stilled, waiting for her answer. When she nodded shakily, his shoulders sagged. Matt used the opportunity to pull his arms behind him again, more securely this time. His hold felt like being encased in iron.

"Hold on, man. Just wait a second," Matt muttered.

"I'm not waiting for anything." Jackson strained against Matt's hold. He glared at Nick, who stood in the opposite corner, wiping the blood from the edge of his mouth.

"What the hell is your problem, Jack?" Nick stared at his bloody hand and then at him. "You'll fight your own brother for *her*?" He glared at Ridley as he said it, making Jackson strain against Matt again.

Jackson couldn't even hear what his brother was saying. He was practically frothing at the mouth, just the image of Nick with his hands on Ridley, *all over* Ridley, making him see red.

"Yes, I would. If you ever touch her again, I will break you."

Matt looked at Nick. "I have no idea what just happened but it's probably better if you go."

"Fine." Nick sent a scathing glance at Ridley.

Jackson lunged forward again and Matt cursed as one of his arms almost slipped free.

"Don't even look at her. I can't believe I almost listened to you. *Just stay away from her!*"

"I'm not Raina!"

Everyone stopped moving at Ridley's shriek.

"God, please stop fighting. Don't fight over me. Not when I've been lying to you all."

Jackson broke away from Matt. "It's okay, Ridley. I already told them your real name and about what happened."

"You don't understand. Raina Winters is my twin sister. She's currently overseas on a modeling job."

Ridley shook her head, tears spilling down her cheeks.

"I've been lying to you, too."

———

RIDLEY GRATEFULLY ACCEPTED the glass of water Mara handed her. Her insides felt as dry as a desert after all the tears she'd shed.

Nick stood in the corner with his arms crossed. "Okay, so run this by me again. You aren't Raina. You're her sister."

Ridley nodded. "Yes. I'm so sorry I lied. I just didn't know what else to do."

Jackson hadn't looked at her since she'd blurted out the news. He sat on the floor with his knees drawn up and his head resting back against the wall. Mara handed him a pack of frozen vegetables, which he rested on his right hand. She handed another pack to Nick. He pressed it against his cheek and flinched.

Matt stood looking out the window. She could understand not wanting to get involved. This whole situation sounded like the plot of a movie. A bad one.

Mara took pity on her and sat next to her on the couch. "You were scared, so you decided to hide out at your sister's house?"

"It seemed like the only option I had at the time. After the accident, weird things started happening. Things weren't in the same place I left them. I'd find my car doors open when I knew I'd locked them. The final straw was when my apartment was trashed. Raina's the only family I have. I didn't have anywhere else to go. Then when her security code didn't work, I was so scared. That's part of the reason I passed out." She looked at her hands, willing herself not to start crying again.

"You really passed out? Before we found you on the ground?" Matt spoke up.

"Yes. I took a train and two buses to get here. I didn't want to take a plane or anything. You can buy a bus ticket with cash. By the time I got here I was exhausted and had been living off vending-machine snacks and gas-station food. When I couldn't get in the house, it all just kind of caught up to me at once."

Jackson sat up and looked at her for the first time. "So, you really were locked out? That wasn't just a ploy to get us to help you?"

"I had no idea anyone else was even outside. Except for the kids, of course. They wanted to know what I was doing in the pond." She smiled at the memory.

"So, you actually were ill. You really were locked out. The only thing you lied about was—"

"My name." She met his eyes. "When you called me Raina, I realized the easiest way to hide would be to literally become someone else for a while. Raina changed her name as soon as she started modeling. No one connects us since our names are different, and I never tell people what she does. She always said it was safer for me not to."

"It's actually a good plan," Nick commented.

Shocked, she looked up. He was the last person she'd expected to defend her.

"Don't look so surprised. I'm not saying it was right. I'm just saying I understand why you did it. You probably figured you wouldn't be here long enough for anyone to have to know the truth."

"Exactly. I didn't count on any of this. I didn't count on liking it here so much," she admitted. She sneaked a glance at Jackson.

He was staring at her. Unable to hold his gaze, she dropped her eyes back to her hands.

"Or on me attacking you like that. I am so sorry about that." Nick hung his head sheepishly. "I'm sure you've guessed that your sister and I have a... complicated relationship."

She grimaced. "Say no more."

"What I don't get is why didn't you just tell me the other day?" Jackson stood and walked over to the couch. He sat next to her and grabbed her hand. "When you told me your real name you could have just told me all of it."

"I was going to. But then you said—"

"How much I hate liars." He pulled her into his arms. She exhaled and grabbed him around the middle. "I'm sorry I said that. I didn't mean about things like this. I'm sorry I made you feel that you couldn't tell me the truth. I seem to have a knack for saying the wrong thing around you. It's like you bring out the worst in me."

There was a moment of silence and then they all started laughing. Nick held up his pack of frozen peas as if toasting them. "Wow, little brother. You really have lost your swag, haven't you?"

Jackson winced and looked at Ridley apologetically. "You know what I mean."

"I do. Besides, it's my own fault. I should have just told you before. Raina is going to get quite a kick out of this when I tell her what happened."

"So, she's okay? Raina, I mean." Nick didn't meet her eyes.

"Yeah, she's fine. The only reason she didn't come back right away is because she's doing a shoot for *Sports Illustrated* and I didn't want her to miss it. It's a big deal for her. Plus, I also wasn't lying when I told you she was matchmaking. I think she was happy I was locked out and stuck here."

"I am officially not mad at her anymore." Jackson smirked and went to pick up the bag of peas he'd left thawing on the floor.

Mara nudged her in the side. "And you officially owe me ten bucks."

Ridley's mind raced trying to figure out what Mara was talking about. Then she remembered their bet. "Oh, geez. Well, you definitely won. But I thought you said five?"

"I did, but I was only betting on you driving Jackson crazy. It looks like you got the two-for-one Alexander special."

———

"I ALREADY GAVE Jackson the FBI surveillance photos on David Finemore. What more do you want?"

Nick pulled the phone away from his ear and regarded it with disbelief. This was Elliott? The most suspicious, cynical person he knew?

"I want you to do a full-scale background investigation on this guy. Not just what's in the FBI file, but everything. I have no doubt that you'll find things on your own that your FBI contact didn't give you."

Elliott sighed. "What are you hoping to find? We already know the guy's a criminal."

"Yes, but I want to know the details of what he's done. And *who* helped him."

"Oh, now I see. Come on, Nick. I already did a preliminary background check on her and she's so clean she squeaks. Why are you trying to find a problem that doesn't exist? Jackson really likes this girl. Leave it alone."

Nick swiveled in his office chair until he was facing the window. After leaving Jackson's house he hadn't felt like going home, so he'd decided to go back to the office. Sometimes he spent more time there than he spent at his condo anyway.

At twenty-seven he had more money than he'd ever imagined,

could travel as he wished, and had a list of women on speed dial who'd happily do anything he asked.

And none of them could stir him like the one woman he couldn't have.

"We need to be thorough on this, Eli. Jackson's not like us. He's already been through so much."

"I know. All right, I'll take another look at Ridley, too. But I doubt it'll be anything more interesting than a speeding ticket and a 'most likely to succeed' award in high school."

"Thanks, bro. And one more thing?"

"What do you need?"

Nick thought long and hard about what he was about to do. It was difficult to be successful in business without developing a thick skin and stepping on more than a few toes. He'd been raised with a strict sense of honor and was careful not to make promises he couldn't keep. But after months of uncertainty, he wasn't any closer to a solution on his own. He was prepared to admit that he needed help.

"Another background check. This time on Raina Winters. The real one."

fifteen

THE NEXT AFTERNOON, Ridley pulled into the first available space she could find in the underground parking garage of MacArthur Center Mall.

Katie had the kids, so she'd decided it was high time she got out of the house. It felt like high school all over again when she'd picked up the phone to invite Mara to lunch. She'd never been that outgoing and after everything that had happened, she wouldn't have been surprised if Mara wanted nothing to do with her. But in the end, Mara had seemed pleasantly surprised to hear from her again and more than happy to meet her at the mall during her lunch break.

Mara worked as an administrative assistant twenty minutes away in the city of Norfolk. She'd suggested that Ridley drive over and meet her since Norfolk had the closest shopping mall to New Haven anyway.

White-knuckling her way through traffic in an unfamiliar area wasn't her idea of fun, especially while driving the ultra-expensive Audi coupe Jackson had insisted she take. It was a small triumph that she'd managed to get there without causing any accidents or getting any scratches on the paint. It had been incredibly kind of Jackson to offer her the use of his car in the first place.

They'd spent the previous night tiptoeing around each other. Even though he'd mentioned the industry party again, she doubted he really wanted to take her. He was just too polite to disinvite her. She sighed.

He was probably counting the days until she left.

She threw her purse over her shoulder carelessly and hopped out of the car. She made a note of where her car was parked and set off.

The smell of pizza, hamburgers, and Chinese food hit her as soon as she entered the mall. Using her nose and a quick glance at the mall map, she was able to find the food court where she was supposed to meet Mara, relatively soon. Spotting Mara sitting alone at a Formica table in the center of the room, she hurried over and plopped down across from her. Her apology for being late died on her lips when she saw the look on Mara's face.

"Is everything all right? You look like you just lost your best friend."

Mara shook her head at the comment, seeming to compose herself in seconds. "It's nothing. I'm just ready to shop. Let's check out the sales in the department stores first."

Bouncing up with renewed vigor, Mara gathered her purse and gestured for Ridley to follow. Ridley got up slowly, unsure of how to respond to the sudden change in atmosphere.

Oh well, if she wants to tell me what's wrong, she will. If not, then maybe shopping will cheer her up.

Ignoring the calls of pushy salespeople hanging out of their shops, they headed straight for the department store closest to the food court. Known for having excellent sales, today was no exception. Signs proclaiming everything thirty percent off seemed to raise Mara's spirits. She made a beeline for the lingerie department.

"So, I was a little surprised to get your call." Mara flipped through a rack of skimpy negligees. "I figured we'd hauled over enough clothes to last you until the apocalypse."

"I just felt like shopping. This has been a crazy week."

"Tell me about it. Hanging out with the guys has never been this much fun!"

Ridley couldn't resist smiling at the other woman's antics.

"So, are you shopping for anything in particular? You need something else for your date with Jackson?" Mara asked.

Heat flooded Ridley's cheeks again but she just shrugged. "It's not a date. He just needs a companion for this dinner and I'm convenient. I already know what I'm going to wear. I just wanted to get out of the house."

"Uh huh. Well, maybe if you take one of these home tonight, being in the house won't be so boring." Mara held up a nightgown with the nipples cut out.

"Mara!" She glanced behind her. "Put that thing down."

Mara winked. "Are you kidding? If you won't get this, then I will."

Ridley picked up a pair of panties from the display table next to her. She flipped them over to see the price tag and then whistled.

Mara looked up. "Oh, yeah. I know. I hate those stupid boy shorts where half your ass cheeks are hanging out."

A girl browsing next to them giggled. "Glad I'm not the only one."

"See! I'm just speaking the truth," Mara declared.

Ridley shook her head and watched as Mara held up night-gown after nightgown, each skimpier than the last.

"I was actually talking about the price. I just can't imagine paying so much for something that doesn't cover anything and feels like a shoestring up your ass."

She flipped through the rack in front of her, then crossed to a table display of panties. It wasn't until she picked them up that she could see the gaping hole in the crotch.

"If you're getting that crazy nightgown you might as well get these, too." Ridley glanced over her shoulder but saw she was all alone. "Mara? Where did she..."

As she turned back around, she caught a flash of movement in the floor-to-ceiling mirror in front of her. A man two rows back staring right at her.

She whipped around. The man now had his back to her and was pawing through the rack of clothes in front of him. *It's just another clueless guy shopping for a present for his girlfriend.* Even though she knew it was ridiculous, her heart was still banging against her ribs when Mara appeared from behind a rack of floor-length silk gowns.

"These are so cute," she said. "Not that I have enough cleavage for them, but still." When she saw Ridley standing in the middle of the aisle, still holding the black lace panties to her chest, she stopped in her tracks. "Are you okay?"

"Fine. I'm fine. Just seeing things, that's all." Ridley stuck the garment back on the table and followed Mara to the other side of the store. When she looked over her shoulder again, the man was still looking at the same rack of clothes. He turned then and looked directly at her.

Her blood chilled.

"I think I need to get some air," she whispered. Mara immediately put down the nightgown she was holding and followed her to the escalators.

"Ridley, you are being so weird. What's going on?" In an effort to keep up with her, Mara pushed past a young couple holding hands, muttering a quick "sorry" over her shoulder as they passed. "You look like you just saw a ghost."

"I'm not sure what I saw. This guy was staring and it kind of gave me the creeps. Is there a middle-aged man with dark hair and a leather jacket following us? I don't want to keep looking."

As they stepped onto the escalator to go down to the first floor, Mara turned and leaned against the rail, looking around her casually. A second later, she turned and faced the front.

"Yeah, there is. He was by the jewelry counter." She turned and looked again, then whipped around. "Um, he's on the escalator behind us now. And I think he saw me looking. Who is that?"

Ridley gripped her hands together so tightly she almost winced. "I have no idea. I don't know what to do. What do we do?"

"At the bottom of the escalator, let's go to the left through the formal wear. It'll be easier for us to hide behind those racks. Then we can make our way back to the parking garage and get the hell out of here."

———

THAT EVENING, Jackson stood at the end of the staircase, shifting his feet impatiently.

He glanced at his watch and wondered for the tenth time what was taking Ridley so long. A lot of women took hours to dress, but he wasn't expecting Ridley to need that much time to get ready. She never seemed to bother much about hair or makeup, which was one of the things that Jackson liked best about her.

He hoped she wasn't having second thoughts. She was probably still shaken after seeing him almost pound his brother into the ground. This night was supposed to be about wooing her. Showing her that he could give her more than just tangled sheets. Instead he'd done nothing lately but go caveman and call her a liar.

Because she was *lying to you and who knows what else she's hiding.*

Jackson had been struggling with it all day. He wanted to believe she'd told him everything, but he'd been fooled by a pretty face before. There was probably more to the story than what Ridley had told him and when the rest came out, he needed to be ready. He wouldn't be blindsided again.

Jackson shook off the dark thoughts when Nick appeared in the doorway of the kitchen. "Are you seriously standing there waiting for her? Have some pride, man."

"Shut up, Nick."

"Hey, free advice comes along with free baby-sitting."

Jackson conceded the point with a nod. "Thank you. I wouldn't have blamed you for saying no."

"Whatever. I didn't do it for you. I just didn't want Mom to get a look at your hand and then give both of us a lecture." Nick waved as he turned and went back to the kitchen.

Jackson flexed his fist, then winced as his sore knuckles protested the movement.

You should have known something was up with him.

They'd never encroached on each other's territory before. If Jackson had shown even the slightest interest in a woman, Nick had respected that. He'd always done the same.

But none of those girls were Ridley.

He knew firsthand that she had the power to make a man lose his sense of reason. A trait she apparently shared with her twin.

It was still a bit of a shock to realize that his brother had been carrying on some kind of affair with Raina ever since he'd introduced them. As a favor to Jackson, she'd accompanied his brother to a charity event. He'd had no idea they'd seen each other after that night. His brother loved being single and had always considered settling down to be something you did when you were too old to do much else.

The sound of high-heeled shoes clicking on the hardwood floor drew his attention back to the staircase and his thoughts stopped in midcourse.

Ridley descended the stairs with her head held high despite the shy look in her eyes. Her long hair had been elaborately braided into an updo fit for a queen. She'd done something to her eyes to make them seem deeper and brighter at the same time. The silk bronze dress clung like a second skin, emphasizing her every curve. The gold fringe on the edge of the hem highlighted her long, copper-skinned legs and tiny ankles. Even her feet, delicately encased in matching heels with tiny straps that wove around her ankles in a crisscross pattern, seemed sexy to him.

Ridley stopped directly in front of him and smoothed her hands down the front of her dress.

"Do you like it? I had a hard time finding something that wasn't too revealing. Raina is a lot more daring than I am."

As an answer, he pulled her to him and lowered his head slowly, giving her time to refuse him. His kiss, while gentle, conveyed his desire as his lips tasted every inch of her mouth. She kissed him back enthusiastically until he had to pull away to catch his breath.

"This is going to be a long night." He pulled open the door and gestured for her to go out.

Ridley smiled knowingly and sashayed past him out into the night air.

"I was worried you didn't want me to come with you tonight. After everything that happened."

His BMW convertible was still in the driveway from when he'd gone out earlier. He opened the door for her and waited until she settled back into the leather seat before he closed the door and crossed to the driver's side.

"I won't deny it was a shock, but I understand why you did it. Now we can start with a clean slate. I'm honored you've agreed to come with me. I was worried you wouldn't want to go out with a Neanderthal who bloodies up his own brother."

She winced. "I still feel awful. How is Nick?"

Jackson laughed. "He's fine. He'll never admit I actually hurt him."

She covered her smile with her hand. "Right. Of course. Because that would mean admitting that his baby brother beat him up, right?" At his shrug, she let out a breath. "So, how was work today?"

"It was great, but I don't want to talk about work. Tonight, we're just two people going on a date." He winked at her and turned the music up before pulling out of the driveway.

"Okay, in that case what should we talk about?"

"How beautiful you are. I knew you would look good, but you are absolutely stunning. I'm going to have to keep you close by tonight. I'm not usually a jealous man, but I think we've already seen that I lose my mind when other men get anywhere near you. It's taking all my control not to turn this car around and haul you upstairs."

Ridley leaned over and trailed a hand over his thigh. Jackson's hands tightened on the wheel and he swerved slightly as he misjudged a curve in the road.

"Not until after the party," she whispered.

———

AFTER THAT, they rode to the restaurant in silence, each absorbed in their own thoughts.

She was really excited to spend an evening out. Hopefully, it would be the perfect distraction to keep her from thinking about her disastrous mall trip.

After they'd left the mall and she'd calmed down some, she realized how silly she'd been. It was probably some kind of posttraumatic thing. She'd run from Florida believing that someone was out to get her. Even though she now knew the Morenos had nothing to do with her case, she was still on edge, imagining things.

The guy in the mall had probably just been staring at them trying to get the courage to ask one of them out. And she'd reacted like he'd been a serial killer or something.

There was no telling what Mara thought of her now.

"We're here."

Jackson brought the car to a smooth stop in front of a busy restaurant. Ridley craned her head and was shocked to see a cluster of what could only be photographers.

Jackson handed his keys to the valet and then jogged around to her side of the car. He opened her door for her and offered his hand. She took it gratefully. As soon as she stepped out flashbulbs went off, blinding her temporarily. She put up a hand to shield her eyes.

Flashbulbs continued to pop as they hurried into the restaurant. There had only been a few photographers but they were as annoying as a crowd.

Several men in dark suits stood just inside the restaurant holding clipboards. Jackson turned to one of them and said, "Jackson Alexander and guest." After he found Jackson's name on his list, they were allowed to enter.

"This is nice. Thanks for inviting me."

"Are you kidding? You're doing me a huge favor by coming. I usually attend these alone and end up listening to some stuffed-suit executive from the label all night."

"Don't try to tell me you don't have a date usually. Because I won't believe you."

"It's not that I can't get a date. I'm just not willing to deal with what comes along with it. Namely, someone who just wants me to introduce her to other people."

"Oh. Well, you definitely don't have to worry about that with me."

"Ah, here we are. Our table." Jackson stopped at a round table and pulled out a chair. She sat gratefully. There were tiny place cards with his name on them in front of their seats. She looked around the table curiously but didn't recognize anyone. There was a redhead across from her with her hair teased up into some kind of eighties-style bouffant who looked slightly familiar, but everyone else at the table was much older.

"Hey, Jackson. Good of you to make it." A man on Jackson's left greeted him with a warm handshake.

"Of course, Scott. Allow me to introduce Ridley Wells."

Ridley smiled politely as the man waved hello and introduced his wife, a bored-looking brunette who appeared to be about three decades younger than he was. The woman just nodded in her direction before flagging down a waiter to ask for more wine.

She leaned over to Jackson and whispered, "Wow, you weren't kidding about these parties. I think she's already drunk."

"Now you see why I needed you to rescue me."

The appetizers were brought before she could even look around. Somehow the restaurant wasn't what she had expected. Although it was obviously classy, she didn't feel at all out of place. Most of the people at their table seemed friendly enough, if a little self-absorbed. Not that she minded, because she definitely didn't want to talk about her life.

"I'm really sorry about all that commotion outside. This part of Virginia is home to quite a few celebrities and some local photographers have started hanging out here trying to catch a glimpse of them."

"Anyone I might have heard of?"

"We have a lot of people from the hip-hop and R&B scene. Timbaland, the Neptunes, Missy Elliott."

"Wow, I had no idea."

"Since you're so into jazz, you're probably already aware that the late, great Ella Fitzgerald was also from this area. She was born in Newport News. Virginia has a rich musical history. Well, anyway... I know photographers are just trying to make a living, but man are they annoying!"

"No apology is needed." She smiled at him behind her hand. He seemed so nervous, and she was sure a man like Jackson Alexander didn't get nervous often. She was flattered that he was going to such lengths to show her a good time.

"So, how long have you been into jazz?" Jackson leaned back in his chair and studied her.

"Ever since I can remember. My mom used to play jazz albums every weekend while cleaning the house. It was usually Coltrane or Miles Davis on Saturdays and then she'd sing along with Ella Fitzgerald on Sundays while cooking dinner." She smiled at the memory. "It was the only time she really seemed happy."

"I'm sorry you didn't get to see her happy more often. I can't even imagine."

"That's because your parents are such happy people. Tell me about what it was like to grow up with three brothers."

"Chaotic. We all had chores on the farm, of course. I was usually able to get out of mine if I was crafty enough."

"So you were a charmer once. What happened?"

"I guess I deserved that." He held up his wineglass. "Touché."

She took a healthy sip of her own drink. "Just teasing."

"My dad would always bring us along while fixing things or repairing fence. We always ate dinner together and then played outside until bedtime. After we got older, my parents cheered us on at our little league and basketball games. Even when I went away to college, they made a point to call every week and check on me. Until I dropped out, anyway." He smiled sheepishly.

"Your parents sound really special, Jackson. I'm sure they're very proud of all their children."

Dinner passed in comfortable silence. Both seemed at a loss for words and spent most of the meal staring into their wineglasses or admiring their surroundings. Usually she felt compelled to at least try to make polite conversation, but with Jackson she felt free to just sit and enjoy her meal in peace. Jackson seemed to share her thoughts as he smiled at her over his wineglass.

"Ladies and gentlemen. Thank you for attending the launch party of Shadowlight Records' newest jazz artist, Simona Raye."

Polite applause broke out around them and Ridley sat up in her seat. "Did he just say Simona Raye? I love her!"

Jackson leaned closer to speak directly into her ear. "You've heard of her?"

Ridley nodded. "I downloaded her single when it first came out and I've been waiting for the album to release. She reminds me of a cross between Ella Fitzgerald and Nina Simone."

The announcer waited until the applause died down completely before continuing. "Ms. Raye got her start in the local theatre before she released her first single independently. It did so well that she was immediately picked up by Shadowlight Records. Her album will be released next week, but tonight, she'll be performing several songs from the album for you. Now without further ado, Ms. Simona Raye!"

Ridley jumped up along with everyone else in the room and clapped as a beautiful, dark-haired woman took the stage.

"I'm glad you're excited. Maybe this'll get me some cool points to cross out all the idiotic things I seem to do and say around you," Jackson said.

"Consider the slate wiped clean," Ridley replied and swayed to the music as the opening notes of the single she'd previously heard were played.

"Would you care to dance?"

Ridley's head shot up. She wasn't much of a dancer and she certainly wasn't willing to risk embarrassing herself in front of all these people. However, Jackson grabbed her hand and led her out to the center of the dance floor where other couples swayed in time to the music. She stopped thinking at all as soon as he pulled her into his arms.

Simona Raye's smooth voice flowed through the sound system and rolled over her in waves. It almost felt like she was floating with Jackson's strong arms as her only anchor. Ignoring the little voice in her head warning her to be careful with her heart, she surrendered to the warmth seeping through her pores and curling sweetly through her veins. Jackson hummed softly along with the music. She felt so safe with him, swaying gently to the music, completely unaware of anyone else's presence.

For just a little while it was their world and she didn't want to let anything or anyone else in.

sixteen

AN HOUR LATER, a band had taken over and Ms. Raye was circulating throughout the crowd. He didn't work with jazz artists but since he knew Ridley would love it, he'd made a point to introduce himself so that Ridley could meet her.

He usually hated participating in the fake socializing that went on at these types of events but with Ridley by his side, it didn't even faze him. As he pulled her against him for another slow dance, he felt a tap on his shoulder.

"Jackson? Hey, it's good to see you!"

Jackson turned and froze when he saw who was behind him.

"Hey, Bill. I didn't think you were on the jazz scene?"

It had been years since he'd seen Bill, but he still looked the same. The older man had been one of his biggest supporters when he was younger and one of the most vocal opponents when he'd decided to take his career in a new direction.

He smiled tightly when his old mentor turned to Ridley.

"Hello there. I'm Bill Witherspoon. I'm an old friend of Jackson's from before he was a superstar. I knew him when he was just another kid with a guitar."

Ridley laughed and shook his hand. "Nice to meet you. Ridley Wells."

"I can see he still has excellent taste." Bill laughed and slapped him on the back. "So, is there any truth to the rumor that you're working on a solo project? You've heard the stuff on the charts lately. That golden voice of yours would be a welcome improvement."

Jackson pasted a smile on his face. "No, that's just a rumor."

Ridley looked up at him, her eyes sparkling. "You sing, too? I didn't know that."

"Oh, yeah he sings. Has the kind of voice that makes me see dollar signs. I was two shakes away from signing him to a deal a few years back."

Ridley raised her eyebrows. "A few years back?"

Jackson coughed. "Well, it was great seeing you, Bill. Tell your wife I said hi."

Bill sobered slightly. "Of course. Take care of those adorable boys of yours. And I meant what I said. I know your label is under Shadowlight, and I don't want to step on any toes, but Interlace Entertainment would ink a deal for you in a heartbeat if you ever decide to give a solo career another shot. That offer is always on the table."

Jackson tugged on Ridley's hand and steered them around the other couples on the floor. He was happy when the song changed to an upbeat number and more people crowded onto the dance floor.

Ridley put a soft hand on his cheek and he looked at her, startled. "Why didn't you tell me you're an artist, too?"

After a moment, he looked away. He'd never been shy. As the youngest of four brothers, he'd quickly learned how to command a room. He'd had to if he wanted any attention at all. But when Ridley looked at him, he felt like she could see everything, even the things he didn't want her to see.

"Because I'm not. I used to be, but I let that dream go. I'm a composer and a producer. That's more than enough for me." Jackson held her close as they swayed to the music.

"I'd still love to hear you sing. I only wish I could sing or play an instrument."

"I'll teach you to play."

"But you can't teach me to sing," she teased. "If I could sing I think I'd be doing it all the time. Around the house, in the shower. Just everywhere."

"It's not that big of a deal, Ridley. Just leave it alone."

She cringed. "Sorry. I didn't mean... Sorry."

The song ended and everyone broke out into applause. He could feel Ridley's eyes on him as they walked back to their table.

"Do you mind if we cut out a little early? I just needed to put in an appearance." He pulled his valet ticket out of his pocket.

"Of course." She collected her wrap and purse and trotted to keep up with him.

He could only hope he'd responded appropriately to everyone who spoke to him on the way out. Once the valet brought his car around, he helped Ridley into the passenger side and then handed the guy a bill.

"Thank you, sir!"

By the young man's wide eyes, he'd probably over tipped by a lot but he didn't even care. Looking for a smaller bill would have taken time. It was worth just about any price to get the hell out of there.

They rode in silence for a few minutes before Ridley said, "Thank you for inviting me tonight."

Jackson stifled a bitter laugh. She was too polite to say what she was really thinking. She shouldn't have been thanking him for treating her like that. It wasn't her fault that he'd rather do almost anything than sing these days.

He was starting to understand why Matt had punched a hole

in his wall. The anger inside him was an ugly, potent thing and it seemed more than happy to shred his insides in lieu of another escape route.

He sat up straighter and gripped the steering wheel tighter. It was raining and he, of all people, knew how treacherous a little water on the roads could be.

"I'm sorry if I bit your head off back there. I just don't like talking about it."

Ridley shrugged. Jackson looked over at her. She continued to stare out the window at the passing scenery.

"Come on, Ridley. I said I was sorry. I'm admitting I was an ass."

"I'm not angry with you," she said finally. "I shouldn't have asked. It's none of my business."

He cursed. The memories roiled around in his brain and he had a feeling they were on the verge of boiling over. It was probably best that they'd left early. It wasn't Ridley's fault that he was in a shitty mood and he didn't want to take it out on her any more than he already had.

Things had started between them with a lie, but there was one thing that couldn't be faked. *Their connection.* They had a bond he hadn't felt with any other woman since his wife's death. He didn't want to expose her to the very worst side of him there was. He didn't ever want her to look at him with condemnation in her eyes.

"I gave up on my solo career when my wife died."

He felt more than saw her turn. Even when he wasn't looking at her, her eyes had the ability to slice his emotions down the middle. Right now, all he could feel was her pity. It was rolling off her in waves.

"It's fine. I didn't tell you so you can feel sorry for me. I just want you to understand why I can't talk about it. It isn't personal."

They rode the rest of the way home in silence.

———

"SO, I guess I'll see you in the morning."

Ridley nodded sadly and turned down the hall to her room. She closed the door behind her and dropped her purse and wrap on the bed.

"So much for my perfect night."

After kicking off her shoes and hanging her dress up, she unhooked her bra with a sigh of relief. She sifted through the array of clothes in the suitcase she'd brought from Raina's house until she found a lacy, silk nightgown. If she was going to be depressed, at least she could wear something pretty.

It was tempting to just drop into the bed but she knew she'd pay the price if she didn't remove her makeup. She walked into the bathroom and took her earrings and necklace off. Her reflection stared back at her. It was crazy that she could look fine when she felt like she'd been kicked in the gut. She pulled the pins out of her hair and massaged her scalp.

There was a knock on the door just as she was soaping her face. "Just a minute," she called out.

She hurriedly rinsed and then dried her face with a hand towel. When she left the bathroom, Jackson was sitting on the bed.

"Hey. I thought you were going to bed."

"I was, but I'm not tired. Not even slightly." He looked up at her and Ridley shivered at the pain in his eyes. "I can't go to sleep with you thinking that I won't talk about it because I don't trust you. Especially when nothing could be further from the truth."

"You don't have to tell me anything." She was suddenly exhausted. Tired of trying to figure out where she stood with him and tired of wondering if he felt anything for her beyond lust. "I just want to go to bed."

He didn't move, just sat staring at his hands. She was just about to tell him to get out when he finally spoke.

"My obsession with my music is the reason my wife is dead."

Ridley gulped, suddenly sure that whatever he was going to tell her, she didn't want to hear. "Jackson, don't—"

"Cynthia was upset that night. I'd been spending so much time holed up in the little closet I used for recording back then. We'd just had Jase and all she wanted was a little time to herself. But I couldn't understand that." He looked up at her. "I accused her of wanting to go out with her friends so she could cheat on me."

"How old were you?"

"I was twenty-two. We were so young. We should have had our whole lives ahead of us. But instead, I picked a fight with her. Said horrible things. It was raining that night, but I didn't care. I told her to go out with her friends if she wanted to so badly. To just leave and not come back. And that's *exactly* how it turned out."

The raw pain in his voice pulled her to his side. She sat on the bed next to him and held his hand. He didn't look at her.

"You were only twenty-two. I had just finished college at that age. I had no responsibility at all. I can't even imagine the things you both had to deal with. You made mistakes, I'm sure but her accident wasn't your fault."

"I've had all the counseling and therapy that money can buy. I know the accident wasn't my fault. But none of it can change the fact that I was a shitty husband. If I had been thinking of anything besides myself, she wouldn't have been out in the rain driving that night. That *was* my fault. My golden voice didn't make my wife very happy, did it?"

She was stunned by the bitterness in his voice.

"I just wanted you to know why I hate talking about it. It's because it reminds me that I failed at one of the most important things in my life."

She pulled him into her arms and didn't let go, even when he tried to pull back. Finally he stopped fighting her and grabbed her tightly. She allowed him to pull her into his lap.

"I want you to listen to me," she whispered. "I'm sure your wife loved you very much, even when you guys were fighting. She wouldn't want you to punish yourself for the rest of your life."

"I know. That was the last thing she asked me to do. To live my life. To love. To be happy." He blinked quickly and wouldn't look at her.

Ridley nodded and held his face in her hands. "That's what she wanted and that's what I want for you, too. For you to give yourself permission to be happy."

She kissed him softly, hoping that she could convey all the comfort and healing she felt to him through her lips. After a few moments, he kissed her back. Then suddenly, his eyes opened. His lashes lowered over his dark eyes as he pulled her closer and kissed her again, an unforgiving clash of tongues and lips and teeth.

"I don't know what you do to me," he panted. "You make me believe anything is possible."

"That's because it is," she whispered.

She pulled him closer and kissed him again, pressing against him. It was strangely arousing to be in his arms when he was fully dressed and she was only wearing a thin, silk nightgown. He held her shoulders still so he could ravage her throat. She shivered at the slightly rough sensation of his stubble against the delicate skin.

He pushed her back on the bed, roughly. One of the straps on her gown snapped when he tugged it aside. She pushed it down, wiggling her hips until she was able to slide out of it. Part of her was surprised at this side of him, but a bigger part was thrilled. It was such a rush to be able to drive a man like Jackson to the point of urgency, where he couldn't get her clothes off fast enough because he couldn't wait to have her.

"I wanted to romance you tonight. To show you a good time. But I can't seem to take it slow with you. You. Drive. Me. *Crazy*."

He punctuated each word with a gentle bite to the soft skin of her breasts. He held them in the palms of his hands, holding them still so he could lick and bite the sensitive tips. She ran her fingers through his curls, trying desperately to keep up.

It was too much, too fast and she could already feel her release bearing down on her. She panted, almost afraid of it.

Jackson fumbled with his belt buckle, growling his frustration against her breast. The rumble of his voice against her nipple made her cry out. He finally got his pants off and then lowered himself between her thighs.

As soon as his erection pressed against her core, she came.

"Yes, come for me. I can't wait to get inside you."

She bit her lip to keep from screaming as she trembled in his arms. When she opened her eyes again, he sat up and ripped his dress shirt down the middle. The *ping, ping, ping* of the buttons hitting the floor would have been amusing if she wasn't just as crazed to get him naked.

She ran her hands over his chest greedily. His muscles contracted beneath her fingers and all she could do was admire as he leaned down and took her mouth in another breath-stealing kiss.

"I promise, the next time we make love it'll be perfect. It'll be romantic. I won't be so rough."

"There's only one thing I need you to do that will make this perfect."

"Anything."

"Get naked. *Now*."

———

JACKSON KNEW he was being too rough but he couldn't seem to slow down. His hands raced over all her enticing curves, dipping into the hollow of her belly button and teasing the silky, soft skin behind her knees.

"Hurry!" She sat up and tugged on the elastic band of his boxers. "I want you naked, too."

There was no way he could ignore a request like that. He probably set a land record for how fast he got the rest of his clothes off.

"That's so much better." She tugged him back down and wrapped herself around him, her long legs curling behind his waist. Her hair flowed beneath them, tangling under her arms as she lay back on the bed. The wild curls made her look like she'd been completely and thoroughly taken and he loved it.

He gritted his teeth and pulled back. "I really hope I have protection with me."

He reached over the side of the bed and pulled his wallet from his pocket. When he found a condom, Ridley leaned over and plucked it from his hand.

"Need some help?"

Her eyes were hot on his as she put the edge of the packet between her teeth and ripped it open gently. The sight of her plump lips on the foil made him shiver with anticipation.

Then she pushed him back on the bed and gripped him firmly, her thumb tracing gentle circles around the tip of his shaft.

"Oh, *shit*."

She took him between her lips, the sight of her pink tongue lapping at him almost enough to push him over the edge. She looked up at him with a wicked grin before taking him deeper, sucking him into the soft, wet cavern of her mouth. She made a little humming sound in the back of her throat that sent jaw-clenching vibrations skittering through him.

Baseball. Musical scales. Little old ladies.

He cursed as she sat back and then rolled the condom slowly down his length, so slowly he thought he'd go mad. His blood raced through his system and he was pretty sure he'd never been so aroused in his life.

Then she proved him wrong when she climbed on top of him and took him deep.

Her head fell back, ecstasy written all over her face. He would do anything to keep that look on her face, to hear her scream, to watch her come.

"Come on. *Come on*," he chanted as she rolled her hips, taking him deeper with every twitch. His palms found her breasts and he cupped the soft weights, then skimmed his thumbs over their tight tips. She moaned at the contact and clenched around him.

"Oh my god," she cried. Her hands came up and tangled in her own hair as she rode him until he knew he was going to come just like this.

Some women faked orgasms but he didn't want Ridley to ever have to fake anything with him. His hands left her hips to stroke between her legs, following her rhythm until she cried out her pleasure. Feeling her enthusiasm made Jackson want to please her more, and he eagerly strummed until her tight, clenching muscles pushed him over the edge, too.

"Yes," she mumbled and fell forward on his chest, shuddering with him as he growled his own release in her ear. He held her close, feeling the rapid fluttering of her heart against his.

An unmistakable sense of warmth stole through him as he looked down at her. He didn't question what he was feeling, just pulled the blanket over them and rested his chin on her head. She let out a soft sigh and cuddled closer, her hand settling right over his heart.

As much as certain less-evolved parts of him wanted her physically, there was another less easily identified desire to see her smile. He wanted to court her—to buy her flowers and take her out to dinner. He wanted her to know how deeply she affected him. He wanted to hear her laugh.

To make her happy.

She could have a good life here. She could start her business; she'd already made some friends and she'd be close to her sister. Plus, they could be together. They were good together and there was no reason they couldn't continue things for as long as they both wanted.

Maybe if he showed her that, she wouldn't go back to Florida. She'd overcome so much already. There was really no reason for her to go back to the life she'd left behind.

And plenty of reasons to stay.

seventeen

"MISS RIDLEY, we got to play in the sprinklers. There was so much water it made *mud!*"

"RiRi, I saw a worm!"

"And now we're going to set up a tent in the backyard!"

Ridley gave up trying to keep track of who said what as each boy tried to talk the loudest. It was amazing how lovely the chaotic sounds of a family could be.

She'd spent the morning with Katie and the kids. The second official day of summer camp had been a resounding success. Chris and Jase had been joined by the Mason boys, Hunter and Matthew, to learn about the life cycle of a plant. Jase had been fascinated by the tiny seeds she'd shown them and they'd each received their own seeds, a small pot, and a packet of soil to practice with.

Afterward, they'd gone to Katie's house for water play in the Masons' backyard while she'd returned to Jackson's house to work on her first column. It was going to be a do-it-yourself guide to planting tomatoes.

"Okay, everybody upstairs! You need to change clothes."

Jackson came up behind them and thumped them each

soundly on their behinds before hauling them up in his arms for kisses. She had never known a man could be so tender with children and be so comfortable interacting with them. He seemed his happiest with the boys.

After their intense lovemaking last night, something seemed to have changed between them, but she couldn't pinpoint exactly what it was. Other than the fact that he had given her the deepest, most arousing kiss before leaving for work this morning. She'd found herself staring off into space and daydreaming about him all day.

Just then he looked up and caught her. Heat curled through her when he raised an eyebrow. She whipped around and busied herself with the containers of food she'd been packing.

"Why don't you guys wash your hands before dinner? I thought we'd have a picnic outside."

"Actually, I told the boys they could have dinner with the Masons. They're setting up a tent in the backyard to pretend like they're camping. I just brought them home so they could change out of their wet clothes. I didn't know you had something planned." He looked sheepish when he noticed the small wicker basket she'd lined with towels.

"I guess that means it'll just be me and you." She glanced in his direction and was shocked at the raw, carnal desire in his eyes.

"Yes. Just the two of us," he replied.

She shivered and tore her eyes from his. Her hands were shaking as she resumed folding napkins to place in the basket with the food.

"I'll go set up outside. We can eat whenever you're ready."

God, I hope my voice doesn't really sound that squeaky and breathless.

She didn't dare risk another glance in Jackson's direction as she scooped up the basket and rushed out the back door. She just prayed she could make it through dinner without climbing in his lap and begging him to make love to her again.

Once she was outside, she spent an unnecessarily long time locating the perfect spot to spread out the blanket. Finding a picturesque nook under a shady elm tree, she began to prepare a cozy nest for them to dine in. She spread the blanket and then made quick work of setting out the various dishes she'd prepared. She heard Jackson walk up behind her but she didn't turn around.

"Did you get the boys settled?" She hated the breathy tone of her voice but was powerless to control it. Trying to keep her hands steady, she continued setting up their picnic, keeping her eyes averted as Jackson sat down beside her, so close her thigh brushed his.

"Yeah, they're really excited. You were right about Katie. And since it's just us, I figured we could have this." He held up a bottle of champagne.

His long, tapered fingers were graceful as he reached over her for the plastic cups she'd brought. He handed her a cup and then poured a little for each of them. He touched his cup to hers, his eyes capturing hers in a heated stare.

"Cheers." He took a healthy sip. "You should try it. It's good." He dipped a finger into the bubbly liquid and dotted it on her lower lip. She licked her lips reflexively. His eyes darkened. Then he leaned over and licked her bottom lip, too.

"See? Delicious."

Ridley sat stunned as Jackson began putting food on his plate, seemingly oblivious to her reaction. She tried to speak but found her mouth was glued together and she just watched mutely as Jackson filled first his plate and then hers.

"Eat. You'll need your energy later."

Ridley gulped and stuffed half her sandwich in her mouth. She made quick work of everything on her plate until it was empty save for a lone, squashed grape.

Jackson laughed. "Relax. No need to rush. We've got more than enough time."

"It's hard to relax when you're looking at me like that."

He was doing it again. He'd finished his food and set his plate aside. Now he was just leaning back on the blanket staring at her. No, not staring, devouring her with his eyes. It was positively indecent the way his eyes lingered over her breasts and hips.

"Are you finished?" he asked silkily. He sat up and moved closer. "Do you want some more champagne?"

Ridley trembled as he moved so he was sitting behind her. She was now in the cradle of his legs. "Jackson? What are you—oh."

He slid his hand up to her right ear, stroking the downy wisps of hair that trailed loose from her ponytail. She gasped as his hand slid down to stroke the sensitive skin on her neck.

The first kiss against the shell of her ear made her sigh. The second kiss made her melt. He pulled her back until she rested against his chest. Then he touched her chin, turning her face toward his.

"I've been waiting to do this all day."

The first touch of his lips to hers was soft, tentative. She didn't even close her eyes as he sweetly tasted her mouth. She didn't want to break the spell, for surely this was magic, the slow swell of desire that was creeping up her thighs and floating in her belly. Jackson slowly pushed her back on the blanket and trailed his hand down her arm in slow circles.

Her eyes fluttered closed as he took her mouth more forcefully this time, his hand coming up to cup her breast. He stroked her through the thin cotton before bending his head and gently biting her through the fabric.

Ridley couldn't breathe. She pulled at Jackson's shirt, wanting to feel his skin next to hers. That was what she needed, the delicious feeling of being skin to skin. His hand moved slowly beneath her skirt, trailing along the sensitive skin of her thighs. When his hand *finally* got to the edge of her panties, she almost cried out in relief.

Suddenly his hand stilled.

"Shit, I'm doing it again," he muttered.

"Jackson," she whispered breathlessly. "What are you doing? Why did you stop?" Boldly she wrapped her legs around his waist. The copper flecks in his eyes darkened before he cursed and let her go.

"I'm always pulling your clothes off like an animal." His breath was still rough but he moved away slightly. "I just can't seem to help myself. I'm supposed to be romancing you."

She grabbed him by the lapels of his shirt and dragged him closer until their breaths mingled. When he groaned, she brushed her lips against his.

"Do you have to?"

This time when he kissed her, he didn't stop.

———

NICK CURSED under his breath as he watched the couple kissing on the blanket jump apart like guilty teenagers. He'd come over hoping he could catch Jackson alone. The manila folder he carried suddenly felt like a brick.

"Nick? What are you doing here?"

To Nick's annoyance, his brother turned back to Ridley and kissed her soundly before getting up. He jogged over to where Nick waited by the back door. "What's up, man? Is everything okay?"

"Not exactly." Ignoring Ridley's interested stare, he grabbed Jackson by the arm and pulled him into the house. Usually the floor was littered with toys and random items of clothing that Jase had removed and left in the middle of the room. Now the area was scrupulously clean. Ridley's influence, he had to assume.

She's already insinuated herself into their everyday lives.

"I hate to just barge in on you, but Elliott found some information that I thought you needed to have right away."

He handed Jackson the manila folder. Call him a coward but he'd thought it would be easier if his brother saw the proof in black and white. He watched as Jackson opened the folder and pulled out the thick sheaf of papers Elliott had e-mailed to him. He'd been surprised by the length of Ridley's boyfriend's rap sheet.

Jackson narrowed his eyes as he read. "What the hell is all this? A background check? You did a background check on *Ridley?*"

"Yeah. And her boyfriend, David."

Jackson's fingers clenched on the stack of paper. "I already asked Eli to look into what David was doing."

"Yeah, but I asked him to look into them both." He continued ignoring Jackson's scowl. "It's a good thing I did, too. It's all there, Jackson. Ridley is the middleman in whatever scheme they've got going. I've found several bank accounts in her name with wire transfers to overseas accounts. From his FBI file, it looks like Mr. Finemore has pulled this scam numerous times with his former girlfriend. But she's in jail now, so of course he had to get a new partner." He motioned outside with his head.

"Wait, you think Ridley was working *with* this guy? Nick, what the hell are you talking about?" Jackson threw the papers down on the kitchen table and glared at him. "You think she made up the whole story? You think she put those bruises on *herself?*"

"I think she really was scared the day we found her. Her partner got killed and maybe the people they scammed are looking for her." At his murderous look, Nick held up his hands. "I'm just saying. It fits the pattern. Finemore always has a female accomplice to get close to the victim, then when they don't suspect anything, he moves in."

"I understand you're just looking out for me, but I think you've got this all wrong." He held up the pages. "Her record was clean up until she met this guy. I know she's probably hiding something else. I've had the same thought myself. But I don't think this is it. She's not a criminal and I don't think she's done anything wrong other than trusting a guy with a rap sheet as long as the Constitution. She thought he was a private investigator; instead he just stole her money and her social security number. She's a victim in this, too."

"She's gotten to you. I can tell. She's already got you defending her." Nick crossed his arms.

"Just leave, Nick, please. I'll look at everything, I promise. I just need to think."

"Okay. Just don't say I didn't warn you." Nick walked out without another word.

He'd accomplished what he'd come for.

———

JACKSON WALKED out of the house, unsure how to behave. Part of him wanted to chase his brother and ask what else he knew and the other part wanted to bury his head in the sand and ignore it. Ridley looked up as he pulled the door closed behind him.

"Is everything okay?" she asked.

He walked back over to the blanket and sat down on the edge. She looked a little hurt that he didn't sit right next to her, where he'd been before the interruption. He wasn't sure how to recapture the carefree feeling of a few minutes ago. Not when all he could see were white pages and black ink.

"Yeah. Nick just wanted to talk business. He has no sense of timing whatsoever."

He looked over at her, watching as she carefully collected

their cups and silverware, placing them neatly back in the picnic basket. Next, she picked up the small containers used to hold their sandwiches and the leftover potato salad and put them in the basket on top. When she was done, everything was arranged neatly with all the similar items grouped together. She hummed to herself softly as she worked. He shook his head.

If Ridley was a criminal she had to be the worst one ever.

When his cell phone started ringing, he gratefully snatched it up.

"We've got a problem, boss."

Jackson closed his eyes and massaged the knot of tension just starting to form between his eyebrows. "What kind of problem?"

"One of the girls is pregnant. She's threatening to drop out of the group."

Jackson groaned. Somehow he had sensed his luck with Divine was too good to be true. However, he had dealt with worse problems in the past. The scandal with Alana flashed through his mind before he could squelch the thought. He wouldn't let it get that bad if it took everything within him.

His eyes shifted over to look at Ridley lying quietly on the blanket, her face serene, seemingly asleep. He smiled confidently. They had been interrupted before things went too far, but he knew it was only a temporary reprieve. A part of him wanted to throw the phone in the pond and bury himself in her forever. After all, whichever group member had gotten herself knocked up, she would be just as pregnant tomorrow as she was today. The papers his brother had brought would still be there, too.

It was tempting to close himself off from the world and revel in what he had found today after a lifetime of searching.

Peace.

But he was a man who believed in keeping his word and he'd told Ridley that the next time they made love it would be perfect. He'd figure out what it was she was hiding, she wouldn't be distraught after a nightmare, he wouldn't be tearing her panties off with his teeth, and they wouldn't rush this time.

He closed his eyes against the memory of her erotic pleadings. A few more moments and he would have said to hell with comfort and taken her right here in the backyard.

Mosquito bites on his ass didn't fit his idea of perfect.

"I'll be there in about twenty minutes. I trust that you can handle things until then." He flipped the phone shut, ignoring Mac's voice still chattering away.

He would have to go into the office to come up with a game plan. There would be difficult decisions to make and he needed time to figure out what direction the group would take.

He sent a quick text to Katie to see if she could keep the boys for a little longer. Once she responded, he dropped down next to Ridley and began kissing his way up her arm. Her girlish giggle let him know she wasn't asleep as he had previously thought and she had probably been listening to his entire conversation.

"I have to go into the office for a little while." She frowned slightly and threw her arms around his neck drawing him down on top of her. He laid his head on her breast and listened to the steady rhythm of her heart beating underneath his ear. "Come with me."

Her eyes met his. "Really? I'd love to go. But wait, what about the kids?"

"We can pick them up after we get back. I already asked Katie if she'd mind them staying a little longer. I want you to meet the new group I'm producing. Besides, I don't want to be away from you right now."

Ridley turned her face into his shoulder and placed her hand in the middle of his chest. The soft touch warmed him unlike anything else. "I don't want to be away from you, either," she finally admitted.

Watching the wind lift her hair and the golden glint of the late evening sun off her smooth cheeks made him realize how vulnerable she was.

"Come on. It doesn't take long to get there but I don't want to be out too late." He held out a hand and pulled her to her feet.

It wasn't her fault that she'd trusted the wrong person in the past. He'd done the same and didn't want anyone judging him for it. Hadn't she already paid the price for her mistake? The night she'd told him about the accident, the emotion in her eyes had been real. She'd been scared and she'd done the only thing she could do. Run.

I don't believe she's a scam artist. I don't care what Nick says.

———

"OKAY, guys, I briefed Jackson on the nature of the problem, so now we have to figure out how to deal with it." Mac, Jackson's assistant, spoke quickly as though he had somewhere else to go.

Ridley sat back in a hard plastic chair and assessed the annoying, albeit beautiful, members of Divine. She was excited to see what Jackson did at work but was a little disappointed that what she'd seen so far didn't look much different than an ordinary office. She'd never been inside a real recording studio and had been expecting something really high-tech and different.

You've been watching too much TV.

"Okay, girls. I'm going to do everything I can to push the single out right away. If we're lucky, it'll catch on and we can book you guys as the opening act on a small tour before Kaylee gets close to her due date."

Jackson looked at Ridley and rolled his eyes. She hid her smile behind her hand. The girls weren't even pretending to listen.

Two of the group members, Mandy Johnson and Christina Milado, were in the corner arguing. Sasha Whitman, a friendly, slim woman with a cocoa complexion and a bright smile, was sitting just to her left. She had been asking Ridley questions about her relationship with Jackson since she'd arrived. There were only so many ways she could play dumb and pretend they were just friends.

Her gaze finally came to rest on the fourth member of the group, standing at the window, distanced from the other members as much in body as she was in spirit. She couldn't figure out how Kaylee Wilhelm had ever hooked up with the other three girls in the first place. She had a sad, sort of haunted look about her, and seemed extremely unaware of her own talent. With her rounded figure she was not the same "bombshell" type as the other girls, but she was beautiful in a unique way. She also had the best voice. Clear as a bell and capable of hitting notes that made her breath catch.

"Okay, why don't we just address the elephant in the room? There's no point in dancing around the problem."

"This is a little more than a problem. This dumb whore got herself knocked up and we haven't even had a chance to shoot our first video," Christina said.

All conversation stopped. Everyone turned to look at Kaylee. She didn't turn from the window.

"Tina, we aren't going to get anywhere by you slinging insults around. If you don't have anything constructive to offer, then you shouldn't be here." Jackson nailed her with a steely look when she opened her mouth to complain. Once he was sure she wasn't going to interfere again, he turned his attention back to Kaylee.

"Kay, look, it's not a big deal. I had a similar problem with another group and we managed to shoot the video around it. I want you to know how important you are to the group and we'll support you no matter what you decide to do."

Ridley thought he had gotten through to her when she turned around. When he saw the tears running down her face, he grabbed the tissues on the desk and offered them to her. She snatched them with a sob.

"My baby is not a *problem*. There's no decision to make. I love this baby and I am not giving it up!"

She hurled each statement as if hoping to pierce him dead through the heart. Suddenly she tossed the box of tissues on the ground and stormed over to the door.

"If she stomps any harder the roof might cave in."

Christina's snide comment was made in a stage whisper, obviously intended for everyone to hear. She didn't even bother to wipe the smirk off her face when Kaylee turned around and slowly walked back in front of her. Instead she met her gaze straight on, even had the nerve to raise an eyebrow as if to say "Whatcha gonna do?"

Ridley had heard enough. She put two fingers in her mouth and let out a piercing whistle. "Everybody shut up!"

They all turned to look at Ridley in disbelief.

"She's about a hundred pounds soaking wet. Does she know she's about to get her ass kicked?" Mac's whisper was loud enough to be heard all the way across the room.

"Uh, ladies, let's all calm down—" Jackson stopped in disbelief when Ridley held up a hand, cutting him off.

"First of all," she said, looking directly at Christina, "no one in here is perfect, but you are the last person who needs to make comments about someone else's appearance. Clearly you've had things you weren't too happy about with your body as well." She looked down at the other woman's obviously fake breasts and widened her eyes theatrically.

Muffled laughter broke out behind Christina and she whipped around. The other girls straightened up and tried, unsuccessfully, to hide their smirks. Kaylee still looked angry but at least she didn't look like she was about to fight anymore.

Ridley turned to Kaylee. "Second of all, Jackson didn't mean anything by what he said. Your baby is not a problem."

"Well, that's what he said."

"Look, I get that you're hormonal, but he's a *guy*. Since when do guys ever say the right thing?" Ridley waited until Kaylee acknowledged that with a small smile before she turned to the rest of the group.

"Baby fever is all over Hollywood right now. Why don't we call in a tip to the paparazzi that a member of the hot new group Divine is pregnant? Kaylee will be photographed shopping for baby clothes with her happy bandmates around her and we'll circulate a rumor that the baby's father is someone famous."

"Only if we say it's Idris Elba," Kaylee interrupted.

"Not him."

"Why not?" Christina asked suspiciously.

"Because he's mine," Ridley shot back. The other girls erupted into a chorus of catcalls. Even Christina gave her a begrudging smile.

Ridley pulled out her cell phone. "I'll ask my sister for some names. If anyone is good at fooling the press, it's her. In the meantime, why don't you all finish recording and I'll figure out the best place for you to be seen shopping for baby clothes."

eighteen

JACKSON WATCHED in amazement as the girls nodded their approval of her plan and started discussing the song. Christina and Kaylee stood on opposite sides of the group, but still. They were there and they weren't fighting.

He walked up to Ridley and laid his hands on her shoulders. "You're really good at that, you know."

"What?" She turned in his arms, snuggling against his chest so her head fit right below his chin.

"Calming people down. Cutting through the drama to the heart of the thing. I'm not sure if there's a name for that but I'd hire you in a heartbeat. Especially since this is the part of the business that I hate, handling different personalities and getting them to all work together."

"I've had a lifetime of dealing with Raina. I consider it on-the-job training."

"Hey, guys? Sorry to interrupt."

They turned to see Kaylee standing directly behind them. "The girls and I decided to record first thing tomorrow. I'm not at my best right now and I think if we try to force it we'll just be wasting your time."

"I agree. Let's call it a night everyone," Jackson said. "I'll expect you back in the morning, ready to work."

Ridley waved at each of the girls as they left. After he gathered a few things from a table in the corner, Mac left, too.

"I thought they'd never leave." Jackson picked up a guitar from a stand in the corner and strummed a few bars. It was a little out of tune. He used to get new song ideas all the time but it had been awhile since he'd played in the office.

"I guess we should go, too. I'm sure the boys will be exhausted." She looked tired but happy.

"Not yet. There's something I want to show you first."

He grabbed her hand and pulled her to the door at the back of the room, walking quickly before he could lose his nerve. He pushed it open and walked in. Ridley followed, her eyes wide.

"Wow. It looks just like I imagined it would."

He could barely contain his excitement as he pointed her to the chair in front of the recording console.

"This is a thirty-two-channel API analog console. I just bought it last year. It's top of the line. I prefer analog because it just gives a better sound. When I want to hear music, I want to hear the real thing."

She sat delicately and swiveled toward the desk. "I'm afraid to touch anything. This looks really expensive."

"Well, yeah, it is. It's about a hundred grand or so."

She gaped at him before folding her hands in her lap. "Oh my god. No wonder it looks like the controls of a spaceship. What does all this do?"

"I'm going to show you." He flipped a few switches. The red light that showed he was recording blinked back at him.

He handed her a pair of earphones. "Here, put these on."

He couldn't look at her as he pushed through another door into the recording room. She sat up straighter and watched him through the glass as he set the old guitar down in the middle of the room.

"This was one of my first guitars." He spoke up slightly even though he knew she could hear him perfectly. Everything in the recording room was being transmitted back to her through the earphones.

She pointed at the earphones in confusion. He ignored her and pulled a short stool from the corner over to the microphone in the middle of the room. After adjusting the microphone, he picked up his guitar and strummed it a few times. He worked his way down the scale, fret by fret, tightening the tuning pegs until it sounded right.

"I bought it at a secondhand shop while I was in college. I have better ones now, of course. Electric ones. Expensive ones. But sometimes when I start hearing the notes of a new song, all I want is to strum bars on this old thing. That's how I know if the song is any good or not. Truly good music doesn't need accompaniment or a lot of studio tricks. It hits you right here." He held his hand over his heart. "Even when it's just a guy on a stool playing a guitar that's older than he is."

She didn't say anything, just watched him with those huge eyes that saw everything. It was just as well, because he had no idea how to explain what he was about to do. So, he just strummed a few more bars and then began to sing.

> Mama always said to me
> You'll know you've found the one
> When every day seems so short
> And you'd give it all up for
>
> Just one more day
>
> Daddy always told me

That love was like a gift
But even gifts come with a price
But I'd pay anything for

Just one more day

For so long I thought I was broken
That I had nothing left inside
Until the day I met you
And all I wanted was

Just one more day

Just one more day with you
My love
Is all I need to survive

One more day

He let the last note fade away before looking up. It was so silent in the room, the only sound his breathing and the fading hum of the guitar strings. Even through the glass, he could tell Ridley had her eyes closed.

He'd made an impulsive decision to play for her but he wasn't sure what had made him play a song he hadn't even finished writing. When she'd asked to hear some of his music, he'd originally been planning to play her one of the songs he'd written in the past. Songs that had been on the radio and billboard charts. Songs he had reason to believe a lot of people thought were good.

But when he'd turned around and seen her watching him and realized they were all alone, the song he'd had swimming around in his head for the past week had been the only thing on his mind.

In that moment, he'd wanted to share it with her. To show her, in a way that nothing else could, what he was feeling.

It felt like an eternity before she opened her eyes. She let out a small breath and then shook her head. When she didn't say anything, his heart sank.

———

"I CAN'T EVEN IMAGINE HAVING that kind of talent."

Jackson gestured to his ears and she realized he couldn't hear her. She pulled the headphones off and set them down gently. She walked through the door into the glass-walled room where Jackson was.

"So, what did you think?"

"I'm blown away. That's what I was saying in there. I can't imagine being so talented."

His shoulders sagged and she realized that he'd been waiting for her approval. This amazing man was waiting for what she thought.

What she felt.

"I'm glad you liked it." He stood and leaned the guitar against the stool.

Ridley followed him as he left the room and pulled the door closed behind them. She was honored that he'd been willing to sing for her when she knew how hard it was for him. It felt like they'd taken another step today, toward what she wasn't sure, but wherever it led, she was willing to find out.

She was hesitant to ask too many questions, afraid he would tense up and pull away from her again, but she found herself asking, "Is that one of the songs Divine is going to record?"

"No. Not every song I write ends up being good enough to

record, unfortunately. I'm probably going to end up scrapping it since I can't quite get the music right."

She met his eyes. "It sounded perfect to me."

He stopped. They stood staring at each other for a moment before he tipped her chin up. He pressed his lips to hers gently. Ridley stood still, completely stunned. He'd kissed her many times. Sudden kisses. Shockingly erotic kisses. Kisses in places she couldn't even say out loud.

But he'd never kissed her like this. Like he just wanted to be close to her. Not for anything sexual but just because he craved her presence.

On the ride home Jackson seemed unusually quiet and Ridley didn't try to fill the silence with small talk. She was too preoccupied with her own thoughts about the events of the night.

They pulled into the Masons' driveway and Jackson left the car running while he jogged up the steps and hit the doorbell. Katie opened the door, juggling a tricycle and a toddler. Jackson grabbed the tricycle before it hit him in the shins and chucked the toddler under the chin. A second later, he came back down the driveway carrying Jase while Chris followed. After he buckled them both into their car seats, they continued down the street.

After they entered the house, the boys ran up the stairs, stomping and shrieking. Jackson waited until they were out of sight before grabbing Ridley around the waist and burying his face in her hair.

"Sorry for all the drama tonight. I should have warned you what we were dealing with before we got there."

She turned in his embrace and wrapped her arms around his neck. She breathed in his earthy scent before turning her face up to his.

"It's okay. I'm just glad I was there. I really think Kaylee is having a hard time."

"I'm glad you were there, too."

Stroking a hand down the side of his cheek, she felt his quick intake of breath. His cheek felt rough against her palm and he turned his head to press a kiss to her fingers.

Ridley sucked in a breath at the look of tenderness that crossed Jackson's face. She swallowed against the sudden lump in her throat. There were so many things she wanted to tell him. That she was sorry for bringing up bad memories. That his wife's accident wasn't his fault.

That she couldn't imagine her life without him.

But what if he wasn't ready to hear it? Things were moving so fast and she had no idea if he would feel the same way. She couldn't take it if she bared her heart only to realize he wasn't capable of returning her feelings.

A door slammed upstairs and they jumped apart.

"I guess I should get the boys ready for bed." Jackson kissed her forehead and then crossed to the stairs. She watched him go, temporarily hypnotized by the sight of his broad shoulders flexing beneath his shirt.

The man didn't know the effect he had on her. She couldn't seem to think about anything other than being with him. Making love to him.

That's because you're falling in love with him.

There had been no words of love spoken between them, just words of passion. She was old enough and wise enough to know the difference. They'd agreed to a "no-strings" arrangement just to avoid these types of entanglements. And she couldn't blame him for that. She'd started this knowing exactly what she was getting into. She wouldn't allow her pride to get in the way of enjoying the time they did have together. She could be cosmopolitan and sophisticated if she had to be. She would act as if it was no big deal and she wouldn't cry her eyes out over a man who obviously didn't love her.

But she couldn't deny that the day he decided he was done with her was going to tear her heart out.

———

JACKSON CLOSED the door to his room and let his head fall back against the wood. It had taken a solid thirty minutes to calm Chris down enough to sleep and Jase had gotten out of bed five times after that. When he'd emerged, the door to the guest room was closed.

He changed into sweatpants and sat on the edge of his bed. It had been an eventful day and he was tired. But the idea of climbing into his bed alone didn't appeal at all.

He hadn't known how intensely personal it would be to play her one of his songs. Especially something that she'd inspired, not that she knew that. Something had happened back at the studio. It had felt like baring himself in a way he wasn't sure he was ready for.

He yanked the covers back angrily and got into the bed. A week. She'd only been here a week and it felt like she was already intricately woven through every area of his life. He couldn't get in his bed, put his children to sleep, or go to the studio without feeling as though she was with him in some way.

After ten minutes he got back up. Ridley was surely already asleep and he wasn't enough of an ass to wake her, he just wanted to see her. He walked down the hallway to her door and knocked lightly before he opened it.

Ridley lay on her back, her long hair splayed out on the pillow like a curtain. One of her hands was flung out to the side and the other was resting on her stomach. He kissed her gently on the forehead and breathed deeply of her scent.

Could he ever get enough of her?

Before he knew what he was doing, he'd crossed to the other

side of the bed and climbed in. As soon as he slid beneath the covers, Ridley turned toward him and opened her eyes.

"Jackson. You're here." She blinked at him sleepily before scooting closer and burrowing next to him.

Was it possible that he was falling for her?

He was already uncharacteristically possessive around her, as though no one else should ever hear her laugh or see her beautiful smile. It was ridiculous, but he wanted to be the only one who made her happy and the only one who brought that smile to her face.

He watched as she took a deep breath and tucked her hand beneath her cheek. Warmth and something he couldn't identify rose in his chest. This was the first time they had spent the night together without making love and somehow he felt closer to her than ever before.

Although he had long felt the need to stay clear of women in general, with Ridley it was different. He didn't feel the need to prove himself when he was with her. She was honest and loving, and he knew he could trust her with his life. He found himself wanting to do things for her, for no apparent reason. He wanted to make her feel special and cherished. He just felt at home.

When he was with her, he felt he was where he belonged.

He eased the covers down so he could see her in the dim light of the moon. Her pouty lips and long lashes made her seem so innocent, but he knew a tigress lurked beneath the seemingly docile exterior. She was everything a woman should be—strong and determined, but sweet and thoughtful. Just the kind of woman he needed in a wife.

Wife—what am I thinking?

They'd only known each other a week and he'd already learned the hard way that he was a bad husband. But somehow, when he looked in her eyes, trying again didn't seem so impossible.

"I love you," he whispered.

He wasn't ready to buy a ring just yet, but he also wasn't willing to let her just walk away. Once Elliott found out who she was running from, they would be closer to resolving the demons of the past and building the perfect future he wanted to create for her. As he looked at her sweet face, gentle with sleep, he made a promise.

I will keep you safe.

Even if it took everything he had.

nineteen

JACKSON SLOWED as he neared the office and turned into The Rush, a popular café on the corner. The small restaurant had been around for as long as he could remember. He'd have to hurry because Mac was probably already in the office waiting for him. His assistant knew he had an addiction to The Rush's sweet potato fries, because he came just about every Saturday for an order of them and a sandwich. Rubbing his stomach, he resolved to hit the gym an extra day this week.

Entering, he grabbed a spot at the counter and waved to the petite, copper-skinned woman behind the counter. She slung the towel that she was using to wipe off the register over her shoulder and came over to kiss his cheek.

"Hey, sweet stuff, I been expecting you. I got your fries on order already and your sandwich should be ready in a few." She moved quickly behind the counter, ringing up orders and shouting back new ones with easy efficiency.

"Thanks, Miss Doris. I can always count on you." She threw him a lazy grin as she counted out change for a portly man with graying hair. Once done with the customer, she came around the counter and hefted herself up onto the stool next to him.

"Are you gonna stay here by yourself or go eat with your friend?" She blew out her breath and swiped a few stray hairs behind her ear. She nodded her head toward the back of the restaurant.

"One of my friends is here?" He craned his neck to see over the head of the woman sitting at the bar next to him. There was a young couple in one of the booths on the back wall. An older man read the newspaper at a center table. A teenaged girl sat in the corner booth, texting.

"I don't see anyone." He turned back to Miss Doris and shrugged.

"That's odd. He was just here a few minutes ago. Same guy came in yesterday looking for you, too. Said he was in town on business and asked if I knew where you lived. I told him I can't remember the name of these fancy communities. Haven's Port. Haven's Peak."

Jackson smiled. "Havensbrooke."

She waved her hands. "Whatever. Oh, there he is!"

He turned and looked out the store's front window. A dark-haired man stood outside on the curb, about to get into an older-model Cadillac. The hair on the back of Jackson's neck stood up.

He'd never seen the guy before.

"He specifically asked for me?" Jackson asked.

Miss Doris thought about it before saying, "Yeah, he definitely said Jackson Alexander. Why? Is everything okay?" She glanced over his shoulder worriedly.

He pulled out some cash from his wallet and put it on the counter. "Can you wrap up my lunch for me? I'll be right back," he said as he rose from his barstool.

He pushed open the front door, the tinkle of the door chime loud in his ears. The man was in his car, backing up.

"Hey! Wait," he called out.

The man lifted his head and their eyes met. He couldn't see

clearly between the car's slightly tinted windows and the blinding noon sun, but he was sure the guy saw him. Only he didn't stop. He gunned the engine and whipped the wheel, his tires spinning in the gravel lining the parking lot.

"What the hell!" Jackson jumped back as a cloud of dust spun from the wheels and enveloped him. He watched the car drive away until it turned right at the closest streetlight.

It never slowed down.

He pulled his cell phone from his pocket and hit one of the speed dials. "Elliott? I need your help."

"Whatever you need."

He looked back at the diner where Miss Doris stood in the doorway watching. "A security detail for Ridley and the kids. I'm not sure why, call it paranoia, but I want to make sure they're protected."

———

JACKSON LED Ridley through the entryway and into the family room at his parents' ranch-style home. After a lazy Saturday with the boys in the park, he'd finally convinced her to come to Sunday dinner. He hadn't told her about the guy he'd seen the previous day. It was probably nothing and he definitely didn't want to worry her, but there was no way he was leaving her alone.

"Come on, I'll give you the grand tour."

He knew she was uncomfortable with the idea of being around his family again. He was, too. A little. If his parents saw him with Ridley again and heard from the boys that they'd been spending so much time together, they would assume they were serious.

He loved Ridley. There was no point hiding from it just because it seemed so sudden. There was no way he'd let her go back to Florida without a fight. But in his parents' opinion, there was only one point to a serious relationship. Marriage. Which he wasn't even ready to think about yet.

Was he?

"The style is similar to your house." Ridley pointed to the draperies and furnishings in the family room, all various shades of blue. The old-fashioned armchairs were passed down from his mom's parents, Jackson knew. Most of the rest of the furniture had been replaced in the past few years.

"Yeah, my mom helped me decorate the house. She's really into all that stuff. I'm practically color-blind."

He and Nick both had been adamant that their successes would give their parents access to whatever they wanted. The only thing his mother had wanted was to redecorate because the family home had pretty much looked the same since he was a child. His father had yet to allow either of them to buy him anything.

Jackson was itching to replace the old pickup truck his father drove. He would have just done it without asking but he secretly thought his dad might have a fondness for the beast. He'd been threatening to replace it for years but never had.

He held in a groan as Ridley crossed to the mantel. His mom still kept all their high school graduation photos displayed.

"Oh my god, you were so cute!"

"Cute? I had a curly mullet thing going on in that photo."

Ridley moved down the line, looking at the other pictures. Bennett had the worst photo of them all—hunched over, his face almost obscured by the massive glasses he'd worn up to college. Eli looked sullen. The only one who looked decent was Nick, who'd been a playboy even then. His hair was cut short and slicked back and he was smiling widely.

"Nick looks exactly the same. Why am I not surprised?"

His chest tightened, thinking of Nick. Despite the circumstances, part of him was still pissed that his brother had kissed her. Especially since he still seemed determined to make trouble for them.

"Do you mind if I use the bathroom? Before everyone gets here?"

"Sure. There's one right here."

She followed him as he walked down the hall leading to the bedrooms. He pointed her to the hall bathroom.

"I'll just go check on the boys. My parents should be back soon."

Jackson continued down the hall to the room his parents kept for the kids. Inside he found toys already strewn across the floor. The room consisted of two sets of bunk beds—which his mother insisted on *just in case* any of his brothers had children—a dresser, and a desk. His parents doted on their grandchildren and liked to keep the kids' bedroom well-equipped for whenever they visited.

His thoughts strayed to his parents. They had been together for almost thirty years and still seemed as in love as ever. That was the kind of relationship that he wanted. Someone he could trust with his whole heart and whom he could respect and admire in return.

His mother and father had been through many ups and downs while raising him and his brothers, but they had always been a team. He hadn't thought he'd been looking for that. He'd had it once and it hurt too much to lose it. But what if the perfect woman passed him by because he had his eyes closed? What if Ridley left him because he was too scared to let himself ask her to stay?

At the sound of footsteps, he turned and was encased in a strong hug. Laughing, he embraced his oldest brother, Elliott, just as warmly. The two had always been close, but lately his hectic work schedule and Eli's constant travel for his job gave them less time to hang out. He missed the time they used to spend together and resolved to make it up in the future.

"Hey, bro, where have you been? I came by yesterday but you weren't home." Elliott smiled warmly as Jase and Chris launched themselves at his legs.

"Oh, Ridley and I took the boys to the park yesterday afternoon."

"You and Ridley, huh? You guys are turning into a regular little family."

He stopped at the speculative look in Eli's eyes. Despite being a confirmed bachelor, Elliott seemed to think that what Jackson needed was a wife. His position was the exact opposite of Nick's, who seemed to think that what he needed was sex—with as many women as possible.

"Hey, don't look like that. Mom is bad enough with all the matchmaking. Where are they, anyway? I would have thought Mom and Dad would be here to meet us."

"They went to pick up a few last-minute necessities for dinner. You know how they insist on cooking everything themselves. I don't know why they don't just buy the food already cooked." Eli shook his head at the baffling idea of doing unnecessary work if you didn't have to.

"Now Elliott, you know that one of the ways I show my love to my family is by preparing the meal with my own two hands."

Eli doubled over with laughter at Jackson's imitation of their mother.

"Ooh, I'm gonna tell Grandma. I'm gonna tell!" Chris laughed and skirted away when Jackson playfully swiped at him.

"Let me just check on Ridley before the rest of the family arrives."

"You brought her with you today?" Eli raised an eyebrow.

"Yes, I brought her with me." Jackson narrowed his eyes.

Eli raised his hands in defense. "I didn't say anything. You're going to get more than enough from everyone else. I'm sure Mom will be planning the wedding by dessert."

———

RIDLEY DROPPED her purse and hurriedly applied lip gloss and a touch of eyeliner. Although she felt very clichéd doing it, she couldn't help wanting to make the best impression she could on the rest of Jackson's family. Judging from the relatives she had already met, everyone in the family had hit the genetic lottery.

Looking at her outfit, she smoothed the front of her dress until the pleated skirt hung just right. She was glad she'd changed into the brightly patterned sundress. It showed off her legs but was still casual.

None of her past boyfriends had been serious enough to warrant a meet-the-parents scenario. Yes, technically, she'd already met them but that was as Jackson's neighbor.

Now she was his girlfriend. Sort of.

Hurrying back out to the hallway, she ignored the quizzical glances she received from Jackson. She hardly ever wore makeup and he was probably wondering why she'd bothered for a simple family gathering. Luckily he didn't comment, he just pulled her to his side.

"Hey, there you are."

Ridley couldn't help admiring again how well Jackson pulled off the weekend-casual look. Instead of looking unkempt, he looked rumpled in a sexy, tousled sort of way. Her thoughts stalled when she saw Jackson wasn't alone. She recognized the DJ from the Memorial Day party. Since she had already met Bennett and Nick, she had to assume this was Elliott.

"I didn't realize that you weren't alone. Hi, I'm Ridley." She extended her hand to the silent man and felt herself melt when he gave her a shy smile. She could tell this one was a heartbreaker.

"Well, hello. I'm Jackson's older brother, Eli. I'm starting to see what all the fighting has been about."

"Um, thanks, I guess." She was surprised into laughing when he refused to let go of her hand.

Jackson scowled at them both.

"Okay, Elliott, if I'd known you were going to hit on her I would've never introduced you. Can you believe the nerve? That's family for you, I guess."

Ridley and Eli chuckled at Jackson's overly dramatic expression and finally Jackson joined in. Gesturing with his head, he motioned for Ridley to follow them.

"We were just going to find everyone. Are you ready or do you need more time?"

"No, I'm done. We can go."

As they walked back to the family room, she was immediately struck by the sheer number of people who had arrived in the past ten minutes.

"Where did all these people come from?" She hadn't meant to speak out loud and hoped she hadn't come off as hopelessly rude. Eli and Jackson just laughed, however.

"Cousins, church members, friends. Sunday dinners around here are kind of a free-for-all. Don't worry if you can't remember anyone's name, they won't expect you to."

Ridley gulped and allowed Jackson to pull her into the middle of the fray. After meeting at least five different cousins, she gave up any hope of ever keeping names and faces straight.

"Let's take a walk. I'll show you some of the property." He led her outside onto a huge back porch. His parents stood next to the railing, looking out into the fading sunlight.

"There you are, son. We've been waiting for you." His father slapped Jackson on the back before turning his bright smile toward Ridley.

"Hello again, Ridley." Julia pulled her into a warm hug. "Jackson never brings anyone home to meet us, but I had a feeling we'd see you again." Beaming, she ran an affectionate hand over Jackson's face.

Ridley could only stare as Jackson blushed and turned away. She had assumed Jackson brought all his girlfriends home. A warm feeling flowed through her as Jackson hugged her to his side.

"Jackson told us about your troubles. We're so sorry to hear that, but glad you're here with us safe and sound. We are both delighted to see our baby has finally met his match." Hooking her arm through Ridley's, she pulled her toward the house. "So, tell me about yourself, Ridley. Do you have family here?"

"Mom, we'll have time to talk later, okay? I was just going to show Ridley the farm." Jackson sent a beseeching look to his father, who luckily seemed to get the hint.

"Come along, Julia. Let's give the lovebirds some time alone." Draping an arm over his wife's shoulders, he silenced her with a kiss before pulling her into the house, the screen door banging shut behind them.

"Sorry about that. Sometimes my parents can get a little carried away."

"Don't be. They're absolutely charming. I can't wait to talk with your mother later and find out all your dirty secrets. Did you suck your thumb like Jase? Maybe she'll show me some of your embarrassing childhood photographs." Ridley couldn't contain her laughter at the stricken look on Jackson's face.

"I'm just kidding. I'm sure your mom just wants to make sure I'm worthy of her baby boy's attention." She smiled sweetly and kissed Jackson playfully on the cheek.

Before she could pull away, Jackson turned his head and

captured her lips in a stirring kiss. Heat climbed from her core and spread outward.

"I don't think I want your parents to know how wild you make me, so maybe we should finish the tour."

He groaned and grabbed her hand. They skipped down the stairs leading from the porch to the backyard. He pointed to the left.

"We have several fields, but I know that's the corn. That was just planted. It should be harvested in August. We used to put the husks on our heads and pretend to be scarecrows as kids."

Ridley laughed. "What about over there?"

He followed her finger. "Those are pastures for the horses and the cows. We only have a few dairy cows. Mom also got some goats a few years back because she wanted to experiment with making goat cheese. She's made some pretty good stuff so far."

They walked farther, hand in hand. Ridley tilted her face up to the sun and took a deep breath. It was the perfect day to tour a farm. The fields spread out before them as far as she could see, rolling acres of lush green and golden hay. They stopped near a fence and Jackson climbed up and sat on the edge.

"Are these berries?" Ridley knelt and peered at a bush laden with black fruit.

He chuckled. "Yes, those are blackberries. We can pick some later if you like. They look ripe." He hopped down and pulled one from the bush, then popped it in his mouth. "Yeah, they're definitely ripe. Really sweet, too."

"Did you just eat that? Without washing it first?"

Jackson chucked her under the chin. "I can tell you're a city girl. Trust me, I'll be fine. My grandmother used to pull apples off that tree right there and bite them as she worked. She got one with a worm once and just ate around it."

She laughed and allowed him to drag her toward the edges of the property. Looking back at the house, Ridley felt a tingle of anticipation. At this distance, she and Jackson essentially were alone.

"Where are you taking me?"

"The barn." His terse answer told her more than what he actually said. He walked faster until they reached the open barn door. The smell of hay hit her first, a warm, sweet smell redolent of earth and nature.

As soon as they were out of sight of the house, Jackson lifted her until she melded against his body, chest to chest, with her legs wrapped around his body. He nestled into the hot space between her thighs. Pressing harder, he was rewarded by a tiny whimper in the back of her throat.

Trailing a line of kisses down the delicate column of her neck, he sucked at the base.

"I thought you were showing me around?"

"I am. This is the barn. Say hello to the horses. Tour over." He toyed with the edge of her earlobe with the tip of his tongue.

"Jackson! Ridley!"

They pulled apart reluctantly at the sound of his mother's voice in the distance.

"It's been a long time since I've been busted making out with a girl in the barn. Feels like old times."

"Oh, is that right?" She pinched him and he laughed, grabbing her hands before she could do any more damage.

"Yeah, you saw what a lady-killer I was back in high school. With my mullet."

They tried to stifle their laughter as they straightened their clothes, but it was nearly impossible. Once they looked somewhat decent, they joined hands and snuck back to the party.

twenty

THE NIGHT SEEMED to drag on. Jackson was desperately trying to keep his mind on the conversation, but he just wasn't interested in hearing about his brother's latest business deal. He was probably being rude, but at the moment he couldn't care less.

His mother had grabbed Ridley after dinner and offered to show her some of the crops they'd just planted. They'd come back a little while ago carrying small baskets of blackberries. Ridley had been smiling from ear to ear.

Now most of the family had migrated out to the large back deck and his dad had brought out a small stereo. His cousin Laura and her husband were twirling around, dancing like they were the only two people in the world. Chris and Jase ran back and forth across the lawn with Laura's two girls, chasing fireflies.

It would be as perfect a summer night as any if Ridley wasn't all the way on the other side of the lawn, deep in conversation with his parents.

It was taking all his willpower not to storm over and drag her back out to the barn. Now that it was almost dark he was about willing to take his chances with getting caught.

"Why don't you just put us all out of our misery and go over there?" Nick grumbled.

"Am I that transparent?" Jackson couldn't keep the smile off his face as he realized just how obvious his thoughts had been. Everyone had probably noticed him ogling Ridley all night. Not that he cared. If he had his way, his family would be seeing a lot more of her.

He grinned and clapped Nick on the shoulder before setting off across the yard. He could only hope his parents hadn't told her anything embarrassing. Knowing his mother, she had probably already offered to show Ridley the family photo albums.

As he approached, he smiled to himself while watching his mom and dad interact. Even after thirty years of marriage, they still held hands and could finish each other's sentences. His father hugged his mother to his side with a possessive arm around her waist. Jackson looked at Ridley and his chest tightened. He could definitely see himself chasing after her like an old dog for the next fifty years or so. The biggest surprise of the night?

It wasn't as scary of a thought as he'd expected.

"I just wanted to see if I could steal this beautiful lady away for a dance."

Jackson surprised himself by leaning down and dropping a kiss on her cheek. His mother's eyebrows shot up under her bangs. Considering how his mother was beaming at them, he was sure she definitely wouldn't mind.

"Well, we've kept these two kids apart long enough. Now I want to dance with my beautiful wife. Come along, Julia. Laura and her husband have been putting us to shame. Let's show these kids how we two-stepped back in our day." He nodded at Jackson and whisked his wife off with a flourish.

"Alone at last." Jackson held his arms open and allowed Ridley to settle herself against his length before gently swaying to the music. He could barely keep up with the rhythm because he was so distracted by the feeling of Ridley's heart beating against his. "I'm so ready to go."

"Jackson! We can't just run off. How will that look?" Her eyes danced as she gazed up at him.

"It'll look like I'm happy to have a kid-free week and want to celebrate. You're not leaving my bed this time."

Her chest shook with silent laughter. "We can't let your parents see us running out. They'll know exactly what we're rushing home to do!"

"Okay, knock it off you two. Get a room." Eli appeared at their left and Jackson scowled at him.

"Everyone in this family has bad timing. Go away."

"I just need to show your lady something. One of the guys I have looking into things just called me. I found out a little more about what David was up to." Elliott pulled out his cell phone and tapped the screen a few times before holding it out to Ridley. "Do these accounts look familiar?"

Her brow crinkled as she read the screen. "No, what are these numbers?"

"They're bank accounts. All in your name," Elliott replied.

Ridley looked up at Jackson, clearly alarmed. "What? But those aren't mine! I only have one bank account."

Jackson froze. He hadn't told her what Nick had shown him, hadn't wanted to give any credence to such ugly accusations. He hoped Eli wasn't going down the same path Nick was.

"I figured that but just wanted to verify it. I'm pretty sure David or someone he was working with was using your identity to wire money to offshore accounts. Ridley is a unisex name so it wouldn't have appeared odd for him to use it."

Jackson exhaled. "So he was using her identity. It makes sense. No one would have looked twice since she has such a clean credit history. "

"I used to, anyway." Ridley rubbed her eyes wearily. Jackson pulled her closer and kissed the top of her head.

"Since your name was on everything, it made it harder for anyone to trace things back to him," Eli continued. "It was the perfect system and if he got caught, he probably would have pretended he had no idea and blamed it all on you."

"That's comforting."

Jackson pulled her closer. "It'll be over soon."

Ridley snorted. "It won't be over until I untangle the mess he made. If he's opened accounts in my name, then I'll have to notify the credit bureaus, but who knows how long it will take before it's all cleared up? What if I end up bankrupt from this?"

"Nick is the financial expert, but I'm sure he'll be happy to help. He knows what paperwork to file so you aren't held responsible for all that stuff." Jackson tipped her chin up until she met his eyes. "You are *not* responsible for anyone else's actions."

"We *will* figure this out," Eli said. "It's possible the break-in at your place was unrelated, but until I figure out exactly who he defrauded and whether any of them were angry enough to retaliate, you're better off keeping a low profile."

"I hope you figure it out. Despite everything David did, I don't think he deserved to die like that," Ridley said.

"Of course. This is why I love my job. I get to right wrongs and help people who need it."

"It sounds really exciting. I'm sure it has downsides, though. I can't imagine putting myself in harm's way for someone else. I would just freeze up. I don't think I'd be able to do it."

"You never know. Sometimes people respond the opposite of what you'd think. I had this one client, real tough biker guy. He hired us to protect his shop when there was a rash of burglaries in the area. We'd been watching the place for weeks. Nothing. Then suddenly, his shop was hit and somehow the guys got the drop on us. The client ended up with a gun to his head. I wasn't sure how it was going to end but it wasn't looking good."

"What happened? Did he fight?" Ridley asked.

"He passed out. Big, tough guy went down like a rock." They all laughed. "It was actually the best thing that could have happened though," Eli continued. "He gave me a shot and I took it."

Ridley exhaled and then pressed her hand against her chest. "So, you saved him?"

"Yeah, he was fine. Woke up and had no idea what had happened. Sometimes the smallest things, the quickest moments, can be the difference between life and death. Things happen for a reason, I guess."

"They definitely do." Jackson clapped Eli on the shoulder. "Thanks for your help. I guess we'd better get home. It's getting late."

Eli smirked. "Mom mentioned she's keeping the kids for a few days. I'm sure you *really* want to get home."

Ridley covered her face with her hands.

"So, how many times did Mom mention weddings tonight?"

Jackson laughed. His mother had definitely dropped more than a few hints but surprisingly it hadn't bothered him in the slightest. "Only a few hundred. Less than I expected."

Elliott's laughter followed them as they crossed the yard to say goodbye to his parents.

———

"I LIKE HER."

Nick turned at the sound of his older brother's voice. He'd been watching Jackson and Ridley from across the yard for the last hour with a burning sensation in his chest that he recognized as envy. He'd deliberately arrived a little late to dinner just so he could limit the amount of time he was required to be social.

He'd thought briefly about not coming but he'd skipped so many Sunday dinners lately that he knew his mother would start getting worried. Momma Julia on a tear was no small matter. The last time she'd been worried about him she'd shown up at his condo early on a Saturday morning and banged on the door until he let her in.

The Brazilian model he'd been entertaining at the time hadn't been amused when he'd forced her to stay hidden in the bedroom for an hour while he convinced his mother he was fine. He could still hear the blistering string of Portuguese she'd let fly with the same fury as the vase she'd thrown at his head.

"I don't know why you don't like her," Elliott continued.

Nick sighed. It seemed his brother wasn't going to give up easily. "I never said I didn't like her. She seems nice enough. I'm just worried about Jackson. He's got her on this pedestal. He has no idea what women like that are capable of."

"And you do?" Elliott moved to stand next to him. His eyes were on the dancing couple as well. Jackson was holding Ridley close and whispering in her ear. "I think they look good together."

Someone get me a barf bag, Nick thought irritably.

"There's no proof she's done anything wrong and I'm inclined to give her the benefit of the doubt just because of the way she looks at Jackson." Elliott smiled at him. His brother was enjoying tormenting him, the little shit.

"I wish I could be as happy about this as you are. But I know a little bit too well how devious beautiful women can be. Especially since her sister—"

"Ah, now we get to the root of the matter. Jackson told me that Raina went with you to the Lupus Foundation dinner a few months ago. He never told me you were this hung up on her."

"I'm not hung up. I'm merely aware of what she's really like," Nick snarled. "It's none of your business."

Elliott shrugged. "Okay, but don't let that influence the way you respond to her sister. Ridley seems really nice and has never had so much as a parking ticket before all this."

"I know. I just hope she's nothing like her sister or Jackson's setting himself up for a world of hurt. Either way, I've washed my hands of it. It's just hard to watch your little brother walk toward a pit that you saw coming a mile away."

"I know. But all we can do is let him fall. Then catch him if it's necessary." Elliott thumped him on the back and then walked away, turning sideways to edge through the crowd.

Nick watched as his mother pulled Ridley into a crushing embrace. His entire family seemed to like her and Jackson hadn't been this happy in years. He turned to go. He didn't even bother saying goodbye to anyone. They would have just wanted to drag him into conversations that he couldn't care less about.

He could admit he was wrong about Ridley, but it didn't mean he was ready to make nice with her. Looking at her reminded him of all the things he couldn't have. Comfort. Companionship.

Raina.

He was glad his brother had finally found someone after years of being alone. He deserved some peace after everything he'd been through.

But Nick didn't want to hang around to watch.

———

RIDLEY CURLED up on the couch and listened to Jackson's footsteps leading to the back door. He'd gone to make sure the house was locked up so they could go upstairs for the night.

So much of their time together had been laced with tension between lying about who she was and worrying about whoever was behind David's death. Tonight had been one of the first times she'd been able to just be a girl out with a guy she was crazy about.

They'd stopped at an ice cream parlor on the way home and had eaten their cones while sitting in the brightly lit interior of the shop. It had been the most romantic, completely normal thing they'd done together.

It didn't mean she hadn't noticed how he'd tensed up when his brother mentioned their mother's matchmaking.

She'd been pleasantly surprised at how friendly and welcoming Jackson's family was and hoped she'd made a good impression. A permanent relationship with Jackson was unlikely, but she still wanted them to like her.

That's because you're still hoping for a miracle. This is how you always get hurt.

The sound of the door opening alerted her to Jackson's presence but she didn't turn around. She closed her eyes and hoped he would think she was asleep and not try to engage her in conversation because, Lord help her, she might just bawl her eyes out if he touched her at that moment.

The soft sweep of his lips over her brow startled her. He lifted her gently out of the chair and held her close. Ridley couldn't resist wrapping an arm around his neck and resting her head in the crook of his shoulder. Words seemed inadequate at the moment and she had no desire to break the mood by questioning him. When she opened her eyes again, they were in Jackson's room. He lowered her onto the king-sized bed and then settled himself gently next to her. He seemed at a loss for words as he looked around the immaculate room.

"I don't want you to leave."

She looked at him in surprise. "What?"

He got down on the floor so he was kneeling before her. She covered her mouth with her hand. He couldn't be proposing. They'd only known each other a little more than a week.

"Jackson, what are you doing? Get up."

He grabbed her hand. "No, I need to say this. You can have a good life here. We're good together. And it doesn't have to end. Stay with me."

Tears sprang to her eyes as he pressed her hand against his heart.

"Say you'll stay."

She shook her head. "This is crazy. I have a life in Florida. I can't just move."

"You can if you want to. I know this seems like it's happening really fast and I'm not saying we need to go out and buy rings tomorrow. I just want the chance to find out. Do you? Do you want *me*?"

His eyes stayed on hers as he waited for her answer. Elation rose in Ridley as her thoughts swirled in a million directions. She had a job and a life in Florida but she didn't have this. A man who was willing to get on his knees before her and tell her he wanted her.

She grabbed his arms and pulled him up on the bed next to her. "I do want you."

"So you'll stay?"

She grinned. "Yes. I'll stay."

He grabbed her and pulled her on top of him.

"Jackson! What are you doing?" She giggled when his lips trailed white-hot kisses down the side of her neck.

"Celebrating," he replied.

She bucked off the bed when he gently nipped at her earlobe. His hot breath in her ear started a tickle that sped all the way down her spine and swirled between her thighs.

He eased himself up enough to pull his shirt over his head, and Ridley took the opportunity to run her hands over his well-developed pectorals and flat abdomen. She brazenly unsnapped his jeans and looked up into his eyes to see his reaction when she cupped him.

He cursed softly before snatching her hand away and roughly tugging the jeans off his body. He reached into the bedside table for a condom and quickly tore the wrapper. She took the package from him.

"Allow me." She straddled him and softly stroked his length as though measuring the thickness. He shuddered when she lingered over the tip, brushing her thumb along the ridge before sheathing him with the protection.

She pushed his hands away when he reached for her and unhooked her bra herself. Flinging it to the floor, she cupped her breasts and saw him fight for breath as he watched her stroke herself. When he reached for her panties, she chuckled softly as she eluded him.

"Uh uh. I'm in control here."

She slipped out of them and dangled them from her pinky finger before letting them drop to the floor next to her bra. When she straddled him this time, she was unprepared for the hard feel of him under her naked heat. She wanted to take it slow, make him want her, but she couldn't deny herself any longer.

She gripped his length with her left hand, satisfied when she heard his cry, then she guided him inside her. The feel of him sliding along her sensitive flesh was so good that she paused for a moment, overwhelmed.

She heard the whimpers, barely realizing she made the sounds as Jackson's strong hands worked her hips against him, over and over until she thought she would burst. She felt the power she had over him at that moment, the way his breath hitched when she stopped her frantic rocking motion. After a few tense moments she saw him bare his teeth in a grimace as he grabbed her hips and held her still above him.

She collapsed on top of him, exhausted from her wild ride, and surrendered herself to his desires. She wanted his lean body pressing tight to hers and she didn't fight him as he flipped her over and sank into her in one thick thrust. She felt him moving against her deepest ache and gripped his ass to pull him in farther.

He reached between them and stroked her in time with his thrusts. She couldn't control her body's reaction to Jackson's fingers on her most intimate body parts. She couldn't even cry out at the exquisite combination.

He seemed to have a thousand fingers, all caressing her at once, inside and outside. Every muscle in her body clenched at the same time as she came, crying out his name.

"Ri, you don't know what you do to me."

He buried his face in her neck and his thrusts started coming harder. Faster. He twined their fingers together and held her down as he came. She bit his shoulder when his last thrust pressed her firmly into the bed. He jerked over her, his fingers gripping hers tightly as his body shook with the last contraction.

He collapsed on top of her and she wrapped him up in her arms. She didn't ever want to let him go. The differences between them probably meant any relationship they tried to have wasn't going to be easy. However, she would always have this moment; she would always have the memory of him inside her, warm and sweet.

twenty-one

"YOU AREN'T GOING to like this."

Raina looked up from her lounger and frowned at Sam. "You're blocking my sun."

"You don't need to soak up rays. You have a natural tan."

Sam moved until he was completely obscuring the sunlight. Raina turned her face in the opposite direction, determined to ignore him. The shoot had ended the previous day and she had a feeling the pictures weren't going to be her best. It sucked to think she might have blown one of the biggest opportunities she'd ever had. Especially since she wasn't sure why.

Liar.

Okay, she knew exactly why she hadn't been able to concentrate. She'd been thinking about Ridley meeting the Alexanders. She'd been thinking about Nick.

"I'm not going away." Sam's voice cut into her thoughts again.

Finally she rolled over and glared at him.

"I have twisted my body into the most unnatural positions for the past three days. Do you know how hard it is to look sexy while wearing a thong bikini and kneeling on gritty sand? I need my sunlight. I've earned the right to lie here and ache in peace."

Sam plopped down next to her lounge chair. "Your sister is on the cover of *Sizzle* and several other major tabloids."

Raina lifted her head. "She's on what?"

He didn't answer, just held up one of the magazines in his hand. She immediately recognized Ridley. She looked amazing and she was wearing one of the sexy little Narciso Rodriguez dresses she'd picked up in Europe a few months ago.

"She's not going to like this." Raina sat up and took the magazine.

Sam pointed at the cover. "It's not a bad picture. It could have been worse."

"*Leggy's Sister Lands A Rich Hottie*," Raina read out loud. "So much for keeping a low profile. I'm surprised they didn't think it was me."

"If it wasn't well publicized that you're here in the Bahamas for the S.I. shoot, they probably would have thought so."

Raina flopped back down with an exaggerated sigh. "She is not only going to hate the fact that her face is plastered on a cheap tabloid, but she'll definitely object to the implication that she's a gold digger. Personally, I don't care, but she will."

"That's because you are a gold digger."

"What good is gold if you don't dig for it? It's not like the men I date are with me for my charming personality." She rolled her eyes and reached a hand over to her beach bag. She rummaged around for a while until she found her cell phone, then typed out a quick text.

"Okay, consider that your good deed for the day. I've warned her so she won't freak out if someone mentions the pictures. Now go away."

Sam got up. "You know you love me."

"That was never in question."

———

RIDLEY GROANED as she read the text message.

Tabloid pictures?

She was downstairs reading a book. Not that she remembered anything she'd read so far. It had mainly been a distraction. Something to keep her mind off the fact that Raina was due back home tomorrow.

One more day and then she'd have to leave.

"It's not like you'll be in a foreign country."

It was silly to feel like she was losing something when she'd only be one street over. This was a good thing. Once she was at Raina's house, she could put a full-sized garden in the backyard. Raina had always loved flowers, too, even if she hadn't the slightest clue how to take care of them.

It would be a fun project and her first official design job under her new business. A business that she would own all by herself. A few months ago she might have turned it down just because she didn't want her first job to come from her sister, but Jackson's words had stayed with her.

That's what people who care about you do. They help you.

She wasn't measuring her success in dollar signs anymore and she definitely wasn't trying to do everything on her own. Having the support of family and friends wasn't something to be ashamed of. If she'd learned that lesson a little earlier she could have saved herself a lot of trouble.

Plus, it would be good for her and Jackson to get back to normal. When she wasn't hiding out at his house and worrying about being stalked. They'd gotten together under very unusual circumstances and if they were ever going to have a chance, they needed to see how their relationship fared under normal conditions.

Either way, it was time for her to stop living in a fantasy world and get back to reality.

She put down her book and walked up the stairs. Jackson had

offered her the use of his laptop many times, but she'd never had any reason to need it. She could access her e-mail and read any news stories that interested her on her phone. Tabloid pictures, however, she needed a laptop to view. If she was going to see tacky photos of herself, she might as well get the full image.

"Jackson? Are you here?" She stuck her head in his office and looked around. He'd been working a lot more lately, bringing things home from the office to review. She hadn't been back with him to watch a recording session yet, something she regretted.

She sat in his office chair and flipped open the lid of the laptop. It powered on immediately and she clicked on the Guest icon. A few minutes later, she had the pictures up on the screen.

Leggy's Sister Lands A Rich Hottie!

Ridley skimmed the article. It was typical tabloid fare, big on insinuations and thin on facts. Somehow they managed to make it seem like both she *and* her sister were opportunistic sluts. Great.

The pictures themselves weren't that bad. One was taken outside Sweeties as they'd entered. Jackson had his arm around her and one hand up as if to ward off the photographers. She'd had her head down but she was peeking up at Jackson with a little smile on her face.

It was probably the happiest she'd looked in a long time.

"Well, I'm glad Raina warned me, but I'm not going to let a stupid tabloid ruin my day." She surfed the web for a little while, reading random news articles and looking at trailers for a few movies that had just come out.

"Maybe Raina and I will go to a movie when she comes back." She could at least write down the names of the ones that looked interesting. Then she could look up the show times for the coming weekend.

She looked around for a pad of paper and a pencil, but there was nothing on the desk. After the first time she'd cleaned in here, Jackson had really been trying to keep it neat. His version of neat appeared to be shoving everything that used to be on the top of the desk into the drawers. She pulled out the closest one and rifled through the papers and folders in her way, lifting them one by one so she could see if there were any pencils or pens beneath.

DAVID RANDALL FINEMORE
RIDLEY ANNE WELLS

Ridley stopped and pulled out the two manila envelopes. She opened the one labeled with her name first. Her mouth fell open as she scanned the documents inside. It looked like a criminal background check along with personal information about her family, her friends, and what she'd accomplished in college. There was even a copy of her driver's license photo from Florida.

"He had me investigated," she whispered. Disappointment crashed through her as she stuffed the pages back into the folder.

She'd known Eli was investigating to see who was messing around with her bank accounts, but she hadn't expected he'd pull up such personal details. This wasn't the type of search you did on an innocent person. This was the type of search you did when you were looking for dirt.

Lots of it.

With trembling fingers she opened the other envelope. This time she flipped straight to the picture.

"David."

She scanned the criminal background check, sickened as she read the list of infractions. She closed the file and didn't even bother to put the papers back into the desk. She left it all out on the surface. Except for her file, which she tucked under her arm.

Part of her could understand why Jackson had done it, but it still hurt that he hadn't just asked her anything he wanted to know. He'd probably just wanted assurance that she wasn't dangerous if she was going to be staying in his house, but she couldn't deny it felt like a violation. Much more so than it had with David.

Mainly because she hadn't loved *him*.

"I love him. And he has a security file on me." She chuckled bitterly. Why couldn't it ever just be simple? Meet a guy. Fall in love. Live happily ever after. Instead, she got identity fraud, hateful brothers, and a background check.

She walked out of the office and went down the hall to Jackson's room. He stood next to the window gazing out.

"I don't believe you. There has to be an explanation." He put a hand to his forehead. "You have proof?"

Proof of what? Ridley wondered. She moved farther into the room until Jackson looked up.

"I guess I should have learned my lesson about eavesdropping by now."

———

RIDLEY STOOD in the doorway watching him. When he turned to look at her, she held up an envelope. Jackson's heart dropped. His brother's voice in his ear suddenly seemed very small.

"Nick, I'll call you back." He hung up the phone, his brother's voice cutting off abruptly.

"It's not what it looks like."

"That's comforting, because it looks a lot like you violated my privacy and did a background check on me. I'm so relieved."

Jackson flinched. "I know you're angry, but I had to know what I was dealing with. You already lied once. I couldn't take the chance of any other surprises. I didn't even ask Eli to do a background check on you. Nick pulled your file mainly so we could find out about David."

"I understand that part, Jackson. I know I lied to you and I'm sorry, but I only lied about my name. I didn't take anything from you or pretend to be Raina so I could spy on you. I only did it to keep myself safe." She shook her head slowly. "You really don't get it, do you? I'm not mad that you have the information. I would have told you anything you wanted to know anyway. I'm upset you didn't tell me about it. Because you had no reason not to."

Fury, white and hot, lanced through him. He crossed the room and got right in her face. The fact that she could be angry with him for breaking trust after what his brother had just told him was the epitome of hypocrisy.

"I can't believe you're lecturing me about honesty after what you did. How could you do it?" he stammered. "How could you steal from me?"

Ridley shoved him in the chest. He grunted and fell back a step. "I would never steal from you. Or anyone," she fumed.

He yanked out his phone. Nick had told him he'd send over the bank information he'd found. When he found the e-mail, he scrolled to the bottom and held it out to her. She took the phone and stared at it.

"But this is my bank account. This is not possible." Ridley shook her head back and forth slowly. "I didn't do this. It has to be the person who tried to kill me. I haven't stolen anything."

"What happened?" He smoothed her hair back from her face. "Did someone threaten you? If you needed money you *know* you could have just asked me."

"I don't understand any of this." She grasped his arms. "Jackson, I don't understand what's happening."

"We don't have time to wait. Eli and Nick are on their way and knowing Nick, he's out for blood. He knows I won't press charges against you but that doesn't mean he won't go to the authorities with everything else he found."

"You won't press charges," she whispered.

"No. I can't see you hurt. Even after everything you've done. The lies. The theft. As angry as I am, I can't see you in prison."

"That's because you know I wouldn't do this," she pleaded. She grasped his face. "Look at me, Jackson. You know I wouldn't do this. You know *me*."

"I don't know anything," he yelled. "Clearly, I don't know *anything* because up until a few minutes ago I knew I was in love with you."

Ridley stilled. "Don't say that. Not now."

He leaned his forehead against hers, his heart racing from his impromptu confession. "I definitely would have preferred to tell you that another way."

"You don't love me." She held a hand over his mouth when he started to protest. "You just feel responsible for me. The truth is that you and I, we just got caught up in the magic. You were there for me during one of the most intense times in my life and I'll never forget that. But it's time for us to stop fooling ourselves."

They both turned at the sound of an engine. He walked to the window and cursed. "They're here. They must have called me while they were on the road."

She was crying and the sight ripped at his heart. He looked down. It wouldn't surprise him to see a gaping hole in his chest.

"What am I supposed to do?"

Jackson pulled out his wallet and peeled off a few bills. It was ridiculous, trying to give her money when she'd already taken so much from him. Fifty thousand to be exact. But he couldn't just send her out there with nothing. He tried to hand it to her but she yanked her hand back.

"I don't want your money!"

"Just take it. You need to go. Hide out. Eli said the FBI has a whole case file on you. This is so much bigger than the money you took from me."

"I'm going to prove I didn't do this. And after I do, I never want to see you again." She said it with such sad finality that it hurt to hear it.

As time stretched between them, a litany of things hung in the air unsaid. He wanted to rage at her, punish her, make her hurt the way he was hurting. He also wanted to tell her that he was worried about her. Worst of all, he wanted to tell her that he didn't care about the money.

He wanted to beg her to stay.

Jackson shook his head. "You know what the most pathetic part is? I would have just given you the money if you'd asked. I loved you that much. I would have given you anything."

Tears shimmered in her eyes. "You can't give me the one thing I need right now. Your trust."

She walked out and left him standing alone.

twenty-two

RIDLEY GLANCED behind her as she crossed the yard to her sister's house. She'd left through the back door and hadn't bothered to rush. Anger made her bold. She almost wished Eli or Nick would try to stop her when she was in this mood.

After punching in the security code, she pushed open the door to Raina's house for the second time that week. After her argument with Jackson, the quiet in the house was unnerving. The air in the kitchen smelled a little stale, so she crossed to one of the windows and pried it open. The breeze was a little too warm to be refreshing but at least it would air things out a bit.

The back edge of the property was dotted with chrysanthemums and there was a pitiful clutch of tulips in a circular bed in the middle of the yard. She smiled to herself at the sight of the tulips. Raina knew they were one of her favorite flowers.

Planting flowers had always been one of the first things Ridley did when they moved to a new place. They'd usually been in small apartments or sharing space in someone else's home, but even the smallest place had room for a window box. Staying in Florida while she finished her master's had been easier than she'd thought due to the beautiful weather and her part-time job at the local nursery.

Just one more thing in her life she'd been forced to leave behind.

I should just go back, she thought as she stood at the window. *I should leave now before I get in any deeper.*

It hurt, being in love with someone who clearly didn't trust her, much more than she could have ever guessed it would. You'd think after being lied to and stolen from by David that this wouldn't even register. But somehow it was worse with Jackson, more personal.

Because you thought he felt the same way you did, you idiot.

Raina's house was done in a clean, modern country style, similar to what Ridley herself would have picked out. She settled at one of the oak chairs at the long farmer's table in the kitchen and looked out into the backyard. It was already close to dusk and it was more than a little weird to think that people outside could look in and see her. Although, knowing Raina, the windows were probably treated with some kind of reflective glass.

A prickle of awareness made the hair on her neck stand up. If she lived here full time, she'd definitely get window treatments. It would obscure some of the view, but at least she could sit on the main level at night without feeling like she was in a fishbowl.

She needed to call Raina. Her sister was going to be pissed, but she also had resources that could be extremely helpful. Whatever other "proof" Elliott had found was clearly damaging. Raina's security team could probably get access to it.

You'll also need a lawyer.

She shuddered. It was crazy that the thought of hiring a lawyer was the final straw that broke her. She swiped at her cheeks angrily. The past month had been overwhelming and instead of things being better, they were worse than when she'd started. Crying hadn't solved anything. Running hadn't solved anything either.

"It's time to stop running and start fighting."

She thought of everything she'd experienced in the past week. Images of Mara holding up the sheer nightgowns at the mall merged with images of discussing business ideas with Katie and digging in the dirt with the kids. She'd finally found something worth fighting for. Friends. Community. Love.

And she wasn't giving it up.

She had friends here now. Her sister was here. Those were good reasons to stay. But most importantly, she liked it here. It would be difficult to be so close to Jackson. It would be difficult to be near him and not be with him. Not love him.

But staying in Virginia didn't have to be about Jackson. The Alexanders had shown her the beauty of community and putting down roots. Not everyone at their family gatherings had been blood relatives, but they were still a part of the clan. Maybe she couldn't find the perfect family she'd always wanted.

But if she was strong enough, maybe she could create one.

———

"I WOULDN'T HAVE BELIEVED it if I hadn't seen the evidence for myself. I still don't want to believe it. But there it is."

Jackson closed his eyes and tried to tune it all out. His brother was still talking but nothing else he was saying really mattered, did it? Not when it all circled around to the same thing.

The woman he loved was a thief.

"I wish I didn't have to be the one to show you this." Elliott sat on the couch next to him. He didn't say anything else.

They both looked up when Nick came in the room. Jackson tensed. Irrational as it was, he especially didn't want to see Nick right now. He didn't feel like hearing what an idiot he was for believing she'd loved him.

"I brought you some water." Nick put the glass down on the coffee table and then sat down behind the piano. He played a string of broken notes.

Jackson took a big gulp of the drink, then coughed violently as it burned all the way down. "What the hell was that?"

"It's water. Tonic water."

Jackson raised an eyebrow.

"Okay, I might have added a bit of vodka," Nick conceded. "I figured you could use it."

Jackson took another sip. Then drained the entire glass. His brother could be an ass but he could also be useful at times. He definitely knew how to nurse him through heartache.

He'd done it before.

"We don't really have to do this now." Elliott picked up the folders he'd brought with him. They'd been sitting on the table mocking him ever since they'd gotten there.

In those folders was more evidence of what a fool he'd been. Pages and pages of transactions, Elliott had said. Evidence of all the scams Ridley had been a part of.

Just the thought made him sick.

"When would be a good time, big brother? When's a good time to learn the woman you love was using you? I need another drink."

He could already feel a warm buzz. His brother had added a little more than a pinch of vodka, but he was okay with it. If he'd ever needed a little liquid amnesia, it was now.

Nick appeared with another glass and Jackson startled. "Shit, you move fast. Or I'm more drunk than I thought."

"I already had it ready. I know the drill."

Jackson took a deep swallow. "Yeah, you do. You helped me

numb out after Cynthia died. What is it about me that makes the women I love want to hurt me, Nick?"

"Is this really the best idea? Do you have to get him drunk?" Eli muttered.

"You have a better idea?" Nick took a deep swallow of his own drink.

"Jack, don't do this to yourself." Eli took the glass out of his hand and finished it for him.

"Cynthia wanted to leave me. Did you know that? We fought that night." Jackson fell back against the arm of the couch with a groan. "I told her to go. Pushed her out the door into the rain. I didn't protect her."

"Jackson. Her accident was not your fault. It was nobody's fault," Eli said. There was no mistaking the pity in his brother's voice. It was there in both of their eyes. The condemnation.

"Just tell me, Eli. I need to know. Maybe it'll make it hurt less."

"All right. The FBI has pending case files for four other women that they suspect were helping David Finemore in a range of fraud schemes." He held up the papers in his hand. "These are just a few of the names I found. Our boy was busy. But I noticed something interesting about his credit history."

"More interesting than wire fraud and just being an all-around douchebag?" Nick asked.

Jackson snorted.

"Yeah. According to David's driver's license, he's twenty-nine. So he should have a good decade of credit history. But he doesn't. There's a period three years ago where he had no activity at all for about six months. I have a theory as to why."

His cell phone rang and he pulled it out and looked at the screen. "Hold on. I have to take this."

Jackson blinked several times. He was starting to feel numb and wasn't sure if it was a good thing or a bad thing.

"Really? No, no, that's good. Send it over." Elliott hung up.

"Who was that?" Nick asked.

Elliott ran a hand over his face. "I had one of my guys check even further back into David's history. I had a hunch and it looks like I was right."

"What did he find?" Jackson asked dispiritedly. It was taking everything within him to act as though he cared. Truthfully, he just wanted them to leave him alone in his misery.

It didn't really matter to him how David had committed his crimes. Ridley had gotten hooked up with him and it had ruined her life. Now his life. But there was nothing he could do about it. He eyed the empty glass on the coffee table.

Eli pulled out his laptop and powered it up. A few clicks later, he sat back on the couch. "See for yourself. He just sent it to me."

Nick got up and stood behind the couch. "Who is that on the left?"

"That's the *real* David Finemore." He turned the laptop around so Jackson could see. Two pictures were displayed. They both looked like driver's license photos.

"The one on the left is from two license renewals ago. We usually only pull what the Division of Motor Vehicles keeps on file. But my guy went further back and pulled some of the old pictures."

"Son of a bitch," Nick whispered.

"He was using an assumed identity. He probably got away with it because the original David Finemore was a lot heavier than he was. The clerk at the DMV probably just thought he looked slightly different in the face due to weight loss."

"How is it possible that the FBI didn't know who he was?" Nick asked. "With all the technology they have access to, between their databases and their facial recognition software, they have to know his real identity."

"It's possible he had surgery to alter his face, but I'm inclined to agree with you. I think they know his real identity and they just don't want to tip off his accomplices. I think they're trying to build their case against all the people who helped him."

Elliott looked over at Jackson. "Including Ridley."

———

"YOU WEREN'T happy with destroying just one Alexander, huh?"

Raina threw her purse down on the sofa in her hotel suite. Nick seemed to have an internal radar for when she was feeling her weakest. He always seemed to call when she was least equipped to deal with hearing his voice.

"Hello, Nick. Lovely of you to call. Who have I supposedly destroyed now?"

Sam hovered just behind her. He nodded at the phone and she shrugged.

"You're really going to pretend you had no idea your sister was fleecing my brother?"

"What?"

"Ridley stole fifty thousand dollars from Jackson. Wired it right out of his account and into hers."

Raina stilled. Sam must have sensed it because he moved closer.

"I don't believe you. Ridley would never steal from anyone."

"Really? Well, tell that to my brother's bank account. She was crafty about it, too. She only took smaller amounts at first. Then, once she realized what the limits were, she jumped to higher amounts. I should have known not to believe her woe-is-me story, but she had us all fooled. She's even better at playing men than you are. Something I thought I'd never see."

Anger rose in Raina's chest at the insult. Not on her own behalf. She didn't care what Nick thought of her. He had good reason to hate her and she wouldn't have expected anything less. But her sister had nothing to do with their feud.

"Insult me all you want, but leave my sister out of it. I don't believe she stole anything. I think you just hate me so much that you want to hate her, too."

"Ask for proof," Sam whispered. He hovered at her shoulder so close he could no doubt hear the entire conversation.

"Send me some proof," Raina demanded.

"Proof? Like a bank statement? Why, so you can get his account number and steal from him, too?"

"Damn it, Nick. Do you want your brother's money back or not? I know Ridley didn't steal from him, but someone did. If I can figure out who it was, maybe we can reverse it somehow."

"It's not about the money. *He loved her*, Raina. But you all don't care about that, do you? That's how you girls do it. Make a man fall for you and then rip his heart out." He paused, his angry breaths coming over the line like static.

Sam raised his eyebrows at her. He'd been with her long enough that he'd pretty much seen and heard it all. He'd handled stalkers, obsessive fans, and jealous boyfriends and she never kept anything from him. In order to keep her safe, there couldn't be secrets.

But this thing with Nick—he didn't even know what had happened the night they were together. She turned her back to Sam and fought to bring her emotions under control. Some things were too personal to share, even with him.

"Are we still talking about Jackson and Ridley?"

The only response was the soft click as he hung up.

Raina squeezed the phone as tightly as she could bear. It was better than giving in to the overwhelming urge to throw it across the room.

"Do you think she did it?"

Raina turned at the question. Sam was at the minibar, which

was cleverly hidden in an alcove in the living room of the suite. He held up one of the bottles and she nodded. She could definitely use a drink.

"No."

"Honestly?" Sam stared at her for a moment before turning back to the drinks. The next thing she heard was the tinkle of ice hitting glass.

Raina heaved a sigh and sank down on the couch. "When we were teenagers, we used to help our mom at the diner where she worked to earn spending money. One day, Ridley had a customer who was particularly flirty. Older guy, nice suit, going bald but still in the comb-over phase of denial. You know the type."

Sam nodded his agreement and turned back to pour a generous amount in each glass.

"Anyway, after an hour or so, he finally left, leaving the money to cover his food on the table. When Ridley went to pick it up, she saw he'd left behind a twenty-dollar bill when he'd only had a cup of coffee and a muffin."

Sam handed her a glass and sat down on the other end of the couch. He didn't interrupt, although she could see his confusion.

"Do you know what I would have done in her position?"

Sam shrugged and took a healthy swallow of his drink.

"I would have pocketed it without a second thought. Do you know what Ridley did?"

Sam sat back, comprehension dawning. "She wanted to give it back?"

"She chased the poor man for two blocks to give him his change. Imagine her surprise when he told her he'd left it on purpose. As a tip. She's always so surprised when men flirt with her." She smiled at the memory.

Sam shook his head. "So, she was a good kid. People can change."

"Sure they can, but I don't think the core of a person changes so easily. You see, she wasn't giving the money back because she thought she'd get in trouble or because someone was watching. She was actually *worried* that he'd need the money. She cares about people. Any of the rest of us would have considered it his loss and our gain. But not Ri."

"So, she's not a thief and this is some kind of mistake."

"It's not a mistake. I don't think someone *mistakenly* wired this money into my sister's account. I think someone did it on purpose and I think I know who. I think it was Nick."

Sam raised his eyebrows. "You think he'd steal from his own brother just to make your sister look guilty?"

"I think he hates me enough to do just about anything. He's a financial genius, so I'm sure a little bit of wire fraud isn't out of the realm of possibility. I just need you to prove it for me."

"It seems a little far-fetched, but I'll see what I can do."

She checked her phone again, surprised to see that Nick had actually sent her the bank statements as she'd asked.

"Look. Here it is." She handed Sam her phone and watched as he scrolled through the e-mail attachment.

"Oh, she definitely didn't do it."

"Well, I know that. But why are you suddenly so certain?"

He leaned over and pointed to something on the screen of her phone. "This is Ridley's regular bank account, right? It's under her real name."

"Yeah, so?"

"So, what kind of criminal uses a bank account in their own name to commit fraud? Not that I doubted your heartwarming story, but I've seen too many nice kids go off the rails when they get older. But this, this is not the move of a fraudster. I was expecting to see a wire transfer to a numbered account. If your sister was actually used to scamming people, she wouldn't be using the same bank account she uses to pay her electric bill."

"I knew it. *That bastard.* This whole thing is so jacked up.

Ridley cared about David and what did that get her? A near-death experience and an FBI profile. She cares about Jackson and look how that's turned out. Being accused of wire fraud? I want so much more for her than this."

"What about you?" Sam asked. "What do you want?"

"Security. It's all I've ever wanted. That's why I have you. You're the only man I need in my life, Sam."

She leaned over and brushed his hair back from his face.

"Now, please find a way to prove that Nick is behind this so I can nail his balls to the wall."

"WHAT ARE YOU DOING STILL UP?"

Jackson had figured he'd be alone at this hour. Nick and Elliott had gone to bed around the same time he had. After hours of poring over the documents they'd brought, he'd been emotionally exhausted.

It was one thing to be told that Ridley had stolen from him but another to see it. If he hadn't seen the wire transfer on the bank printout, he wouldn't have believed it.

"Just looking at the information I received earlier."

Elliott held up the pages he was reading. Even from across the room Jackson recognized the photo of David Finemore.

"Why are you still looking at that? We already know he and Ridley were scamming people. It's over, Eli. Let it go."

His brother made a frustrated sound and dropped the papers on the coffee table.

"What?" Jackson asked. It was hard to believe but his brother seemed almost more pissed off by the turn of events than he did.

"I feel like I'm missing something. Or maybe I just don't want to admit that I didn't see this coming."

Suddenly Jackson understood. All his older brothers looked

out for him, but security was Elliott's specialty. Of course he felt guilty for not protecting him.

"None of us saw this coming. You can't blame yourself for that."

"I agree."

They both turned to see Nick standing in the doorway. His brother had removed his dress shirt and tie and wore just a white tee shirt and slacks.

"You can't sleep either, huh?"

Nick shook his head. He crossed the room and sat on the couch next to Eli, propping his feet on the coffee table in front of him.

"I'm surprised you haven't said I told you so. It'd actually be justified for once."

Nick leaned back and crossed his arms behind his head. "Somehow, I'm not enjoying this as much as I thought I would."

Jackson observed his brother from across the room. They all had stubble and looked tired but Nick looked the worst of them, easily. It made him feel marginally better that his brother wasn't gloating. Especially since he'd tried to warn him about Ridley from the beginning.

"I just can't believe she would do this. I would have just given her the money if she'd asked."

Jackson gritted his teeth. He'd told himself that he wasn't going to think about it but he'd been doing nothing but all night. Turning it over and over in his mind. He still had no explanations for why Ridley would steal from him. She had to have known that he was *gone* over her. So infatuated that it was embarrassing.

And why steal the money when she'd refused everything else he tried to give her? He'd offered to be a landscaping client and she could have easily billed him an outrageous amount for that. Instead she'd pulled weeds in his backyard and dug a spot for a garden for free. The day she'd gone to the mall he'd practically had to beg her to take the Audi. She could have just driven off with it and not come back. She'd even refused the money he'd offered her the previous day when he told her to leave.

It just didn't make sense. He *needed* it to make sense. Maybe if he could understand it he could stop seeing her face when he'd told her to leave.

"Wait a minute," Nick interrupted. "What do you mean 'if she'd asked?' You're saying she never asked you for money?"

Eli narrowed his eyes.

"No. I already told you guys. She hated the idea of charity. She didn't even want to have her sister as a landscaping client because she wanted to do it on her own. She didn't want people thinking her success was due to her sister's fame."

Nick steepled his fingers. "What kind of scam artist doesn't even *try* to scam you out of the money first? Why come here and get all cozy with you if she wasn't buttering you up?"

"She wasn't buttering me up for anything." Jackson glared at them both. *She was just burying herself so deeply in my life that I can't function without her.*

"Well, if she wasn't trying to scam you, then what the hell was she doing? If all she wanted was your banking information, she didn't need to stay this long to get it." Nick spoke so softly that Jackson wondered if he knew he'd said the words aloud.

Elliott sat up, a grim look of determination on his face. "Something about this doesn't add up for me. We need to figure this out. Fast."

"How?" Jackson ran his hands over his hair and blew out a breath.

"By going back to the beginning. Everything started with the car accident, right? The authorities indicated that it wasn't an accident."

"If you say she's a murderer, then I'm going to hurt you. I don't believe Ridley killed David."

"I don't believe she killed him either, but someone did. Which leads me to wonder what they hoped to accomplish? Were they actually trying to kill the guy or just scare him? And how does Ridley fit into the picture? If she's not involved, then why are they coming after her?"

Jackson sat up straight. "The necklace!"

"The what?" Nick and Eli spoke in unison.

Ignoring their puzzled looks, Jackson ran upstairs to his room. He opened the door to his closet and pushed aside the row of black suits in front of his wall safe.

"Jackson, what the hell is going on?" Eli's voice floated from behind him.

Jackson ignored him and punched in the electronic code. The numbers flashed and then a soft click indicated the unit was open. He pulled the door open and reached behind the pile of documents he kept on the bottom row. When he turned around, he held the necklace up to the light.

"I think I know what they're after."

Eli took it and ran his hands over the front. "What is this?"

"Ridley said David gave her this for safekeeping the day he died. That he was chasing down a lead and didn't want it to get stolen. Do you think the jewels are what they're after?"

Eli flipped it over and then grinned. "That's not a necklace." He yanked on the ends. It snapped in two.

"Wait... Did you just break it?"

His brother held up the two ends triumphantly. Jackson stopped in his tracks. One end looked like a jeweled pendant. The other end looked like a computer port.

"What is that?" he asked.

"This, little brother, is a flash drive. Now let's go see what the hell was worth killing for."

———

"I DON'T WANT you to worry. I've got Sam working on it and we are going to figure out who's behind all this. I still think I should have changed my flight."

Ridley sat on the edge of her sister's bed and smoothed a hand over the luxurious counterpane.

"I still can't believe this is happening."

Ridley knew she needed to just go to bed. There wasn't anything else she could do tonight and Raina was furious enough for the both of them. She was already scheduled to come back late the following day, but it had been a fight to convince her not to change her flight to that very night. It seemed ridiculous to go to all that trouble and expense when she would be here within a day anyway.

"It's fine. I'm not going to let them intimidate me. I know my rights and since I haven't done anything wrong, whatever evidence they claim to have must be bogus."

"You bet your ass it is. I already have my suspicions about who's behind this nonsense," Raina snarled. "Nick hates me enough to do just about anything."

"You think Nick did this?"

"Sam is going to prove it. He's already working on tracing the IP address used to make the transactions. Nick is smart, so I'm sure he didn't do it from his own computer."

It was horrifying to imagine someone hating her so much that he'd be willing to frame her for something she didn't do.

"I don't understand any of this. What happened between you two that was so bad?"

Raina was quiet for so long that Ridley figured she wasn't going to answer her.

"As a favor to Jackson, I went to a charity dinner with Nick a few months ago. It was a high-profile event. The publicity was good for both our careers."

Raina had dated so many men over the years that Ridley

had stopped trying to keep track. She knew some of the guys weren't real boyfriends but just people her sister spent time with to bolster her public profile. The more she was photographed, the more famous she became and the more money she could command when companies wanted to book her.

Ridley couldn't imagine dating someone just to get photographed for the tabloids, but Raina had explained the tabloids were a necessary evil and having a strategy to deal with them was just smart PR.

"So, you dated him for a while then?"

"No, it was just one night. We only spent one night together but that was all it took. I fell for him, Ri. I think I fell in love with him the moment we met."

Ridley stood, a million questions swirling through her brain. Nick's fevered kiss had told her that his relationship with Raina was more than just casual, but this? She hadn't expected this.

"If you love him, then why aren't you with him? I know he feels something for you, too. He may not want to admit it, but he does. I can tell."

"I can't be with him." Raina let out a soft sound. A moment later she cleared her throat and when she spoke again, her voice was stronger. "Nick is not the kind of man you settle down with."

Neither of them spoke for a minute and Ridley was suddenly incredibly depressed. They were both in love and they were both sitting by themselves, lonely.

"I'm sorry, Ray."

"It's fine. I was just being melodramatic. Plenty of women have fancied themselves in love with Nicholas Alexander. I'm not the first and I doubt I'll be the last. But I'm the smartest because I'm not wasting my time."

"Ray—"

"I'm going to check with Sam to see where he is on this. But

I'm sure he'll have it figured out by tomorrow. You need to get some sleep, baby sis."

Raina's voice was firm and Ridley knew she'd gotten all she was going to get out of her. Raina was hardly the sharing type so it was a minor miracle she'd opened up at all. Plus, she didn't really want to dissect her own feelings either. What she really wanted was to fall asleep and dream of a simpler time.

A time when she'd never even heard the name Jackson Alexander.

"Okay, I'm going to go to bed. Just call me if you find out anything. Night."

After they hung up, she moved around the room in a fog. Her brain sent directions that her body followed blindly.

Open drawers.

Find nightgown.

Get undressed.

She could have been a robot for all the emotion she invested in what she was doing.

She moved into the bathroom and turned the light on. Her reflection in the mirror was even grimmer than she felt. Her hair was sticking out of her ponytail in various directions, so she just pulled the band from her hair and let it go wild. There was no one here she needed to look cute for.

Her toiletry bag was still on the counter where she'd put it earlier. She dug around in the bag until she found her toothbrush. Her toothpaste should have been there, too but the bag was filled with all the other things she'd left on the counter earlier. Ponytail holders, her hairbrush, and some of Raina's makeup that had been sitting out on the counter.

"I'm not this much of a slob."

She shoved the bag aside wearily. It was a waste of time trying to remember why she'd shoved all that stuff in there. Considering how emotional she'd been after leaving Jackson's house, she was lucky she hadn't thrown the thing in the trash without realizing it. Growing up, they'd always kept extra toothpaste and mouthwash below the counter. She bent to look under the cabinet. Nothing.

"Damn."

When she stood up, she saw a dark shape moving from the corner of her eye. She spun around, her heart beating wildly.

"Hello, Ridley."

A man stood in the doorway. He held up her toothpaste and waved it back and forth. As she stared at him, all the pieces fell into place. Humiliation, anger and finally fear swirled around before settling in her stomach with the force of a blow to the gut.

"Oh my god, it's you."

———

"THIS IS A LOT OF MONEY."

Nick held up the pages in his hand. "Over a million dollars moved through this one account in just a month."

They'd been up for hours sorting through all the information on the flash drive. It had taken three of Elliott's best guys an hour to crack the encryption on the files saved on the drive. Now that they were in, Elliott had printed some of it so they could help him sort through it all.

Jackson had gotten up a few times to bring drinks and nuke some food. He wanted them fueled so they could keep working. It was almost three in the morning, but he didn't want to go to bed. Going to bed felt like admitting defeat.

It was ridiculous, but he was strangely hopeful. He tried to squelch the feeling before it could take hold. What they found likely wouldn't change anything, but he couldn't help hoping there was an explanation.

Maybe Ridley had taken the money because she was being

blackmailed? Maybe David had gotten her into something that she couldn't get out of and she'd panicked.

He knew it probably made him a stupid sap, but if she'd just needed money to get away from whoever was chasing her, he could forgive that. What he really wanted was just to know that she was okay.

Elliott handed him another stack of paper. Most of it appeared to be bank transactions, so Jackson gave it to Nick. "You'll be able to decipher this before I will."

Nick looked through the top few sheets and frowned.

"Most of this stuff seems to be confirmations of wire transfers. But it's to a lot of different accounts. It would help if we could figure out who the accounts belong to, but I can tell you one thing —all the transactions appear to have started roughly three years ago."

Elliott grunted. "Has anyone else noticed that three years seems to be a recurring theme here?"

"You think it's important?" Jackson asked. "Or just a coincidence?"

"I don't believe in coincidence." Elliott stood and paced a bit before cracking his knuckles. "Let's look at everything we know. This guy was into something shady, he had dealings with the Morenos, and it all started three years ago."

"What the hell happened three years ago?" Nick threw his pile of paper on the floor.

Elliott sat back down behind his laptop and tapped the mouse to wake it up. "Let's find out."

Nick and Jackson exchanged looks before moving closer. When Elliott had a hunch about something, he was rarely wrong. He could take bits and pieces of random information and use them to chase almost any lead down. It was what made him so good at what he did.

"What are you going to do? E-mail one of your military buddies?" Jackson asked eagerly.

"No."

Nick snapped his fingers. "Hack into the FBI database?"

Elliott gave him a quelling look. "Hell, no."

Jackson leaned forward. "So, what's your brilliant plan?"

"Google it."

"What? Eli, this is serious."

"I'm serious, too. I would have done it earlier if I'd made the connection. I just have a feeling that if we do a search on the Morenos and filter the results by year, we'll get an idea of what's going on."

His fingers flew over the keys. Finally, he hit "Enter" and sat back.

Nick had moved next to him so all he had to do was lean over to see the screen. His eyes widened before he glanced at Eli. "Does that mean what I think it means? *Jesus.*"

Eli stood and pulled his cell phone out. "Danner? I need an eye on Ridley Wells."

Jackson jumped up and crossed to the computer. He peered at the articles on the screen. There were tons of listings about the Morenos.

"She's in the house. Was anyone monitoring the property before she went in? *Christ.* Tell Rothwell, Holmes, and Maddox to meet me out front." Elliott hung up and strode to the door.

"What's going on? Nick?"

His brother wouldn't look at him and just clicked on one of the articles. It loaded and the headline screamed out at them in big bold letters.

- - Heir To The - -

- - Moreno Crime Syndicate - -

- - DEAD AT 33 - -

"What the hell is this?" He stood as Elliott withdrew his Glock from its holster and did a quick check of his ammunition.

"Alberto Moreno only had one child. I should have remembered this case. It was huge news at the time. It was rumored that the FBI was closing in, getting ready to take them down. Most of their evidence was against the son. Then he suddenly died. *Three years ago.*"

Jackson's heart dropped. "Three years?"

"You want to guess how he died?"

"Don't say a car crash. Please don't say it."

Elliott put a gentle hand on his shoulder. "Not a car crash, but it was a fire. The body was too burned to identify using the usual methods. Now we know why."

Jackson shook his head, fear gripping him so hard he could barely get the words out. He'd sent her out there alone with nothing more than a weak apology and an offer of cash. He couldn't have failed another woman he loved.

Jackson raced for the door. "Oh God. *Ridley.*"

twenty-four

"YOU'RE SMARTER than I gave you credit for."

Ridley watched as David poked through the contents of Raina's dresser. He had forced her to walk from the bathroom back to the bedroom. He hadn't raised his voice or said anything threatening. Then again, he hadn't needed to.

The gun in his hand was more than motivation enough for her.

"Apparently I'm not smart enough. I actually thought you were helping me." She backed up a few steps and leaned against the wall. "How did you get here?"

He glanced back at her, seemingly amused by her attempt at polite conversation.

"I got a sweet deal on a bus pass. You know you should really sign up for that CoupOn site. I've saved so much money." Finished with the bottom drawer of the dresser, he shoved it closed before moving to the nightstand and picking up one of the books stacked on top. He flipped through its pages carefully before moving to the next.

"I'll pass. I doubt I'll be traveling much anymore. So, you're alive."

Ridley clenched her fists. He was looking at the books so leisurely, as if trying to decide which one he wanted to read. *Arrogant bastard.* She'd spent the past week agonizing over his death and he was acting like he didn't have a care in the world.

He cursed suddenly and then swiped the stack of books to the floor before picking up the lamp and looking under the base. When he looked back at her there wasn't a trace of anger on his face. If she hadn't just witnessed his little outburst she wouldn't have known anything was wrong.

What the hell is he looking for?

"Do you know how easy it is to fake your death? When people find a mangled car with a body in it, they tend to assume it's you."

"Don't they check fingerprints or dental records? Something?"

He just laughed. "Someone's been watching *CSI* reruns again. Sure they look for that stuff, but since the body I left in the car belongs to the real David Finemore, I'm sure the coroner found nothing amiss."

He smirked at her before running his hands over the comforter.

"Even if there had been something to find, the body would have likely been too burned to give them much to work with. Fire covers a multitude of sins."

Ridley shook her head in disgust. "Good to know. I'll remember that if I ever decide to become a criminal."

"Haven't you heard? You already are. Tsk tsk, tsk, now why would you steal fifty grand from your new boyfriend?"

Oh God, what if he'd done something to Jackson?

It took everything within her not to ask. So far, he hadn't done anything overtly violent. He'd just stolen money and stalked her until she thought she was going crazy. The last thing she wanted to do was bring Jackson to his attention.

"It was you." Ridley swallowed the tears in her throat.

"Yes, it was me." He laughed—a cold, hard sound. "I had to do something to get you away from him. I'm not sure why you're so shocked. No matter how much evidence you have to the contrary, you always want to believe the best of people."

His eyes met hers and she shrank back against the wall. How could she have ever been attracted to him? Had his eyes always been so empty? Maybe it was the hair. He looked so different with dark hair. Forbidding.

"I like that about you, Ridley. You almost make me want to be a better man." He winked at her before kneeling to look under the bed.

Ridley glanced at the window as soon as his head was out of sight. It was early morning and there was no one to hear her if she screamed. She didn't dare try to run. He'd only catch her and then he'd be even more pissed off. There wasn't anything nearby she could grab as a weapon, either. Her best bet was to keep him talking as long as possible.

As long as he was talking, she was still alive.

"Okay, you win. You got the money. Everyone thinks you're dead. I don't understand why you're here. Shouldn't you stay hidden?"

He sat on the edge of the bed casually, as if they were just hanging out. "That was the plan. Little setback though. I need my necklace. It wasn't in your apartment in Florida or your car or anywhere in this *fucking* house! So, where is it?"

"I don't know."

David hissed in a breath. "I've been really nice so far, Ridley, my dear, but I'm losing patience."

She couldn't understand why he'd come all this way for a piece of jewelry, but then again all her jewelry was fake. The jewels on the necklace he'd given her were probably real.

"Why would you even care about that now? With all the money you stole, you can just buy another one." Ridley edged toward the side of the bed, frantically trying to think of a plan. As soon as he realized she didn't have the necklace anymore, she'd have nothing to bargain with.

And he'd no longer have any reason to keep her alive.

"It doesn't matter why I need it. I gave it to you because I figured it would be easy to come back and relieve you of it later."

David sighed and then stood. He raised his arm and pointed his gun directly at her chest. "But you had to make this difficult."

———

"DROP THE GUN, MORENO."

When they turned the corner into the master bedroom, Jackson knelt down so he could see around his brother. His heart almost stopped. Eli had convinced him that it was better if he went in with his guys first. They were licensed bodyguards and if someone had to take a shot, it was better if it was one of his team instead of a civilian.

He'd agreed mainly because he'd still been hoping his brother's theory was wrong. But clearly they'd figured it out too late. Moreno held Ridley in a chokehold, his gun pointed at her temple.

"Not a chance. Not until I get what I want."

Jackson nodded to Nick. Now that they were sure Moreno was here, they could alert Eli's contact at the FBI. Nick raised his chin and pulled out his phone and walked back down the stairs.

"What is it that you want?" Jackson spoke up. "I'll give you whatever you want if you let her go."

"Who is that? Show yourself!" Moreno screamed.

Jackson stepped to the side so he was visible. He held his hands up in the air, showing he wasn't armed. "I'm right here."

"Jackson, what are you doing?" Eli muttered.

"I'm just trying to deal," Jackson said loud enough for everyone to hear. "If you want money, I can do that. You need a car to get away from here, you can have mine. Nobody needs to get hurt."

"I don't need any of that. All I need is the necklace."

"Oh, you mean this?" Jackson pulled the necklace from his pocket and held it up to the light. The crystals on the front caught the light as it spun on its chain. "You can definitely have this if you let her go."

"What about them? You expect me to believe you'll just hand it over and let me walk out of here? I'm not an idiot."

Jackson looked at Eli. Eli turned to the other men and motioned for them to hang back. They fanned out to the edges of the left side of the room, leaving the center open.

"Tell them to drop their weapons."

After a momentary hesitation, Eli nodded. The three men bent down and placed their weapons on the ground.

"We're not going to stop you from leaving. Just let Ridley go. You walk away and so does she. Everyone's happy," Jackson said.

Moreno walked forward, Ridley stumbling to keep up. He maneuvered them until they were close to the door. "You all think you're so smart. Let me guess, you've got more guys downstairs waiting to bust me when I leave."

"There's no one downstairs," Eli said.

Moreno shook his head. "It doesn't matter. There's only one way I'm getting out of this alive and that's if she comes with me. So this is what we're going to do. Ridley, you go get the necklace. Keep it high in the air where I can see it. You try to run, you die. You say anything to lover boy over there, you die. Got it?"

She nodded and bit her lip. He let her go slowly and she walked toward Jackson. He gave her the necklace and as instructed, she held it over her head as she walked back.

Eli kept his weapon pointed at Moreno. His brow furrowed as he watched Ridley take each slow step. His brother looked frustrated and Jackson didn't need security training to know why. If

Moreno got her out of this room, the chances of him seeing Ridley alive again were slim. The police were on their way and once Moreno realized he was surrounded it was unlikely he'd just surrender.

It was much more likely that he'd panic and start shooting.

"It was an honor meeting you, Ridley," Eli said. "I really enjoyed getting to know you on Sunday. I've never had such a connection with a woman before—I feel like I really taught you a lot."

Jackson looked at his brother in confusion. What the hell was Eli doing? Was he saying goodbye? Was he giving up?

"Me too!" Ridley was staring at Eli and the sound of her voice drew Jackson's attention. "I remember everything you told me."

Eli nodded at her.

"Sorry to interrupt your touching reunion, but we have to go." Moreno prodded Ridley in the head with the gun and she flinched. "Now!"

"Okay. I just wanted to say goodbye," Ridley stammered.

"Well, say it and then move!"

Ridley's eyes met Jackson's. For a moment, it could have been just the two of them in the room. There were so many things he wanted to say.

It's going to be okay.

I'm sorry I didn't believe in you.

I love you.

But he couldn't say anything. All he could do was watch help-lessly as she inched backward until Moreno put his arm around her neck again. As he tugged her backward toward the door, she looked at him and said, "Goodbye."

Then she dropped to the ground.

———

FOR THE FIRST harrowing moment after the shot rang out, Jackson wasn't sure what had happened. One moment he was looking at Ridley and the next, she was on the ground. Time seemed to compress before Moreno's eyes widened. He looked down at his chest, then back up at Eli. A red bloom appeared on the front of his shirt. Time sped up as Elliott rushed toward them. Just before he got there, Moreno raised his arm.

Another loud sound rent the air.

"Oh, shit!" Elliott tackled him, sending Moreno's gun skittering across the floor. The team of guards who'd been waiting behind them surged forward. Jackson could only see one thing.

Ridley was still on the floor. Unmoving.

He raced forward and cradled her in his arms. "Ridley? Baby, wake up. It's over." The skin on her neck was red and inflamed but otherwise she looked okay. He held her tighter, overcome with emotion. Her eyes were closed and she looked almost as if she were asleep.

"Jackson? You have to give her to me."

Jackson looked up wildly at his brother. The room was suddenly filled with people. People he didn't know. A few men stood behind his brother. They had a gurney with them. *Paramedics*, he thought dimly. He startled as someone tried to pull Ridley from his arms. He looked up into Elliott's concerned face. His brother. His brother was trying to take her away.

"No, she's mine. Don't take her away from me."

Elliott grasped his face between his hands. "Jackson, she's been shot. You have to give her to me. Now." His brother's voice was calm but firm.

Jackson gripped her tighter, noticing for the first time the sticky wetness on her side. "She was shot? Oh God..."

"It's okay. Just let me help her."

He watched numbly as Elliott laid her back on the floor and pulled him out of the way. Emergency personnel immediately started working on her. The next thing he knew, she was on a stretcher and being rolled out.

"Where are they taking her?"

Elliott grasped his shoulders. "New Haven General. Go ahead and follow her. I'll give a statement to the police."

"I'll drive him." Nick appeared at his left side.

"I didn't keep her safe. She was scared and I didn't keep her safe." All he could see was her face as she'd said goodbye. She'd been terrified but she'd still been smart enough to do what was necessary. His brave, beautiful girl had been strong enough to do what he hadn't.

"Jackson. Listen to me." Elliott grabbed his face so hard it hurt. "We figured it out in time and Ridley was very smart to do what she did. She gave me a shot and I took it. Moreno is in custody. She's going to be fine. She has to be."

"Did you see where she was hit?" Jackson demanded.

Eli looked pained. "It looked like she got hit in the side. I'm hoping it was her arm."

"Hoping won't keep her alive."

twenty-five

THERE WERE moments when life seemed to repeat itself, like a movie stuck on instant replay. Jackson sat in an uncomfortably rigid chair in the waiting room of New Haven General Hospital feeling like he'd time traveled back three years. The same bland, blue color scheme. The same worn, plush chairs. The same bad artwork.

It didn't look any different than when he'd been here after Cynthia's accident. He just had to hope the news he would receive would be better than last time.

"You're still here. I told you I wasn't going to let you see my sister."

Raina stood in front of him, arms crossed. Her security officer stood behind her. She'd introduced him last night but Jackson didn't remember his name. All he remembered was Raina telling him that Mr. Muscle's only task was to keep him and Nick away from her sister.

"And I told you I wasn't leaving until I do."

He sucked in a deep breath and clasped his head between his hands. Nick had been on the phone practically all night. He'd called every number he had for Raina until he found her. Then he'd stayed on the line listening as she cursed him every way possible until she'd arrived at the airport for her flight.

"She wouldn't be in here if it wasn't for you."

She had all the power in this circumstance and he knew it. She was Ridley's next of kin and could deny him access to her until Ridley woke up. But damned if he was going home without a fight. Eventually Ridley would be ready to leave the hospital. He was prepared to sit there for days if that was how long it took.

"We agree on that."

He hung his head again, shame twisting his stomach into knots. He'd thrown her out, hadn't even given her the benefit of the doubt until they could look into things. He could have let her stay until her sister came back. He could have done any number of things other than send her out on her own. Moreno hadn't even had to work for it. Jackson had practically gift wrapped his prey and handed her to him.

"At least Moreno isn't your father." At her surprised look, he added, "Eli figured it all out. That's how we knew she was in trouble."

"Too late, though. You figured it out too late, or my sister wouldn't be lying in a hospital bed fighting for her life."

"I know." There was nothing else for him to say.

"Moreno isn't our father." She paused. "According to the FBI, there was never any lead in the first place. He was just playing on her hopes and dreams so she'd keep the flash drive for him. Ridley's always been a soft touch."

A family came in and sat in the chairs next to Jackson. He got up and moved so they could use his chair. The mother nodded at him gratefully before plopping her oversized diaper bag in the seat he'd vacated.

"I'm glad he's not. She deserves better than that."

Raina crossed her arms and stared at him. He held her eye, not to challenge her but because he knew he deserved her scorn.

When she'd arrived, perfectly made up with her hair arranged in a stylish updo, she'd looked like the Raina he remembered. Now, hours later, she'd shed the top layer of her outfit and taken her hair down. Her makeup had worn off, so she looked softer. More like Ridley.

It was painful just to look at her.

"She's going to be fine," Raina said finally. "She's out of surgery. The bullet missed her lungs so she'll be okay."

Jackson let out the breath he hadn't realized he was holding. He wanted to thank her for letting him know but the words wouldn't come, so he just nodded. She seemed to understand though because for a second, her expression softened just a little bit.

She motioned for him to follow her. "I'm only letting you see her because I'm sure the nurses are tired of seeing you."

He followed as she strode down the hall and turned left at the nurses' station. Her security officer trailed him. Jackson looked back at the other man. He raised an eyebrow at him, so Jackson turned around and jogged to catch up with Raina. She stopped outside the second-to-last room on the hall and pointed at him, her finger almost jabbing him in the chest.

"You said you just wanted to see her, so go see her and then get out of here. The nurse gave her a sedative and she's sleeping, which is the only reason I'm agreeing to this. I don't want her to see you and get upset all over again. You've done enough damage as it is."

"I understand." Now that he was here, his heart was beating wildly at the thought of seeing her again. He ducked into the room. It was dimly lit, the only sound the soft beep of the machines next to the bed. As he approached, his breath caught at the sight of Ridley motionless against the stark white sheets.

Jackson took in her calm features, trying desperately to memorize her face. He looked up at the machine connected to her IV and let the comforting sound of the rhythmic beeping wash over him. It hurt to think of her being sustained on machines, but at least she was here. She was alive.

He stroked her cheek gently. "I told you before that I loved you. I'm so sorry I didn't love you enough to believe you when you needed me to."

I would have given you anything, he'd said. He was such a fool. All he'd been able to see was the money. He'd been so worried about being taken advantage of that he hadn't been able to give her the one thing she'd needed. His trust. Something that didn't cost anything other than faith.

"Two minutes," Raina hissed from the doorway.

If Raina was expecting a fight from him, she wasn't getting one. He fully agreed with everything she'd said. It was his fault Ridley had been in harm's way in the first place. His fault. He just kept failing the women he loved. Ridley deserved better than that. Better than him.

He leaned down and pressed his lips to Ridley's forehead.

"Goodbye."

"WHEN CAN I get out of here?" Three days later, Ridley was beyond ready to leave the hospital. Unfortunately, until her doctor decided she was strong enough to go home, she was stuck.

Stuck in a stupid hospital bed watching stupid TV while her sister held her stupid phone hostage.

"The doctor should be around soon. He usually checks on you right before lunch." Raina folded the blanket she'd been using in half.

"Aren't you ready to get out of here? That chair can't be comfortable."

The nurses had offered to bring her a cot but the chair in the room was big enough that Raina had been able to prop a pillow against the back and sleep there. Still, she was going to end up in traction if she slept all cramped up for much longer.

"I'm fine. I'm just worried about you."

"Is that why you won't give my phone back?" Ridley asked.

Raina wouldn't meet her eyes. She picked at the edge of the blanket until a few long, white strands came out. "I forgot it."

"Again? That's what you said yesterday."

Raina crossed her arms and glared at Ridley. "You are supposed to be recuperating, not socializing."

Ridley held in a groan. She'd thought Raina had been insufferable before, but she'd had no idea. Ever since the shooting, Raina had been in hyperdrive. The poor nurses on the floor were no doubt ready for her to leave so they wouldn't have to deal with Raina questioning everything they did. It had been endearing the first day or two, but she was about ready to shake her sister silly.

If she was strong enough to get out of this damn bed.

There was a brisk knock at the door and Ridley turned toward the sound. Elliott stood in the doorway holding a small teddy bear and looking extremely uncomfortable. She wondered how much he'd heard. He looked back and forth between them.

"Is this a bad time?"

Raina looked like she was about to protest when Ridley motioned him forward eagerly.

"Elliott! Come in, come in. I'm so glad you came to see me."

Eli stepped in and set the teddy bear on the edge of the bed. "Hey, how are you feeling?"

"Like crap. But I'm alive. Thanks to you. So what happened, you know, after everything? I don't really remember."

Elliott perched on the edge of the bed carefully. "Well, I figured out David's identity on a hunch. I knew he'd been using an assumed name for about three years, but it wasn't until I looked at the information on the flash drive that I put it all together."

"The flash drive?"

He reached in the pocket of his jacket and pulled out a stack of photos. He flipped through them and then pulled one out.

"That's the necklace he gave me." Ridley took the picture and ran her thumb over the image. It was hard to believe something so small had been at the heart of everything.

"It opens to conceal a flash drive." Eli held up another picture. In this one the necklace was in two parts.

"That's why he wanted it back. What was on it?"

"Confirmations of payoffs. The wire transfers we noticed going through the accounts he had set up in your name were just the beginning. He's been borrowing identities for a while now. He uses them to set up accounts to funnel mob payouts to his father's offshore accounts. Then after a few months he closes the accounts and moves on."

Ridley tried to sit up a little but pain lanced through her side.

"Wait, I'll help you." Raina rushed over and pushed the button to raise the bed.

"Thanks. So, that's why he needed it back so badly. Because it has all the account numbers and payoff information?"

Eli nodded. "I'm sure he's got bits and pieces of information saved other places, but a lot of criminals keep their information offline. That way it can't be hacked. He must have known the FBI was on to him again. So, before staging his car accident he hid the flash drive somewhere no one would ever find it. With you."

"And I ruined his plan by running." Ridley closed her eyes.

"Yes. You put quite a kink in his plans by doing what you did. Moreno is a great tracker, but you literally disappeared for a while. He admitted that Raina's house was the first place he looked. But when it stayed empty, he had no idea where to go. It wasn't until he saw the tabloid pictures of you and Jackson that he knew for sure you were in Virginia."

"You know I almost left the necklace behind that day."

At Elliott's puzzled look, she continued. "He saw me put it in the drawer of my front hall table the day he gave it to me. Right before the accident. I took it out at the last minute because I was going to the bank. I thought it would be safer in my safe-deposit box. If I hadn't done that, he would have gotten it when he broke into my apartment. None of this would have happened. I would still be in Florida living my life."

Ridley swiped at her eyes, embarrassed to find her cheeks were wet. Part of her wished it had happened that way. She'd still have been a victim of identity theft, but at least she wouldn't have been injured.

She wouldn't be heartbroken.

"Maybe you should go," Raina said gently. "She shouldn't be getting upset."

Elliott started to stand but Ridley grabbed his hand. "No, don't leave. Please. Just stay and talk for a little while longer. I've been stuck in this bed for three days. I'd love to know how everyone is doing. How are your parents?"

"Worried about you. I filled them in on what happened. I think my mom was ready to storm the hospital because she thought you were in here alone." He turned to Raina. "She didn't realize you were back in town."

He pointed to the cluster of flower arrangements that Raina had corralled next to the window. "Anyway, they sent flowers. It's one of those. Nick sent flowers, too."

"Hmm. Fat lot of good that does," Raina muttered.

"Raina! Don't start anything. Eli saved my life."

Raina immediately looked chagrined. "I know, and I'm so grateful he was there." She looked at Eli. "If I was the touchy-feely type I would hug you for that. Thank you for saving my sister."

Eli shrugged but Ridley could tell he was a little embarrassed at the praise. "In all honesty, Ridley saved herself. That was a brave thing you did. You carried it off like a pro, too."

Ridley snorted. "You were the one who told me what to do. If I hadn't talked to you on Sunday, I wouldn't have thought of that on my own. I guess things really do happen for a reason, huh?"

A nurse came in the room then and Elliott moved back so she could get to Ridley's side. She knew it was necessary but hated the constant poking and prodding. Ever since she'd woken up, it seemed like there was someone there taking her temperature and blood pressure every hour.

How was she supposed to get strong enough to leave the hospital when she couldn't get any sleep? She waited, impatiently, for the nurse to take the temperature bulb out of her mouth before she turned back to Eli.

"So, how's everyone else?"

"We're all fine. Mara and Matt came to the hospital afterward but you were in surgery so we told them to come back."

Ridley sighed. "You're really going to make me ask how he's doing?"

Elliott looked down at his hands but didn't say anything else. "I don't know," he said finally.

"Eli—"

"Honestly," he added. "I haven't heard from him since. None of us have. He won't talk to us."

They sat quietly for a few minutes. Raina shifted in her chair, picked up a magazine, and held it up in front of her face.

"There's no point pretending you can't hear us, Raina. It doesn't matter."

Eli tried unsuccessfully to hide his smile. "Oh, before I leave, I have a present for you." He reached in his jacket again and pulled out another photograph. He held it out to her. She leaned forward and then did a double take.

"Hey! That's him. That's the guy that was following me at the mall!"

Raina got up and leaned over so she could see the picture. "Are you sure? Who is this?" she asked Elliott.

"That is William Rainier-Ridley. Your father."

Ridley gaped at him. "What?"

"It appears David wasn't lying when he said he found your father. Unfortunately, David pretended to be you and blackmailed the guy out of about a hundred thousand before he went underground. That's why he was following you. He was trying to figure out why his own daughter was blackmailing him."

"This is too much." Ridley lay back against the pillows and sighed.

"I know, and you don't have to do anything with this information if you don't want to. I just wanted you to have the choice. There's been enough secrets lately."

Elliott stood and then tapped her on the nose. "By the way, if my idiot brother hasn't told you, he loves you, Ridley. Now, get better so you can kick his ass personally."

———

JACKSON HAD NEVER KNOWN how empty a house could seem despite being occupied by three people. The one thing he wanted to do was off limits—visit Ridley to see how she was doing. According to Eli, she'd been released from the hospital a week ago.

He'd called probably hundreds of times and she'd ignored every one. He was already in stalker territory. He had to keep his dignity if nothing else.

The house below seemed unnaturally quiet. The boys were starting to adjust to Ridley's absence. He could hear it in the rare peal of laughter or the sound of commotion coming from the playroom. They were trying to be on their best behavior, having sensed that Ridley's "vacation" was especially trying for Jackson.

He tried to put on a nonchalant face but as perceptive as they were, they could probably see right through it.

Pushing back from his desk, he decided to call it quits for the day. He hadn't gotten any work done anyway, so he might as well go down and spend some quality time with the boys. Since Ridley had come, he had seen a lot of positive changes in both boys, but especially Jase. Normally quiet and introspective, Jase had said more in the last two weeks than he had in the previous two months. But ever since Ridley had left, Jase had barely said two words to him.

The sound of the doorbell stopped him in his tracks. He turned around and peered through the peephole. Shocked by what he saw, he immediately pulled the door open.

"What the... Eli? I thought you'd gone home?" The two brothers clasped hands and slapped each other on the back.

"I heard from a little birdie that you might need some comfort, so I came to see you. Now that I'm here, I can see for myself they were right." Shocked, Jackson didn't speak until he noticed Chris's head peeping around the corner. He had a feeling it had been two little birdies that had called their uncle Elliott to come and spy on him.

"Well, I don't know who your sources are, but I'm fine. However, I'm always happy to see my big bro."

Eli's eyes lingered on Jackson's face, taking in his unkempt hair and unshaven face. "So, how are things with the new group you're producing?"

"Slow, but it's going. Anyway, come on in and make yourself comfortable. The boys are around here somewhere. I'm sure they'll be happy to see you."

Eli clamped a hand down on his shoulder. "Actually, the little birdie that called was named Nick. He wants to take you somewhere."

Nick appeared in the doorway behind Eli. "Can I come in?"

It was funny how he'd been mainly fine for the past week. He still got choked up at random intervals and he hadn't been able to sleep in his bed anymore. He'd taken to sleeping in the chair in his office. But more than anything, seeing his brother seemed to bring it all back. He took a deep breath.

"You're my brother. You don't need an invitation."

His brother pulled him into a hug before cradling his face in his hands. "I wasn't sure if you'd feel that way. I really screwed things up this time."

Jackson closed the door behind them and walked to the living room. "You didn't screw up, I did. I was the one she trusted. I'm the one who let her down."

"But this whole thing started because of my feud with Raina. So, I want to fix it. At the source."

"How do you plan to do that? Raina isn't going to forgive you."

"I'm not looking for forgiveness from her, little bro." Nick slapped him on the cheeks lightly. "I just want the dragon to take a step back so you can get to the princess. After that, you're on your own."

Eli settled back on the couch and heaved a sigh. "I'm sorry to miss the groveling, but I'm going to stay here with the boys. Just make sure you video it when Raina decks him. That's so going on YouTube."

Jackson followed Nick out of the house. He had no idea what his brother planned to do to get Raina to let them in but he knew he'd only have one shot at this.

He was miserable without Ridley. She might not give him another chance, but at least he could tell her how he felt and apologize. He owed her at least that.

He looked at his brother. "Tell me you have a plan."

Nick smirked. "Of course I do. Watch and learn."

twenty-six

"I DON'T NEED another magazine, Raina."

Raina stood at the foot of the bed wringing her hands. "Maybe some water? Or some lunch?"

They'd left the hospital a week ago under the cover of night. It had seemed ridiculous to go through such measures to keep it secret but Raina had insisted it was necessary. The story of the Moreno family's only son rising from the dead was too good for the media to ignore.

Sam, Raina's chief of security, had arranged an elaborate ruse involving several models hired to impersonate them in order to get her out of the hospital undetected. She hadn't had the energy to care back then. They'd gotten her home without microphones and cameras in her face and that was all she'd wanted.

Well, that wasn't *all* she wanted. But the other thing she wanted hadn't called in a week.

"What about a movie? Or we can see what's on TV?"

It had been years since she'd seen her sister plain-faced, but Raina hadn't left her side for the past few days. It was kind of sweet, actually. In the beginning she'd been so tired she hadn't been good for much else besides sleeping. But the last few days they'd talked. A lot. She'd had the chance to apologize for some of the things she'd said and Raina had apologized for trying to run her life. They were on the right track for the first time in months.

But now her sister's hovering was getting on her nerves.

"I don't want magazines or food or anything. I'm tired." Ridley knew she was being rude but she couldn't take it anymore.

"Okay. I'll let you sleep." Raina kissed her forehead and left, pulling the door closed behind her.

Ridley sighed and looked out the window, the late afternoon sunlight like a beacon drawing her attention outside. Since leaving the hospital she'd been pampered and coddled, slept what felt like a million hours, and taken more pain medication than she was sure was safe.

What she hadn't done was call Jackson.

Raina had told her about his visit when she'd been asleep at the hospital. It didn't make her feel good to imagine him hurting but damn it, he'd hurt *her*. Tears welled in her eyes again and she gritted her teeth. Crying wouldn't erase the humiliation of being pushed out the door. Of being accused of being a thief. As much as she'd tried to understand things from his perspective, part of her couldn't let go of the fact that he simply hadn't believed her. He'd honestly thought she'd just been after his money.

But now a week had gone by and she had to wonder if her pride was worth this misery. He'd hurt her more than she knew it was possible to be hurt, but she couldn't deny that she loved him. So, who was she really punishing? Jackson or herself?

"Maybe I should just go over there."

She pushed the covers back and sat up gingerly. The doctors had said she was a lucky girl because the bullet hadn't hit her lungs. Intellectually, she understood that she was fortunate not to be dead. But every move she made exhausted her, the skin around her wound still burned like crazy, and she could barely shower without help. She didn't feel lucky yet.

She just felt miserable.

"Raina," she called. She cursed as her energy flagged and she sagged back against the pillows. How was she supposed to go track Jackson down and fuss at him when she could barely sit up without needing a nap?

A door slammed downstairs. Then she heard the sound of voices. They hadn't had many visitors over the last week since Raina didn't want anyone to know they were here. One of the voices was unmistakably male.

Who is that?

Maybe it was one of the security guys? The voices got louder as they came toward the stairs. The closer they got, the more familiar they sounded.

"Is that Jackson?"

A rush of elation gave her the energy to sit up again. He was here. He'd finally come to see her. She was still kind of mad at him but every part of her was suddenly overjoyed, too. A week ago, she'd been standing in this very room with a gun to her head, wondering if it would be the last time she saw his face. Now he was downstairs and she wasn't waiting another minute. Ridley put her legs over the side of the bed and stood up gingerly.

Then she took her first shaky step.

———

"RAINA! OPEN THE DOOR!"

Raina sat in her living room and blithely turned the pages of a magazine. The sound of yelling outside ceased for a few minutes before resuming.

"I'm not leaving until you talk to me. You know I'll make a scene."

"Ugh! He is so irritating." Raina groaned and slammed the magazine down on the couch next to her. Sam had offered to delay his own vacation and stay if she needed him. She hadn't wanted to ruin his fun when she didn't plan on doing much other than keeping her sister company while she recuperated.

The guards he'd posted to watch her house from outside had seemed like more than enough, but they were trained to prevent anyone from coming in. They couldn't do anything about someone who was bothering her from the street.

It was petty, but now she kind of wished she'd asked Sam to stay. He was creative. He'd have found a way to take care of the extremely annoying pest outside her window.

"Okay, Raina. If you don't open the door I'm going to video this and put it online."

She marched over to the front door and snatched it open. "What the hell do you want?"

"I just want to talk." He motioned to the guards standing between them. "Can you call off the goon squad?"

She nodded. The guards moved aside. Nick shook his head as he walked by them. As soon as he crossed the threshold, she slammed the door. "I don't know why you're here. I have nothing to say to you."

Nick stood in the middle of her living room and stared at her couch. They'd done some pretty inventive things on that couch. Raina blushed. It shouldn't embarrass her but somehow it did. She'd been someone totally different that night, and as much trouble as it had caused her, she couldn't find it in her to regret it.

"How is Ridley doing?" Nick asked. He looked faintly guilty.

"Better. Nothing that rest and a little peace and quiet won't cure. Which is why I'd appreciate it if you'd go bother someone else."

"She hasn't returned any of Jackson's calls."

"Maybe she doesn't want to talk to him."

Nick ran his hands over his hair. "Is she even getting his calls?"

Raina thought about lying, but knowing him he'd already figured out what she'd done. Part of the reason they loved to hate each other so much was because they were alike in a lot of ways.

"Not unless he knows her new number. I had it changed before she even left the hospital."

Nick shook his head. "I figured it was something like that."

"I'm just trying to protect my sister. She's been hurt enough."

"You're right. She's been hurt and it's mainly my fault. *My fault.* Not Jackson's. I screwed this up because of what happened between us. But unlike us, Jackson and Ridley are good for each other. Let's fix this."

Raina squeezed her eyes shut against a sudden rush of emotion. She whipped around, horrified when tears welled in her eyes.

"All my life, I've worked so hard to make sure that we're safe and we're never vulnerable again. I thought if I had enough money, everything would be perfect. But everything I have wasn't enough to keep the only person who loves me safe."

The hand that settled on her shoulder was as unexpected as it was comforting.

"She's not the only person who loves you."

She shivered and tried to pull the emotion back in, to lock it up before she became an inconsolable, sobbing mess. It actually *hurt* to tamp it back down, a literal crushing pain in her chest, to ignore his offer of comfort. But if she ever made the mistake of allowing anyone in, she feared she'd simply break apart—all her insecurities and fears spreading her into a million tiny fragments.

"You're right," she admitted, "Jackson and Ridley do belong together. So, just tell him to come over and I'll let him in. Someone deserves a happy ending." She wiped her cheeks and faced him.

Nick went to the door and opened it. A second later, Jackson appeared.

He waved from the doorway, a sheepish smile on his face. "I was hoping you'd say yes."

Raina shook her head, unable to resist smiling back. "Let me just go see if she's awake."

There was a loud crash right above them. Raina looked up, dread racing through her.

"What was that? Ridley!"

———

RIDLEY FELL against the dresser and dropped her head down to the wood. Going to get her man was not supposed to be this hard.

The door flew open and she was scooped into a pair of strong arms. Her gaze met Jackson's. Everything that had happened over the past week fell away and suddenly all the pain, fear, and heartache didn't exist. There was just the pure, incandescent joy of being in the arms of the man she loved.

"This reminds me of how we met," he said.

Ridley sucked in a breath, suddenly overcome with some emotion she couldn't define. It seemed crazy that she could be so happy to see him after only a week apart. How could someone she hadn't even known existed last month suddenly hold the difference between happiness and misery?

"Yeah, except this time we don't have an audience."

"Well, not exactly." He looked over his shoulder and turned slightly. Raina and Nick came into view. Nick waved.

She smiled through her tears. "Oh, you're right. This is just like old times."

He carried her to the bed and put her down gently on top of the covers. "Are you hurt?"

She shook her head. "No, but that picture frame can't say the same. Sorry, Ray."

Raina knelt and picked up the pieces of the frame that had broken when it fell. "I never liked this one anyway. I'll just go throw this away and leave you two to talk."

Ridley watched as Raina left the room and Nick followed, pulling the door shut behind him. For a long moment, they sat in silence just gazing at each other.

"What? You're staring," she whispered.

"I am. You're beautiful."

She smiled at the familiar words.

"I just want to look at you for a minute," he continued. "I thought I was never going to see you again."

She understood. It felt as if she could look at him for hours, just soaking up his scent and memorizing the lines of his face.

"I came to apologize. When you didn't answer any of my calls I figured you meant what you said when you left. That after you proved you were innocent, you never wanted to see me again." His bowed his head for a moment.

"Wait? You called me?" Ridley pointed to her phone on the nightstand. "I never got any calls."

Jackson picked up her phone and handed it to her. She tapped the screen a few times and then showed him the missed-calls log His number wasn't there.

"I probably called a hundred times. Wait, call me."

She tapped the screen. His phone rang in his pocket. He pulled it out and looked at the unfamiliar number.

"You changed your number?"

"No. When would I have had time to change my number?" She thought for a moment, then groaned. "But Raina had plenty of time to change it without me knowing. I knew there was a reason she wouldn't give me my phone back!"

"She's just trying to protect you. I don't blame her. I'm not good for you. I'm not a good bet for anyone. I'm damaged and even if you give me another chance I'm sure I'll make mistakes over and over again."

"I lied to you. And I'm not sure if I would have believed me either if that much money showed up missing from my account. We both made mistakes."

"I finished our song."

Ridley squinted at the sudden change in subject. "You did?"

"It's called 'One More Day.' I'm going to record it."

"Jackson, that's wonderful! But I thought you said it would never be recorded? That you were scrapping it."

"Some things are worth saving." He got off the bed and knelt on the floor in front of her. For a moment, Ridley felt weak again and leaned against the pillows for support.

"Working on the lyrics really made me think about my mom's advice. About wanting one more day. The thing is, sometimes you don't have one more day. Sometimes all you have is the moment. And if you don't take it, it's gone forever."

"What are you saying, Jackson?"

"I'm saying I love you. And I really hope you love me, too."

Ridley bit her lips. "Is this crazy? Is it just completely crazy that I felt like I'd lost a limb just because I didn't see you for a week? Is this even logical?"

"Screw logic. *I love you.* I love the way your forehead crinkles when you laugh. I love how you put everyone at ease—my mom, my brothers, even the kids. I love waking up and looking over at you and being the happiest I've ever been. Even if you find someone else, someone who isn't all damaged and scarred, he'll never feel the way about you that I do."

"I love you, too. So much." Tears spilled down her cheeks as she smiled at him.

"Give me one more day, Ridley. Marry me?"

The sound of whooping in the hallway made him scowl. The

door to her room swung open and she saw Nick and Raina cheering and dancing in the hallway.

"If I'd known you were going to propose, little brother, we could have stopped at a jewelry store on the way," Nick said.

Jackson looked down. "I guess this would be a great time for me to have a ring, huh?"

"Say yes, Ri!" Raina yelled.

Jackson's lips twitched. He lowered his voice so that only Ridley could hear him. "You realize it's always going to be like this, right? Just wait until the rest of my family hears about this."

Ridley laughed, the beauty of the moment so overwhelming it had no way out of her system except through laughter. The past month had been the worst and best of her life. She'd been stalked, terrified, and shot at. But she'd also been cherished. She'd fallen in love. She'd made friends. Most importantly, she'd gained a family.

"I'm not sure laughter during a marriage proposal is a good sign," Jackson said.

Ridley cupped his face. "Oh, yes it is. Our lives are going to be filled with laughter and joy and love. So, *yes*. I'll give you one more day. Every day." She kissed him gently.

"For the rest of our lives."

I hope you enjoyed *One More Day*.

Keep reading for a special excerpt of Nick & Raina's book.

THE THINGS I DO FOR YOU

Nicholas Alexander finally has something the woman of his dreams needs. He'll give Raina a baby if she gives him what he wants. Her.

The Things I Do for You is available now!
mmalonebooks.com/thethingsido

Nick leaned forward. "Is that why having a baby is so important to you?"

She immediately tensed up and set her drink down on the table. "You are relentless!"

"That's why you should just tell me. The faster you tell me, the faster we can move on to finding a solution."

"Not everything has a solution, Nick. This isn't a business deal." She pushed her hair back and rubbed her hands over her face. It killed him to see her looking so tired. So defeated.

"If you don't tell me, then I'm just going to work with the facts I have. Let's see..." He pretended to think. "I find a brochure for a sperm bank that *does not* belong to my brother and Ridley. Since you were the only other person on the patio that day, it must have been yours. But that doesn't make sense since last I knew you were engaged. What am I missing?"

Raina glared at him. "Fine. Since you apparently aren't going to stop until I tell you everything, consider yourself warned. I hope you're not the type to get squeamish when talking about girl stuff."

Nick leaned over and took her hand again and held it fast when she tried to pull back. "Raina, this is not high school. Despite our past, I want to know that you're okay. If that involves talking about feminine stuff, then so be it. So, why would you need a sperm donor when you had a fiancé?"

Raina stood and he let her. She didn't look at him as she walked over to the window. She stood there so long that he wondered if she was reconsidering her decision to talk. She finally turned to face him.

"I have a condition called endometriosis. I won't bore you with the details."

"Nothing about you bores me, Raina."

"Anyway, bottom line is that I'm a ticking time bomb. Every month that passes where I'm not pregnant means it's less likely I'll get to be a mother. A baby is all I want."

"Did Steven not want children?"

"No, he said he did. We weren't in love but we both wanted the same things. Partnership. Family. Children. Marriages built on common goals have higher success rates. It made sense to get married and start trying right away. My doctor gave me a bunch of brochures about in vitro fertilization, egg donation, and surrogacy just so that I could be informed. Turns out I'll actually need them now."

She turned away and he realized she was wiping away tears. The sight of her crying sent a paralyzing wave of fear through Nick.

"Oh, sweetheart. Please don't cry." The endearment slipped out before he could catch himself.

"Sorry. Ugh, I hate crying. As awful as it sounds, I'm less upset about Steven and more heartbroken over losing my dream."

"What if you could still have it?"

"I don't think Steven is going to change his mind." Raina laughed bitterly. "Not that I'd want him to. We were supposed to have a relationship based on mutual respect and trust. If I wanted someone who'd cheat and lie I could just have a normal relationship."

It was all he could do not to growl. "I'm not talking about Steven. And we'll have to talk about your shitty relationship expectations later. But I'm saying what if someone else offered to help you out?"

He debated the best way to present his idea to her. He could do what he really wanted to do, which was fall to one knee and tell her he adored her. But their interactions had proven time and time again that Raina didn't respond well to romantic gestures from him. If he told her he loved her, she'd probably just assume he was trying to get in her panties and just saying what he thought she wanted to hear.

There was only one thing he hadn't tried. She freely admitted that she hadn't loved her fiancé and was just marrying him because it "made sense." Well, Nick would be damned if she considered that guy a better bet than him. It was going to kill him to play it cool, but if pretending their interaction was just a business deal got him what he wanted, then he wasn't above a little deception.

"Help me out? How likely is that? It's not like I'm asking to borrow a cup of sugar, Nick! How many men would offer to father my child?"

Nick stood and thrust his hands in his pockets, aware that his next words would change his life forever.

"You're looking at one."

———

***The Things I Do for You* is available now!**
mmalonebooks.com/thethingsido

MILO

Time to get our game faces on.

As we approach the table, everyone stands, and the introductions are made all around. Maybe it's because I'm watching Mr. Lavin so closely that I see how his eyes follow Mya after she shakes his hand and then walks around the table to greet the other members of his team. She knows all of their names, as do I. Then she takes a seat right next to me.

Before I can even sit down, James is already ordering a scotch from the waitress. Then I see why.

Elizabeth is sitting two tables away.

She raises her glass of wine in our direction. I turn to see James give a begrudging wave. I'm not sure if anyone else has noticed her yet, but she's already accomplished her goal. There's no way James can focus completely on the client tonight with his ex-wife sitting right in his line of vision.

Christ.

"Thank you all for traveling to meet with me. I've had this week scheduled with potential investors for months, so it's been helpful that you could come to me while I'm already in the States."

"When do you go back to Italy?" Wallace asks. "I follow you on Instagram. You guys, his page is *lit.* Fast cars, beautiful clothes. You're living the dream, man." He sighs before digging into his salad course enthusiastically.

Andre just laughs. "Thank you. This is our goal, to be as the kids say, *fire.* Why is all of the American slang centered around temperature, I wonder? It used to be that things were *cool,* now they're *hot, fire, bomb* or *lit.* Fascinating. I have an entire team of people who study the social media trends."

James looks like he has no idea what is happening. But I strongly suspect that Wallace in his own unique, bumbling way has just broken the ice for us.

Well, if he's broken the ice, I might as well jump in first.

"Mirage employs a lot of talented young designers. It's why our ad campaigns are so on trend. We combine years of experience in understanding what makes people buy with the fresh perspective of different generations."

Mya grins over at me. "Wallace is on Milo's team. He's been with us for almost a year now and graduated from Columbia with honors. He's also an amateur photographer and is pretty popular on Instagram, too."

I glance over at her. *He is?* How does she know all that? Maybe there is something to paying attention in those bullshit icebreaker sessions at work after all.

Wallace looks shocked, too. "My account has nowhere near the numbers some of my friends have, but I just passed ten thousand."

Mr. Lavin actually looks impressed. "That's quite an accomplishment, especially for a hobbyist." He clears his throat. "I'm happy to meet with you all in person after hearing about you from Mr. Lawson."

James gives him a tight smile. "I'm extremely proud of my team."

"It shows," Andre replies.

Dinner proceeds with the typical pleasantries. Wallace looks a little confused, but I can only pray the kid can hold his tongue. With these types of clients, you never rush right into business. You need to woo them, almost like a woman you're trying to convince to come back to your place after dinner. She's not just going to come with you if you ask within the first ten minutes. She needs you to show her that you're worth her time. Are you going to savor her the same way you do the ten-inch porterhouse on your plate? Or will you rush through the act like a kid scarfing down an ice cream cone?

I can't imagine a man like Andre Lavin scarfing anything. He needs to see that we're not only the best team to take over his marketing but also that we're people he can work with.

We need him to *like* us.

As the waitress is clearing the entrees, Andre looks around the table with satisfaction. "Perhaps it is old-fashioned, but I care to meet with any agencies that work on our marketing directly. It's important that the people crafting our image understand what we're about here at Lavin Fashions."

Everyone instantly ceases their side conversations and pays attention. Now we're getting to the good stuff. The reason we're all here.

"What is your vision of Lavin Fashions, Mr. Lavin?" Mya asks. "I've read the official company mission statement, but I would love to hear it from you."

"Please, call me Andre."

The way he's looking at her makes it seem like he just wants to hear her say his name. My hand sitting on top of the table curls into a fist. It's unsettling that this bothers me. He's just a client, throwing a little charm at the pretty ad executive. I've seen it plenty of times, and I've had my fair share of clients, male and female, attempt to flirt with me.

None of those made me want to growl in frustration. Or made me worry that Mya might actually want to flirt back.

"It's much more than just the clothes," Andre begins after a brief pause. "Our brand creates the garments that become part of people's memories. And for our newest venture, we're looking for a partner that understands the importance of family, friendship, love."

The woman sitting next to him sniffs. *Cristiane Laveque.* From my research on the Lavin team, I know that she's a top designer for Lavin Fashions.

"Apologies, but this is not a strength of American companies, we have found. So few understand *l'amore.*" She shakes her head ruefully as if the vulgar ways of the American market are just too much.

Mentally, I'm rolling my eyes, but this could be a real obstacle to winning their business. If they think that we're not cultured enough, it will be difficult to change that opinion. Granted, Mirage does plenty of "American" commercials and brands, but it's not like we're all racecars and beer. We have plenty of upper-echelon brands in the jewelry, hotel and entertainment industries.

"I believe Mirage can handle anything. We have such a diverse workforce that all of our clients find someone they can relate to. We also have more women in leadership roles than many of our competitors."

Maybe that'll calm her fears that we don't get *l'amore*. Mya in particular handles a lot of brands that cater to women, including a high-profile lingerie line.

Andre sits back in his chair and seems to be considering her words. "I must admit we've been approached by other firms that are run by people who are married. They understand what brides want."

James sits up straighter. "So, it is a bridal line?"

Andre laughs lightly. "Yes, the rumors are true. Lavin Fashions will introduce a new line called Lavin Bridal next year. It will be a separate division of the company which is why I'm meeting with investors. I didn't want word to get out until it was all finalized."

James looks like he's going to be sick. This is why Elizabeth has been so smug. She must have heard the Lavin group wanted someone who has been through the process of planning a wedding. Just another way for her to rub her recent marriage in James's face.

"I'm sure all the women on our team have mentally planned their dream wedding, even if they aren't married." I send a panicked glance at Mya.

This would be a really good fucking time for her to pipe in with some story of how she's been dreaming of her wedding dress since she was a little girl.

Unfortunately, Andre seems to be following my line of thought because he turns directly to Mya, too. "If you were planning a wedding, for example," he says, "wouldn't you want a wedding planner who was married?"

Mya pauses with her water glass halfway to her mouth. "Well, yes. I suppose I would."

James just blinks. Wallace pauses mid-chew with a piece of iceberg lettuce hanging from his lip. The whole table seems stunned into silence. She didn't mean to say that, and everyone can see it on her face. But in a rare, caught-off-guard moment, Mya has done the unforgivable.

She's been honest.

An awkward silence descends over the table. James takes another gulp from his scotch. Across from me, members of the Lavin team exchange significant glances before taking an interest in their plates. Worst of all, Andre Lavin just looks amused.

While Mya looks devastated.

You know how sometimes you can look back and identify the precise moment you fucked up? Well, later tonight I'm sure I'll be remembering the exact second I pushed us all off the cliff together.

"I agree," I state loudly.

James chokes slightly, and Wallace pounds him on the back. I ignore his panicked look and keep my eyes on Mr. Lavin.

"I agree with Mya," I repeat in case anyone at the table missed it the first time I pushed my career in front of a bus. "Having a married wedding planner would be great. Although I'd be more concerned about the people actually doing the work. That's really what sets Mirage apart."

By now, everyone is staring at me, especially James, probably wondering where the hell I'm going with this.

Mya, however, is watching me with a small, tremulous smile on her face. Like she can't believe that I'm backing her up right now. And damn if that smile isn't what does me in. Because I don't just bet on distracting Mr. Lavin; I double down and take it all the way to the bank.

"Mirage is really the best fit for anything to do with weddings. After all, it's the only agency I know with two team leads that are in love and engaged to be married." I turn to Mya and whisper, "Just go with it."

Then I tilt my head slightly and brush my lips over hers.

———

Download BEG ME now
at minxmalone.com/begme

acknowledgments

This book wouldn't be possible without the support of my friends and family. Thank you, especially to my friend Zaki Shabazz, an amazing musician with a golden voice of his own.

As always, thank you to my husband, Andre, for putting up with my special brand of crazy as I wrote this book.

reformed con artist and a perfect little princess don't belong together. But I still can't leave her alone.

Zack : She's my brother's ex. Off limits. But she needs a nude model for her show so I'm taking one for the team. Turns out she needs more than just my picture...

Luke : My online BFF is the only hacker better than I am. Then I'm asked to consult on a hacking case for the FBI and the hauntingly beautiful suspect seems to know a lot about me. Things I've only told one other person...

Bad Business (The Kingsleys)
Contemporary Romance

Bad King: My parents just put a gold diggers target on my back. But if all they want is a wedding, I'll find the fiancee of their nightmares. *Who Wants to Marry a Billionaire? Must be completely inappropriate.*

Bad Blood : I'd do anything for my best friend's little sister. Until she asks for the one thing I can't give. One night. No rules. ***RITA® Award Winner!***

The Alexanders
Contemporary Romance

One More Day : "Good girl" Ridley has always attracted bad guys. Now she's on the run and has nowhere to hide. So when Jackson Alexander mistakes her for her twin, she decides to do something she knows is wrong. *She lies.*

The Things I Do for You : Nick Alexander finally has what the woman of his dreams needs. He'll give Raina a baby if she gives him what he wants. *Her.*

All I Want: The only gift Kaylee wants is for Elliott Alexander to stop treating her like she's invisible. When her car skids out of control on

Christmas Eve, she's forced to reach out to the only man she trusts to save her. **(VIP List only)**

All I Need is You : When the man she loves leaves town after their steamy kiss, Kaylee Wilhelm is done. But when she's targeted by a stalker, Eli is the only one who can protect her.

Just One Thing : Bennett Alexander is a bona fide genius but he still can't figure out how to "get the girl". So he hires a dating tutor. What could go wrong? Other than falling for his teacher, of course.

One More Chance : Now that Ridley is expecting, everything is different. All she needs is for Jackson to pretend that he finds her as sexy as he used to, even if it's not true. But with a little advice from her meddlesome twin, she has a plan to seduce her own husband.

<u>* Join my VIP list for FREE books *</u>

newsletter.mmalonebooks.com

M. Malone is a RITA® Award winner and a NYT & USA Today Bestselling author of completely inappropriate romantic comedy. She lives with her husband and their two sons in the picturesque mountains of Northern Virginia even though she is afraid of insects, birds, butterflies and other humans.

She also holds a Master's degree in Business from a prestigious college that would no doubt be scandalized at how she's using her expensive education.

instagram.com/minxmalone

bookbub.com/authors/m-malone

patreon.com/minxmalone

amazon.com/author/mmalone

tiktok.com/@minxmalone

The sexual chemistry between the hero and heroine was off the charts."

--BookKraze Reviews on *The Things I Do for You*

"The book is full of great characters - my favorite had to be Jackson - he is sweet and sexy yet cautious with his heart...The story is well written with plenty of twists. I can't wait to read the next installment of the Alexander brothers."

--Fairy Tale Ending Reviews on *The Things I Do for You*